HIS EYES DILATED WITH AWE
AT THE SPECTACLE APPROACHING
FROM THE HORIZON

A thousand Jovan warships decelerated into Earth orbit. Despite the distance and the ocean of atmosphere, Jon knew that staring into those intense lights could damage his eyes.

"Is there any way to hide from them?" he asked. "Those people don't own me. I'm not a piece of property for them to dispose of at their leisure."

They continued walking. In a day or two they'd reach the foothills of a mountain range where perhaps they could find some rugged terrain that would protect them from a landing craft. If not . . . Jon was well aware that his capture would start a chain of events that could lead civilization to the brink of catastrophe.

We will send you a free catalog on request. Any titles not in your local book store can be purchased by mail. Send the price of the book plus 50¢ shipping charge to Leisure Books, P.O. Box 270, Norwalk, Connecticut 06852.

Titles currently in print are available for industrial and sales promotion at reduced rates. Address inquiries to Nordon Publications, Inc., Two Park Avenue, New York, New York 10016, Attention: Premium Sales Department.

SILENT GALAXY

William Tedford

author of
The Timequest Trilogy

LEISURE BOOKS ❧ NEW YORK CITY

A LEISURE BOOK

Published by

Nordon Publications, Inc.
Two Park Avenue
New York, N.Y. 10016

Copyright © 1981 by Nordon Publications, Inc.

Humanity held off on the final Holocaust long enough to put a tiny fraction of its population into space. With the developed nations struggling from the wreckage of economic collapse during the last decade of the century, two-thirds of the world's population had no resources to cope with the interlinking crises of energy, food, and pollution. Ideological conflicts turned mindlessly destructive, dozens of cities and the last of the major oilfields in the Mideast falling prey to nuclear terrorists. A final, convulsive conflagration engulfed the world and destroyed civilization between dawn and dusk of June 5, 1998 A.D.

Earth-orbiting factories, research laboratories, and the Luna mining facilities had the capability of returning their populations home, but only to a contaminated world. Instead, they joined forces in the desperate struggle to become fully self-sufficient. During the first year, not a single colonist escaped near-starvation. But within five years, man's only remaining technological society stabilized. Within one century, it doubled its population and within five centuries, civilization spread outward as far as the dark worlds beyond Pluto.

Humanity did not return to the surface of the Earth.

5

During the first century, the space colonies did not have the resources nor the motivation to launch a reconnaissance mission to the surface and return. From lower Earth orbit, observers could watch cities dying and falling into ruin in gruesome detail. When the first expedition did return after an absence of 150 years, society discovered what a minority had preached all along. Man had lost all tolerance to Earth's natural environment. For too long, man had controlled his environment to suit technical needs and personal preferences, adapting to near-sterile conditions, low air pressure, and low gravitational fields. Slowly and willingly, man became an alien to the world of his biological origin.

CHAPTER ONE

The curved rise of Earth loomed in the forward view-screen, an awesome destination for a man who had never stepped foot upon the face of a planet. Especially this particular world, the origin of the human species, humanity's abandoned cradle of civilization.

"Cobra Ten, this is Squadron Command," a metallic voice sounded over the radio. "We have your optimum ejection trajectory coming up in four minutes, thirty-two seconds."

"Acknowledged," Jon said quietly, preoccupied by the cloud-swirled and vivid blue of the Pacific Ocean far below. He took note of how the atmosphere hazed the horizon in a halo of light giving way to the velvet blackness of star-dusted vacuum. The sun flashed briefly through the quiet cabin of his Cobra fighter, shadows swinging once from left to right. A solitary pilot light flickered in the dark on his control panel, futile commands transmitted by a computer aboard the approaching Jovan battleship ordering his damaged fighter to automatically self-destruct. His own damaged computer had yet to respond.

He estimated that he would strike atmosphere on the dark side of Earth. It wouldn't be a pleasant way to die. Much better to eject as Squadron Command ordered, to let the battleship coming up on the far side of the horizon burn him out in a quick and painless laser beam. The warfleet from Luna Nation would be upon them both within minutes. He could not be rescued in time. Neither could his own forces afford to have him fall into enemy hands.

A green-lit chronometer counted down the seconds to ejection. Jon gripped the handles of the attitude controls on the armrests of his acceleration couch. He had sat at the controls of a dead fighter many times before, waiting patiently for rescue. There'd be no rescue this time, not within days or even years in the secure, dreamless sleep of suspended animation.

Jon caressed the ejection button on the right attitude-control handle with his thumb as the numbers counted down and flashed zero. He drew back with sudden irritation. Why bother expending the energy to ensure the inevitable?

"Unable to comply with ejection," Jon radioed. "I have an ejection system failure."

He used his attitude thrusters to angle the Cobra to strike atmosphere belly first to demonstrate his intention of assuring the destruction of himself and his fighter.

The battleship returned a mechanical beep of acknowledgment. In the same moment, it appeared in the rear viewscreen on the hazy, distant horizon of Earth, its fusion engines glaring like a cluster of miniature stars. Breaking orbit, the huge craft accelerated on its long journey home.

The sun passed behind the horizon. Darkness fell and the outer fringes of atmosphere began heating the underbelly of the Cobra to dull red.

Jon had never disobeyed a military order in his life. Neither had he ever lied. Now he committed his crimes with a grim apathy, angling the crippled fighter's nose toward the edge of the horizon. After all, many battles had been fought in the region of Earth with Luna Nation forces. Hadn't the doomed in their ruined fighters captured by the gravity of Earth ever attempted a safe entry to the surface of that mysterious and beautiful world?

The crackling of the radio startled him.

"Jovan Nation warcraft, this is Luna Nation Defense. Entry of your craft into Earth's atmosphere is imminent. It appears that you are attempting a survival entry trajectory. You will not, however, survive exposure to the Earth environment. If you choose to live, eject immediately. We have a shuttle on standby and will attempt rescue. Please reply."

He feared the voice of his enemy, but suffered his guilt to give the offer a moment's consideration.

"Luna Nation, defection is not a viable alternative to death."

"If that's your decision, Jovan, good luck."

The note of compassion surprised him. His own people hadn't wished him luck. The loss of a Cobra Ten and an expert-class fighter pilot had called for nothing but quick and automatic destruction to keep him and the technology of his craft out of the hands of the enemy. But if his life had belonged to the government, his death belonged to him alone, this one moment of freedom too precious to share with anyone.

Odd, to think that even in defying certain death he violated directives backed up by the threat of death. Who might understand that he played games in a realm where logic contradicted itself and freed him from life-long bondage? He was curious about his one-way journey into the gravity well of Earth. After all, men had lived down there at one time.

Upon initial impact with the dense layers of atmosphere, the forward shields designed to deflect head-on laser beams shattered and fell away in a pyrotechnic display of sparks and flame. The monatomic

9

hydrogen stabilizers held the attitude of the ship steady by brute force, the deep-space craft possessing hardly a square millimeter of aerodynamics.

An incredible vibration racked the ship. In the sudden blaze of heat, Jon had an instant of consciousness remaining and barely the strength against an inhuman deceleration to finger the eject button. Bound within his cocoon of safety webbing, it was the only motion allowed him, the only one necessary for an outside chance of survival.

The meteor that streaked through the night skies of Earth trailed a kilometer's long tail of glowing ionization and flame. It broke into several pieces, multicolored glare rippling through the tumbling debris. In a final shower of sparks, most of the wreckage burned out. But tons of glowing debris plowed into forests, a desert, and an ocean. Over one small portion of the western coast of the North American continent, thunder rolled in clear skies across an early-morning sunrise. A dark sphere of metal descended upon four brilliant columns of fire.

Jon regained consciousness in pain and darkness. Cracked ribs sent tendrils of pain shooting through his chest and back. His right shoulder felt dislocated, and singed lung tissue made it hard to breath. He probed the contours of his burning face with gentle fingertips. His eyebrows and eyelashes were gone. His skin felt raw, but was dry and unbroken.

He thought he suffered severe neurological damage when he tried to move, but the enormous pressure he felt was only his own weight. He would enjoy no more freefall. Earth's gravity would burden him for whatever remained of his life. Without the utmost care in moving about, his bones would snap and his joints would dislocate. It wouldn't take much of an accident to cripple him.

Jon checked to ensure the capsule was intact and

airtight, then estimated his remaining electrical supply. The fuel cells operating the life support and recycling systems would last a week, his week being ten days, but his days close to the time period of Earth's rotation. His screens were dead, but leaning forward in the acceleration couch, Jon caught sight of light and color through a slender horizontal port in the side of the cabin. He gasped with surprise and wonder. Even knowing he'd never leave this place alive, he discovered one small compensation to his exile, one single initiative to survival. He caught a glimpse of his first view of Earth's landscape.

Jon had never seen one living tree and here were thousands. Individual green leaves and twigs sparkling with dew swayed against the purple morning sky. The sun, muted to a near-tolerable glare of yellow-orange, filtered through an emerald forest in flickering bits of brilliant light. His mind balked at the impossible beauty, accustomed to a contrived environment and a life-long habit of analyzing the effects of color, size, and perspective in the architecture of the space colonies. Nothing of what he saw could have been engineered, but he had never seen a planetary landscape except in films and visits to the ice and rock carvings on the barren satellites of the outer planets. Forbidding clouds raced through the dark skies of Titan, but nothing like the clouds of water vapor billowing, towering and tinged with color on Earth's distant horizon. Shafts of sunlight silhouetted insects and birds airborne in the dawn. Through the speakers, he listened to the sounds of a world more alive than anything imaginable. Open space had its own kind of panoramic beauty, but Earth promised beauty employing all of his senses— if he could but survive long enough to sample even a tiny portion of it.

He barely survived the pain and distress of that first day. Awake, the discipline of training and the

11

experience of hardship served him well, but the nightmarish, half-delirium of sleep edged him toward the temptation of suicide. Nurtured by childhood memories of photographs and films taken by robot tractors plying the face of the Earth in past centuries, he decided to play a game of life-and-death with himself. For each hour of pain, he would expect, anticipate, demand a moment of that impossible beauty to compensate. The game demanded that if beauty and pain could not be balanced in their extremes, then he would open the airlock and let Earth's microorganisms relieve him of further suffering.

Just after dawn of the second day, he raised the stakes. He could not sleep during the night and viewed films of his descent taken by automated cameras. He made an unexpected discovery. The shore of the Pacific Ocean lay less than three kilometers to the west. He had been so intent on surviving atmospheric entry, he hadn't given a thought to the probability of landing on the three-fifths of the Earth's surface covered by water. Setting down a few kilometers to the west would have crushed his capsule in the ocean's depths.

Earth scenes had haunted him as a child. As an adult, he had ignored them as irrelevant to life as he knew it. But he remembered spending hours watching a film of a surf rushing and retreating across the white sands of some unknown shore. Now he reconsidered: What would it take for him to walk those three kilometers? After all, it need be only a one-way journey.

To begin with, he'd have to heal, to be able to stand, bear his own weight and walk. He'd have to build up the necessary strength before his power failed. He had sufficient food concentrates and water distilled from outside air to last several weeks. Next? The dense atmosphere. A sudden increase of air pressure

12

would suffocate him. Adapting would be no problem, however. He could increase air pressure within the capsule a small amount each day until it equalized with exterior pressure. But even if he could adapt to the gravity field and the air density, could he survive Earth's microbiological wildlife?

There were microorganisms symbiotic, beneficial and even essential to health. Space colonies were disease-free, but not sterile environments. In fact, he would have died of radiation exposure many years ago had it not been for a biologically engineered virus that rebuilt damaged chromosomes and stimulated cellular reproduction. However, colonies in space tended to be isolated for long periods of time, insignificant mutations of microorganisms in one population group sometimes posing a threat to individuals in another. Antibiotics were used to prevent adverse reactions. Jon carried a supply of antibiotics geared specifically to his body chemistry, an arrangement that allowed a Cobra pilot drifting in a damaged fighter to be rescued by any friendly agent in a position to do so.

His strategy, then, would be to expose himself to unfiltered air, administer a dose of antibiotics and simply hope that it would suffice. Success of the entire adaption program might give him extra time, perhaps as much as several days outside the capsule. Then, he would die.

Jon entertained no hope of indefinite survival. He had been born and raised and had lived in a carefully controlled environment for the thirty-five years of his life. What lay beyond the prison of his metal walls Jon found to be shockingly beautiful, but utterly alien, alive in nonhuman ways and deadly. He did not doubt but that the Earth would kill him rather quickly.

Jon didn't exert himself at first, allowing several days to pass within which to heal and to give his body

13

time to strengthen against the gravity. He hardly noticed the increased air pressure. When he figured his singed lungs had healed, he breathed unfiltered air and waited for a reaction. An hour later, he vomited. His temperature soared. Panicked by sensations he had never before experienced, he quickly took his dose of antibiotics and waited. And grew ill.

He developed diarrhea, not knowing what it was, grew delirious, nauseous and aching, facing a death he could never have anticipated. He had never been ill for a single moment of his life. Maybe it could never have worked as he had planned. He'd die without ever seeing his ocean or knowing Earth as man had known it for millions of years.

A day later, he felt better. He increased the air pressure to fully equalize exterior density and stood unsupported for twenty minutes.

He took another breath of unfiltered air—and developed boils. His eyes itched and his ears ached. His muscles cramped, knotting him into a fetal position on the acceleration couch for long hours. He lost track of time, struggling for each breath. The constant low level of illness sapped his strength and initiative. He grew weaker, finally unable to stand at all. In moments of clarity he knew that if the aches and pains and nausea didn't subside soon, there would be no capacity left in him to appreciate beauty, nothing left of him but a shell of misery.

He had read about illness and knew on an intellectual level what disease meant. He could even name a few of the plagues that had once preyed upon humanity on Earth. But he had never known that sickness hurt and made it impossible to think clearly. His nausea and diarrhea contaminated his environment. They now threatened his continued survival worse than the illness itself.

On the dawn of an uncounted day since his arrival, Jon opened the airlock. He crawled outside one full meter and spent the day without moving from that spot.

He felt the sun on his skin and a breeze that cooled his fever. He smelled odors of things living and dying and the salt air from the ocean. He heard sounds echoing from vast distances. He touched dirt for the first time, got wet in an afternoon shower, picked a flower and studied an insect—all without moving from the spot where he sat.

An animal emerged from a wall of trees less than thirty meters away. It was small, hairy, and unattractive, the first nonhuman form of life he had ever met. It shied from him as he shied from it. He retreated to the security of the capsule for the night.

Jon smiled as he closed the airlock behind him. He felt sick, but oddly content, frightened and tense, but strangely exhilarated. If this was to be his death, he would regret nothing. It took no time at all to feel at home in this strange world. Useless and ignorant perhaps, but at home beneath the dome of the blue sky, sharing the Earth with rustling, creeping living things. Earth touched the ancient part of his brain that enabled life to function within the natural environment. Jon responded like a tuning fork—and the illness passed.

He had long since abandoned his original schedule. He began walking around the capsule during the day, his laser pistol clenched in his right hand, the battery pack strapped to his wrist. He slept in the capsule at night with the airlock closed, but with the vents open. Days, maybe weeks later, the fuel cells failed. But with his food and water supplies dwindling, shelter was no real priority. He still had his ocean to see.

Jon had studied his history. Men had taken the ancient game of chess, had given it three dimensions and a wider variety of pieces and moves and had turned warfare into a game. The basics remained the same. The Command Ship replaced the king, invested with the power to control the pieces on the three-dimensional board of space-time. Destroy the opponents' Command Ship and the battle ends in victory. The only major difference was that men still moved the pieces, but moved them from the inside— and men died if they were lost.

A large cometary mass had entered the solar system. Once it had been determined to be of interstellar origin and a genuine scientific find, the Jovan and Lunan governments could not risk hostilities breaking out among competing exploration parties conducting a space race to claim the find in the name of a single government.

Even by Jon's standards, the ideal solution would have been to mix crews aboard an international exploration caravan. But the Jovans considered Lunan lighting harsh and distracting, the air too dense and hot. The Lunans considered Jovan gravity preferences unnecessarily stressful and the side effects of the antibiotics necessary to prevent cross-biological contamination too uncomfortable. It took little more than minor grievances to result in a challenge by the Outer System Federation to armed combat, the winner to take possession of the cometary mass, the loser to trust that all findings would be fairly shared by all the nations. But Jon not only knew the real reason for the challenge, he had anticipated it. It had been six years since the last major confrontation between the two greatest powers in space. Both were eager to probe the developing war technology of the other side.

On Earth, prior to the Holocaust, a growing population had forced different races and cultures to learn tolerance of one another or face the stress and destruction of constant war. Humanity had almost succeeded. But once free in the vastness of space, the process had reversed itself, two major and a myriad of minor racial and cultural variations developing by the process of fission, a new addition to the growing variety as each colony left the shipbuilding yards of Jupiter or the inner system, each colony seeded with the minorities of other societies and each moving into space to find its own place in the scheme of this new civilization.

Economically, the two major spheres of humanity complemented one another. The colonies among the outer worlds specialized in the mining and processing of the lighter elements. Icebergs of insulated gases, liquids, and solids spiraled constantly down into the inner system. The outer system colonies considered themselves independent, but organized economically and militarily under the leadership of the Jovans, the outer system's largest society orbiting the four major moons of Jupiter.

The colonies of the Inner System Alliance also considered themselves independent, but, again, organized under the leadership of the Lunans, the largest inner-system colony based on Earth's single moon. Given the abundance of free solar energy close in to the sun and the heavier elements mined from Mercury, Luna, and Mars, the Inner System Alliance specialized in heavy construction and manufacturing.

Early in the days of the thriving space colonies, humanity learned three important facts and worked quickly to incorporate them usefully into the structure of a burgeoning society. First, a highly technical civilization meant increased specialization and interdependence between its parts. Second, the psychological distance between cultures in space would surpass anything seen on Earth in mankind's history. And, third, as long as man could bunch his hand into a fist, violence as a viable alternative to negotiation would remain too great a temptation to ignore. The

17

rules of the wargames had been established by the Ganymede Convention less than two centuries after the Holocaust.

The Outer System Federation voiced the initial challenge. Therefore, the Inner System Alliance had the choice of a defending position. Luna Nation chose Earth as a backdrop to their defensive position, forcing the Jovan forces to attack at a shallow angle across the interference provided by the face of a full-sized planet. Every nation in the system waited with eager anticipation for the Jovan forces to arrive. War no longer threatened civilian populations. In fact, the struggle of two opposing warfleets to destroy the Command Ship of the opposition made the wargames the most intensely fascinating and challenging sport man had ever known. Directly or indirectly, entire populations eagerly participated in the outcome.

The Jovan fighter squadrons had been brought in by the carrier *Saratoga*. Jon's squadron had been assigned to defend the battleship *Ganymede*. The *Ganymede* engaged early in the apparently suicidal attack upon the Lunan Command Ship *Brystol*. But the battleship deflected at the last instant, attacking the fortress defending the *Brystol*. The maneuver forced the *Brystol* to take evasive action, a move to place more of the mass of the Earth directly behind it in relation to the incoming Jovan forces.

The wargames would have been little more than mass destruction of automated equipment without the deliberately imposed handicap of human-piloted machinery. Because of their human pilots and crews, the Jovans couldn't move directly against the Lunan formations. At velocities of hundreds of kilometers per second, the human body couldn't survive the G forces necessary to pull away from the bulk of the planet lying behind the Lunans. Automated vessels were legal, but limited in firepower. Still, in the excitement of battle, the Lunan forces panicked in the face of the onslaught of the carrier *Saratoga* barreling in on a full-frontal attack, decelerating engines of over fifty billion tons of thrust burning like full-fledged supernovas.

Long before the *Saratoga* reached maximum deceleration, swarms of fighters fell away from the craft, blossoming outward to attack the flanks of the Lunan fleet on the horizons of Earth, the hurtling *Saratoga* little more than a weapon of fear, a lightweight shell never intended for combat worthiness. The *Brystol* had only seconds to analyze the bizarre strategy and respond. As the juggernaut deflected from its suicidal trajectory, skimming the Earth's atmosphere and disintegrating from numerous missile hits, the *Brystol* moved out of harm's way— directly into the firing trajectory of a Jovan weapons barge that had moved into position during the confusion.

Jon studied the entire battle and its subtly shifting strategy during the seconds it took to engage, fire, and pass from the scene on his own individual mission. The *Brystol* should have vanished in a fireball of thermonuclear fury. It somehow survived, the Lunan formation reorganizing for its offense and a tighter defense around its Command Ship. The Jovan forces had incurred high losses in order to accomplish a probable victory. Knowing they would not survive another pass, Jon heard the concession to victory an instant before a random proximity mine detonated a few kilometers away. The blast reduced the underbelly of his Cobra to slag.

His computer assessed the damage as terminal, blew off the shell of armor and ignited the emergency retrorockets to kill as much of his forward velocity as possible. Crippled fighters spinning into deep space at several hundred kilometers per second were not prime candidates for immediate rescue in the after battle cleanup.

A pilot in a fighter too heavily damaged to decelerate always had the option of entering a state of suspended animation and be rescued at convenience in the outer system. Jon had slept twice under such circumstances. He would have preferred to sleep again. The procedure designed to save him the inconvenience of attending update classes after a year or two of absence doomed him. Captured by the gravitational field of Earth, he orbited the planet once, sweeping inward to skim tenuous atmosphere. He lost orbital velocity. The fighter skipped once into space and arced back down for a final confrontation with the unknown.

Perhaps a dozen or so fighters and one or two battleships died their fiery deaths in Earth's atmosphere, an acceptable contamination level that would not harm the Earth's biosphere. Hadn't others been in a position to attempt a safe entry and landing? Jon knew himself to have a reputation for eccentricity, another reason why men still flew the fighters instead of the predictable computers. Jon often wondered why so many chose immediate death during battle rather than allowing fate to run its unpredictable course.

He had stumbled upon a real mystery. Why did so many believe Earth to be the antithesis to human life? Certainly no space-born citizen would ever lead a comfortable, long, or healthy life on the surface of this world, nor would rescue missions ever be economically feasible on a routine basis. But neither did the environment spell instant death.

Jon left the capsule in the first light of dawn carrying his laser pistol, a pouch of antibiotics, a canteen, and a small satchel of concentrate tubes. He reached the beach at noon.

There were footprints in the sand. Absorbed by the

panorama of sky and water and the sound of the crashing waves, he did not notice them right away. They stretched the length of the beach as far as he could see in either direction, a single set of human footprints. Jon knew about tides. The prints were recent, running close to the water's edge at low tide.

Jon didn't know a whole lot about Earth beyond what a quick indoctrination course had taught him prior to the launch of the warfleet. He had learned that between one and two hundred million primitives were scattered across the face of the globe. He hadn't known that. Now he didn't particularly care to meet one. They'd be too primitive to communicate with and possibly hostile. Jon had never confronted violence outside of the cockpit of a Cobra. Space wars were bloodless. You survived unscathed or died in clouds of superheated vapor.

As the day passed, he saw nothing moving other than the grasses on the beach tipping to a seaward breeze and gulls crying and wheeling out over the water. The hypnotic roar of the surf put him in a peaceful revelry broken finally by a twinge of fear ignited by a spectacular sunset fading to twilight. He rose slowly, turned, and started on his way back through the grassland toward the forest, moving with infinite caution.

Stars in space were clouds of discrete bits of light both steady and eternal. Here, they twinkled and glowed through an ocean of air, a very select few of the brightest visible in the dusk. They moved slowly along with the setting sun and the rising, orange and bloated moon as the Earth turned. Jon could almost see the lights of civilization scattered about the moon's surface. He most definitely saw a number of Luna Nation satellites orbiting overhead. They'd be communications and research stations along with a few military outposts. There'd be more than a few anthropologists aboard those stations studying nomadic tribes and fishermen plying rivers and the shores of oceans. Despite the odds, the possibility existed that at some time he would look upward and into the direct, startled gaze of a Lunan scientist. He'd see only sky, but from overhead, looking through telescopes or cameras, there'd be no mistaking the blue-and-gold uniform of an Outer System Federation fighter pilot.

Jon's absentmindedness amused him. In space, a momentary lapse of attention could easily prove fatal. Here, he could afford to overlook hours. It would be midnight before he'd return to the capsule. If he didn't lose himself in the increasing darkness, he would totally exhaust himself. Although he endangered his life by walking in the twilight so ignorant of the hazards of his environment, he didn't really seem to care.

He picked out each footstep carefully, resting often. He noticed that the more noise he made, the less wildlife rustled in the underbrush. Not at all anxious to encounter anything larger than the birds and the tree rodents chattering about him, he made a point of stirring dried leaves and stepping on brittle twigs whenever possible. He tensed while crossing a mossy area of ground, acutely aware of the sudden stillness. Anything could come crashing through the underbrush. In that moment, he imagined creatures as he had seen them in photographs, the wildlife from various continents that had given him the impression of a hostile world of sudden death.

He gripped his laser pistol tightly, but had given no consideration to the effects of firing it in an atmosphere. It was a weapon designed for use in a vacuum, a last-ditch defense against being captured and boarded by enemy forces. He had fired it only once as a part of a familiarization course five years ago.

Given a fraction of a second of secure observation,

he would have recognized the creature that stepped from the trees as a harmless herbivore. But his mind perceived only a large, nonhuman entity confronting him in the twilight. Jon fired by reflex, a millisecond thread of light turning dusk into an eye-searing glare. The creature standing fifty meters away exploded in a crack of superheated steam. Bits of carbon hissed at high velocity through the surrounding foliage.

Blinded by the flash, knowing he had endangered his life in a mindless act of stupidity, Jon froze and waited for the effects to pass. Birds killed by shock and debris tumbled through the trees and fell around him. The odor of burnt organic matter drifted through the clearing. He stood in one spot for what seemed like hours, wondering if he had permanently blinded himself or exposed himself to a dangerous level of secondary radiation.

Jon tried to put the incident into perspective. He could no longer afford to unconsciously equate every unknown with danger. He'd be encountering far too many unknowns to react in blind fear. If the animal had been a few meters closer, he would have killed himself in the blast.

When his vision returned, he continued on. Little more than the flow of adrenaline prodded him on through the night. When he reached the capsule near daybreak, the sharp pains in his joints and the aches in his very bones convinced him that he had seriously injured himself. He was too tall, frail, and weak to cope with the constant stress of Earth's gravity. Still shaken by the incident, he shut himself up in the capsule in the heat of the day and caught himself thinking about snakes and spiders, things tiny and deadly crawling through the vents. His overstressed arms and legs twitched with a life of their own as he tried to sleep. His imagination kept replaying the incident in every conceivable variation. If he had thrown himself to the ground, he'd be dead by now or helpless with shattered bones and torn tendons. What truly amazed him was the fact that he had run across no real threat to his life so far. He had been told that death would be immediate, that adaption to the face of a hostile Earth would be impossible. Given adequate supplies, what specific danger did Earth pose to him? He could breath contaminated air at full density. His frame could support him in a one gravity for short periods of time. Even the microscopic creatures teeming inside his body had yet to kill him.

Jon felt like an uninvited visitor with an expired visa ready to rush home with his stories of paradise lost. But it had been a one-way trip from the beginning. A new kind of fear began gnawing at him, a quiet paranoia that his death would be the product of his own blundering. But the threat of imminent death had retreated and along with it, his apathy. Self-preservation reasserted itself as an immediate priority. Tomorrow would bring a fresh set of challenges to dull his carefree appreciation of Earth's beauty. If this world would support his life, then it would be his responsibility to be resourceful and survive. The most primitive lifeforms living around him managed to provide for themselves. Would Earth's most intelligent product fail among such abundance?

Jon had no idea of how man had once lived upon the face of the world. He had no idea of how to provide himself with shelter, food, tools, weapons, or fresh water other than what he had on hand. Nor did he feel he had the physical strength or stamina to provide for himself. Within another week or so, he'd be out of food concentrates. That need would be insurmountable. Generations of breeding as well as life-long eating habits had adapted his digestive system to handle concentrates. Even if he could adapt rapidly enough to the bulk of natural food and locate food supplies without poisoning himself, could he ever

24

force himself to eat the flesh of a living creature? He'd need that source of protein, but it had been 200 years since man had eaten foods other than synthetics.

He walked the seashore often, growing to need the white noise of the surf to calm and block out his thoughts. Otherwise, the inner chatter fed by his imagination formed vicious cycles of fantasies of countless forms of death bearing down on him. Calmed by the serene competence of nature, he took inventory of his surroundings, studying the plants and wildlife to determine what might be eatable and how he would go about preparing food. He formed his tentative plans and waited, drawing out his concentrates as much as possible. But he consumed them at an alarming rate, his body demanding the fuel to thrive in this dense gravity field.

At first, the three-kilometer walk to the ocean took many hours. Soon he could walk the distance and return in half a day. He refused to walk the forest at night and occasionally trapped himself into spending a night on the beach, always carrying a canteen of water, a day's supply of concentrates, and the small satchel of indispensable antibiotics he administered to himself whenever illness threatened to return.

It had rained three times since his landing, once during daylight hours and twice at night. Once, he had seen distant lightning and heard the slow, broken tumble of thunder. But after a lifetime of fighting on silent battlefields of vacuum, he had no fear of this open living environment. The day he sauntered along the water's edge, captivated by the ominous beauty of a steel-gray wall of clouds moving in from the ocean, he identified with the approaching storm reflecting his own inner turmoil. The clouds boiled as they neared, constant flickerings of lightning glowing in their depths. He grew concerned only when the ocean turned dark and violent. The temperature dropped and the surf seethed high onto the beach.

Jon moved in the rising wind for the trees overlooking the beach. The wind rose to a howl, tearing bits of foliage from trees thrashing above him. He curled into a ball at the base of a stout, ancient tree and withdrew into the depths of his own psyche while the storm raged.

Ships in space moving through the invisible solar winds could pick up enormous electrical charges. Docking vessels neutralized those charges before making physical contact. Jon had often watched lightning flickering between approaching spacecraft in columns of ionized gas. As a child he had spend countless hours watching electrical storms rage on the face of Jupiter. He understood lightning.

But through the blinding flashes, the breathtaking sizzling of nearby strikes and the sharp crack and roll of thunder, he gave no thought to the capsule lying in the forest clearing three kilometers away. Jon saw the explosion a fraction of a second before the shockwave struck. The glare of silver-white reduced the thunderstorm to insignificance. Intense shadows flickered and lashed about on the ground like tormented, living entities. The ground thudded once hard beneath him. The sound of trees tearing and crashing to the ground rose above the dull echo of the explosion.

Jon lay secure against the wet earth in his waterproof, insulated uniform. In the hard and cold void of emotional shock, he understood what had happened. He hadn't even thought of providing a simple ground for the capsule to protect the unstable monatomic hydrogen fuel supply of the attitude thrusters. That slight oversight had cost him most of his food concentrates, his only secure shelter against the night, and the last tangible contact with the world he had once known. Sometime later, he rolled over and unhooked his canteen from his belt. By the flicker of

26

lightning, he replenished his water supply with rain water pouring from the foliage overhead.

The rain tapered off during the night. By daylight, dense clouds were rushing inland from the ocean. Jon sat shivering, his arms wrapped around his legs folded against his chest, waiting for the sun to appear. When the clouds failed to dissipate near noon, he climbed to his feet and returned to the beach and began walking to the south along the storm-littered shoreline.

Jon threw his life to fate, to whatever combination of circumstance might fall his way. Once, it had felt as if he determined his own fate. But that had been in the world of man and his technology moving about in a dead, static environment, not the complex, animate environment of Earth. Jon did not feel belittled by the impersonal forces stirring around him. He wasn't yet dead or even in the process of dying. As long as he lived, he would choose his next best course of action and move on.

By late afternoon, he reached an odd place of beauty. The sands were white, the sea glass-calm. Gigantic water-worn boulders crouched in the waters off shore. Sheer rock-faced cliffs rose from the beach. Gnarled trees with green needles for leaves hung out over the cliffs, several twisted limbs almost closing the gap to the nearest of the boulders. It formed a portal through which he had to pass. Beyond, the mirror-calm water of a bay faded into ground fog. The vapor hazed everything beyond a short distance to uniform gray-white. In the unusual calm, Jon stopped. The portal struck some deep chord of significance at a level of mind that had little respect for waking reason or logic. Behind him, his footprints disappeared into invisibility. Before him stretched beaches just as endless. His unending trek had exhausted his concentrates and his water. He could spend a comfortable night in this place of beauty, but tomorrow, the end of it all would begin.

A large round stone smacked into the sand less than two meters in front of him. Jon glanced up the face of the cliff, bothered more by his own lack of reaction than by the threat to his life. A line of squat human figures stood on the cliff's edge raising more of the stones over their heads. The rocks fell at an incredible speed.

Jon dodged the first salvo, backing to the surf. But even ankle deep in the tumbling water, he stood within range of a barrage of smaller rocks. Unholstering his laser, Jon searched for an effective way of using it: It never occurred to him to kill.

He considered firing into the face of the cliff, but could imagine the spray of molten rock he would send cascading over the beach. Instead, he took aim toward the beach a half kilometer behind him. Averting his eyes, he fired. The line of sun-brilliant white sliced along exploding sand to the surf. A section of the beach exploded with white-hot fury followed by a geyser of steam. A concussion of hot air almost threw Jon to the ground.

The shrill screams that followed the explosion threw him off balance in a different way. The screams rose in volume, sounds of utter terror cut off by dull thuds he felt through the soles of his boots. When he could see through the after-image of the glare, there were two bodies lying at the base of the cliff.

Jon walked over to them, stopping far enough away to avoid having to view the details of bone protruding through torn flesh. One body was male, ancient-looking and bearded, the other a small female child. They were dressed in animal skins, their long hair unkempt and tangled, their skin dark and coarse.

They had fallen further than from the height of a cliff. They had fallen back through centuries of civilization. Jon had not meant to harm them.

Through a haze of fatigue and hunger, he realized that he had not be walking the beaches alone. From a distance, others would be following and waiting.

CHAPTER TWO

The space station fell through vacuum, a carousel rolling through the skies of Earth. The turning wheel fell in an arc that matched the curve of the landscape below, gravity and velocity balancing in an unending orbit. The turning of the wheel provided centrifugal force, an illusion of the same gravity the satellite used in its polar orbit freefall.

"He's not dead yet."

Base Commander Isaac Harper looked up from a desk screen at the slender, towering figure he had only vaguely sensed standing before him. He shifted mental gears, running a hand across a balding pate. Small dark eyes that still showed traces of an ancient oriental heritage betrayed no emotion.

"You told me he couldn't survive."

Coordinator Ida Moore looked down at the expressionless face through ice-blue eyes set against flat black skin. "I believe psychological factors play an important role in his survival to this point. That and his training in high-G fields."

Commander Harper leaned back in his seat, giving Moore his full attention. "Expand on that, Moore."

"Fighter pilots live with death," Moore said. "They function independently. We've seen pilots try to go

31

down in damaged fighters from time to time. This one made it. He landed uninjured and with his wits about him. We know the effect the Earth environment has on the human psyche. He'll survive as long as he can to experience as much of it as possible."

"How did he survive bacterial and viral contamination? A team of pathologists and a pharmaceutical lab would have trouble keeping a man alive down there."

"I'm an anthropologist," Moore said. "Expecting me to double as a pathologist is pushing a bit far. Commander, I don't know how he managed to survive. All I can say is that our Jovan fighter pilot is trying to survive, and he's had some luck on his side so far. But he can't make it much longer. He'll starve. Or he'll be killed by natives."

"Do you still have him under surveillance?"

"We lost him during some storm activity and thought he had been killed when his capsule was struck by lightning and exploded. But we kept a computer scan on the area. He fired a hand laser, probably in defense against a native attack. He's walking south along the beach. He's being tailed by a coastal tribe."

Commander Harper fell silent, his gaze shifting to a blank data screen. Ida Moore braced himself for the inevitable question.

"What are the chances that he'll stumble across the Valthyn?"

Moore felt a sudden influx of fear and anger. "Sir, I've suggested time and time again that you convince Luna Authority to play their wargames elsewhere. For as long as they've used Earth as a backdrop to their defenses in the wargames, they've risked just this sort of incident happening."

Harper glanced up sharply. "And I've told you what Luna Authority's response has been. It would be too much of a self-imposed handicap. It would be suspicious behavior."

"Perhaps. Fortunately, the Jovan won't survive long enough to cause us trouble. His concentrates must be exhausted by now."

"Let's hope so. I don't think either one of us enjoys the thought of being stationed on this base the day the Outer System Federation learns about the Valthyn. Keep me updated on the Jovan's movements. Let me know the moment there are further developments."

Ida Moore gave a curt nod. He turned and strolled from the office. The corridors outside were deserted, the station halfway through a sleep cycle. For him, sleep would not be possible.

Moore stopped off at the observation deck on the way back to his own office. The door slid open for him, the rush of cool air smelling stale. He stepped inside and the door slid shut behind him.

He stood on the inside of a rotating torus. Up was toward the hub of the station. He looked down through a transparent deck at the slowly turning stars, waiting for the bright globe of the Earth to swing into view. The planet had once looked like a very lonely world to him. Moore didn't know whether he pitied or envied the Jovan. He envied him for what he was experiencing, but pitied him knowing he must die soon. But he understood Luna authorities' panic at hearing of the Jovan survivor on Earth. Once, even he had felt secure knowing Earth to be uninhabited for all practical purposes, serving as little more than a large, nostalgic knick-knack of the solar system and reminding them all of their heritage and what they had lost and gained by their exile into space. The Jovan survivor made him feel unsettled and anxious, but the Valthyn made him feel bitter and directly frightened. Strangers had no right to be there. Earth didn't belong to them.

The savages following him grew bold. Several of the youngsters mock-stalked him, pressing close to the wall of the cliff and pretending that they couldn't be seen. Jon walked on and tried to ignore them.

His concentrates were gone, his canteen empty. Already he had tried drinking sea water to quench his fiery thirst. More and more often he staggered and dropped to his knees in the soft sand, taking the opportunity to rest for a moment before trying to stand and continue. During longer rest periods, he turned around and watched the group of primitives.

The children soared like birds confined to two dimensions, chasing and being chased by dogs emitting sharp barks of excitement. The adults stood scattered across the beach in small groups, the men leaning on their spears, engaging one another in animated conversation. The elderly sat in the shade of the cliff overhang and gazed out to sea. A group of young women were staring at him with open curiosity.

The squat stocky physiques of the natives were freakish, but he respected the sheer quantity of muscle necessary to cope with the gravity. He stood almost twice the height of the tallest of them, yet probably weighed less. He could take one full stride to their four, moving with a exaggerated slowness in contrast. Long and heavy hair covered the faces of the older males. Jon's thin, colorless hair seldom needed trimming. Interfering with a few genes had ended the need to shave.

These were the beginnings of racial differences. With man taking a hand in his own genetic makeup, the gulf between different peoples would widen rapidly. But Jon felt a kinship with rather than antipathy toward these simple people, hoping only that they'd do him the honor of letting him die by natural causes. Within hours, he'd be too weak to defend himself.

Despite his suffering, the world impacted with full

34

strength upon his senses. He and the world blended into a unity. He couldn't tell where he ended and the sky began or the tracings of clouds high in the stratosphere or the gulls wheeling and crying out over the ocean. Each creature that scurried from his path startled him like a chord of a symphony that struck with sharp clarity. In a way, his would be a death by ecstasy, not as futile as dying in super-heated vapors of a laser beam nor as tragic as streaking through Earth's skies as a burning meteor, so close to experiencing all of this and yet as far from it as the most distant star.

Jon tried to rise, then decided that this would be about as far as he could go. Consciousness deserted him by slow degrees. When the savages clustered around him, he could no longer separate reality from hallucinations of color and sensation plying his senses. He waited for the death they would give him, but instead, they lifted him from the sand and carried him forward along the beach. Bits and pieces of consciousness followed, but never connected into logical patterns.

Sometime later, dark walls of rock enclosed him. Sunlight glared through an oval opening like a large port in the passenger section of a transport. He lay on a bedding of something soft, but smelling of decay. His weight pressed on him and the dense air made it hard to breath. He tried desperately to rise, to get to the controls of his ship to adjust centrifugal spin and the life-support parameters.

At regular intervals, he drank cool, clear water. It came from nowhere and he had only to turn his head aside to stop the flow. At other times, the liquid tasted warm and thick with a strong odor. He drank desperately of it in an effort to satiate his unending hunger. The cool water remained water, but the warm liquid grew thicker, like concentrate, but inadequate. He spit out an occasional solid bit of substance in the broth with disgust. But approaching starvation made adaptation to some solid material easy.

He noticed eventually that a woman tended him— an old, gnarled, smelly woman with tangled, waist-length hair, the flesh of her face lined and pitted like the hull of an ancient cargo barge. One eye was missing, the other twinkling black beneath heavy brows. Her touch was always gentle and coaching. She displayed more patience and humanity than Jon had ever known.

He lay in a small cave, its entrance overlooking the ocean. Day and night, the surf roared incessantly, but that sound more than any other factor aided his recovery. The sea would be an intimate part of him for as long as fate allowed him to live.

The savages nursed him to health intuitively, by a patient process of trial and error. Feeding him became their most perplexing problem. He gagged reflexively on solid bits of food, but drank the thick broth they fed him. It never sufficed, even when it bloated his stomach. Always, the old woman remained alert to even his most intimate discomfort.

Others crept into the cave from time to time, standing against the far wall of the cave in the shadows and watching him for hours on end. Jon sensed their curiosity, sometimes a mild hostility, but always the same kind of reserved awe the old woman demonstrated. He knew himself to be on display, an item of curiosity and probably community property. From the beginning he worried about his laser pistol: It was missing from his belt.

They did not try to stop him when he finally rose from his bed of grass and stepped outside the cave to stand on a low ledge overlooking the beach. Obviously, he posed no physical threat to them standing like a slender giant. The entire tribe gathered around, clapping, laughing, calling, and chanting to him. Jon smiled. They were congratulating him on his recovery.

Off to one side, an outcropping of rock provided a convenient seat, Jon sat down in the sunlight, appreciative of the view. The glittering ocean stretched to the horizons before him, the surf surging and retreating at the base of a long, sloping beach. One by one, the beach people grew weary of the sideshow and went about their business, satisfied with an occasional glance to ensure that he hadn't wandered off. Leaving was the furthest thing on Jon's mind.

They were an unattractive, brutally strong, and massive people. Jon couldn't get over the way the children churned sand with their powerful legs. They ran incessantly and played games of physical prowess rather than the quiet, mental activities he would have expected of children absorbing the science and technology of civilization. The men easily carried loads that he could never have moved a single millimeter. Driftwood burned in circles of rocks every few meters along the cave entrances. Jon spent the remainder of the day watching the activities of his unexpected hosts.

Men constantly entered and left the camp, returning with small dead animals dangling in one hand, their spears grasped in the other. Women went to and fro with them, gathering driftwood along the beach or wooden buckets of fresh water, and selected pieces of vegetable matter from the forest above the cliffs. The older women hovered about the fires, horrifying Jon with the kinds of food they prepared and the way they prepared it. In the evening, the tribe waded waist-deep into the ocean with nets and spears, pulling fish from about the rocks offshore. Jon knew about fish, but had never seen one, not even on film.

Jon had already decided that there was no real purpose to life. Freed of the necessity of single-handedly providing for themselves with the basics of life, his people lived in a black vacuum and special-

37

ized in war. Why had they forgotton about Earth and its environment? These people were born fit simply because the defective did not survive. They relied upon their own wits for survival and life rewarded them with simple, all-encompassing pleasures. For what purpose would a self-maintaining, automated food factory free the beach people? Primitives? Savages? Perhaps. But Jon also saw another kind and another innate intelligence inherent in this environment. It existed at the level that gave rise to a natural world vastly superior to the technology of the space colonies. How long would it take technology to self-consciously recreate the given? His thoughts depressed him. Despite his intellectualizations, he still felt out of place and helpless.

From the first day, he stopped worrying about the laser pistol. The tribe built a vertical alter of stones of diminishing size. Upon the edifice they placed his pistol and battery pack. When Jon took to strolling the beach in the days to follow, he quickly learned to steer clear of it. The men were not frightened of him, but they were clearly terrified of allowing him to regain possession of the weapon.

Also from the first day, they tried to communicate with him. Everyone took a hand in the attempt at one time or another. They'd wander close by as if passing by coincidence, turn, and ask a question. Jon would reply to demonstrate that they spoke two entirely different languages. They taught him a new kind of language, one he intuitively understood, but had seldom used in a world where people communicated more often with computers than with other people—the language of expression and gesture. The beach people were good at it. It would suffice without undertaking a special effort to learn their spoken language or to teach them his.

When darkness fell, they made music and danced around the campfires. The music was simple, but with surprisingly complex rhythms beat out with sticks on hollow logs or stretched animal skins. The women often danced solo and nude, and did not manage to rekindle his desires for sex. At first, Jon assumed that he just found the women unattractive, but in the hypnotic beat of the dances, he came to realize that they frightened him with their power of life. He felt physically inferior to them despite his height and regal bearing. As well, a light depression had set in. Nothing could match the beauty of computer-generated and computer-synthesized music. Nothing could match the beauty of freefall ballet performed by slender, graceful colony women. But Jon had never before lived in the past. Trying to do so now would accomplish nothing. He couldn't go back to what had been. Instead of learning to live in this world, Jon soon discovered that he would be relearning his old way of life from new perspectives.

Jon learned about different kinds of ignorance. The beach people could live with theirs, but perhaps he'd not survive his. Not in their world.

Several young women were afflicted by stomach tumors. Jon avoided them in fear and disgust, classifying deviations of that kind with the mysterious word *disease*. But during one clear night, he heard a woman scream and an infant wail in the early-morning stillness. And in daylight, the young girl who had carried the largest tumor was flat-bellied and nursing a tiny infant at her breast. His blindness appalled and frightened him. What in Jupiter's name had he expected? Did he believe that even here the world couldn't function on its own without man's intervention and technology?

One hundred billion people lived off-earth, cultures and ways of life without end. Jon had been born on Phenomedon, the military fortress-city orbiting *Ganymede*, born and raised to perform one function in society—fighting. His first mission had sterilized him, only the engineered viral activity repairing what would have been lethal cellular damage. But his chromosomal pattern had been safely stored from birth in the digital symbology of computers to be synthesized and modified at will by the genetic engineers responsible for balancing whole populations. The women Jon had known, women he had considered normal in every respect, had not been physically capable of giving birth to their own children. In Jon's world, sex was social intercourse and children were born in state-operated baby factories. He had known that, theoretically, a man and a woman alone could give birth to a new life. He had just never taken the theory seriously.

Among the beach people, mated couples shared a deep emotional bond with each other and the children they produced. They lived with an intensity that insulted the emotional impoverishment that he had considered normal. But they suffered just as intensely. Two deaths occured only days apart. A child drowned, and the mourning and the depth of their anguish and bitterness alarmed Jon. An old man died, but by then, Jon felt sorrow and regret himself. The old man had smiled and nodded to him at every opportunity. Jon had recognized the inner wisdom accumulated by a man who had lived so long as to grow wrinkled and crippled. Nobody aged in Phenomedon. An individual losing that edge of mental and physical acuity that meant survival in a military society took a small, inexpensive craft into space and did not return.

Jon was beyond the standards of judgment of the beach people as they were beyond his. As time passed, Jon learned a compassion for them that stopped just short of fondness. They continued to forbid him to approach the laser pistol, but otherwise, he figured his entertainment value exceeded the cost of his upkeep. They enjoyed the giant that strolled their beaches.

Once, over two centuries ago, the space colonists had maintained zoos and living curiosities from Earth until it occurred to them that a species became a travesty separated from its ecology and environment. When it occurred to him that he fit the definition of a pet, the last of his feelings of superiority ended.

A commotion one night weeks after his arrival roused Jon to consciousness—human screams of pain and terror, cries of alarm and anger—and noises that no human could have made. Jon rolled from his grass mattress to his feet and ducked through the cave entrance to stand on the ledge overlooking the beach. A snarl and a howl of utter malignancy arose from within a semicircle of whirling, jabbing torches in the night. Jon had never seen the likes of the massive, four-footed animal with the twitching tail, but the fangs gleaming in the torchlight and the vicious swiping of claw-studded forepaws told the whole story at a glance.

A body lay on the sand in front of the animal. The tribesmen were stabbing desperately with spears and torches in an effort to rescue the young woman sprawled before the creature. It would not retreat, crouching and slipping forward to clamp its jaws on the girl's leg in an attempt to drag her into the shadows beyond the torches. A spear arcing from darkness skimmed the skull of the predator and rebounded. In a scream of pain and unutterable rage, the animal leaped and took one of the men down in a flurry of claws and fangs.

Jon dropped the meter height from the ledge to the sand without thinking. He hit the sand with a shock that sent him to his hands and knees. Regaining his footing, he limped toward the altar and the unguard-

41

ed laser. In one smooth motion, he slipped his hand over the stock of the weapon and clamped the battery pack to his wrist. He held his left arm across his eyes and fired into the air.

With an ear-splitting crack and a sharp hiss of ionization, the night fell abruptly silent. After-images swirled behind his closed eyes. When they faded, Jon opened his eyes. The animal stood alone, outlined in a fading, ultraviolet light, its eyes two mirrors of brilliant silver. Jon took careful, accurate aim, fired and fell to the sand before the blast of the explosion tore over him.

An eternity passed, his skin burning and itching furiously from the sandblasting his arms and back had taken. His field of vision was a mass of colored flame. The sound of the surf returned to his consciousness, then the darkness and the odors of the torches smoldering in the damp sand. Gradually, he heard muffled voices and children crying in the caves, finally a scream and a sobbing and an increasing chorus of frightened and excited voices.

Until he was sure he hadn't injured himself, Jon remained prone on the sand, convinced that it would be best to leave the tribe to their simple and yet complex lives. They could cope with death and go on living, but how could they live with the destruction he carried with him, a weapon that spoke of the blinding lights in the night skies of Earth when the gods fought in the heavens?

He returned to his cave before dawn, not knowing what to expect of the beach people. He thought they might slip off quietly in the night or chance surrounding him in the darkness in hope that a silent spear might rid them of the terror of the giant alien and his stick of lightning.

He puzzled over the women emerging from the caves at dawn. The fires had gone out and they bent to the tedious task of relighting them with dry kindling and slivers of shiny stone. Without looking in the direction of his cave, the hunting parties and gatherers of firewood and shellfish emerged. Only the children gave indication that anything unusual had happened during the night. They remained inside the caves.

The old woman prepared his morning meal. She placed a shell of steaming paste and a gourd of fresh water near the cave entrance. She kept her eyes averted and backed away in a silence that pervaded the whole camp.

Jon returned the laser to the altar. He took his bowl and gourd and retreated back to his cave. By late afternoon, the burial and mourning of the dead in the forest above the cliff had ended. Everything returned to normal—except that the guards at the altar were missing. The camp fell silent if he passed too closely. Jon avoided doing so. At least he had discovered a service he could render in exchange for sustenance. Each night the pistol was gently carried on a flat stone and placed at the entrance to his cave. Each morning before dawn it was returned to the altar.

Twin sisters took to dancing for him each night by the campfires. The camp fell silent while they danced, the music slow and haunting and all eyes focused on his reaction. He no longer shied away from the cautious attention paid to him by several of the women in camp, the sisters included. As his past life drifted into distances of time, the world of the beach people becoming an increasingly familiar reality, he experienced a gradual re-emergence of what had once been a modestly active sex life among the female fighter pilots of his squadron.

Sensing when they'd be accepted, the sisters entered his cave one night, standing before the small fire in the center. They tossed their fur clothing into the shadows, the rapid rise and fall of their breasts

43

assuring Jon that they weren't merely rendering him an obligatory service. Jon stalled his decision for a time, cherishing the way the fire cast shadows across the rich contours of their bodies. Later, when he learned to tell one from the other, he took care to alternate between the two of them.

When the newness of their relationship wore off, the sisters began taking turns, visiting him one at a time on alternate nights. It would have been an idyllic existence dulling the routine of his exile, but just as sex had its ritualistic obligations in his world, so apparently did it have among the beach people.

The entire camp turned out for the confrontation between Jon and an older woman escorting her two daughters to his cave early one morning. The old, one-eyed woman took up her position at Jon's side, the two women arguing in curt tones that spoke of some hurt or embarrassment. The mother of the twins had little trouble making herself understood. She used a bird egg and pointed with it to the bellies of her daughters, demanding to know why they hadn't become pregnant.

How could he explain sterility to these people? How could he tell them that his seed lay in storage near a bright star often visible in the night sky? He took the egg from the mother of the twins. He held the egg out to indicate a small brown bird on the beach, then a white gull wheeling out over the ocean.

The one-eyed woman caught on before the others. She shook her head and pointed to two brown birds on the beach to reveal her awareness that the brown and white birds could not interbreed. She did so with a tear in her one eye, already suspecting the truth. And Jon stood tall, towering above the tribe like a graceful tree swaying in the breeze. He pointed again to the gull and the brown bird and crushed the egg in his fist.

The sisters cried together in his arms for one final

night. The following day he saw them in the company of young men who had taken an interest in them long before they had considered mating together with the man from the stars.

Alone, he had as much of a life among these people as he would ever have. He felt isolated knowing the differences between them could never be fully bridged. Because of his size and his frailty, he could not hunt or trap or wade knee-deep in the ocean without being thrown off balance by the pull of the surf. The women would not allow him to perform their work.

His lanky frame filled out slightly, supporting as much muscle as it ever would. He could walk long distances, slowly and ponderously, but he could not run. He could not even afford to fall without risking injury. Dependent upon these strangers for his continued survival, Jon grouped together the assets of his life and concentrated on enjoying them. He grouped together the liabilities and estimated the suffering he would have to endure. Stoically, he settled into a daily routine and assumed that it would last until disease or injury or old age ended his life.

He seldom missed a sunrise or a sunset on a clear day. He walked the beach in the early mornings, napped in the early afternoons and reminisced late at night when the moon glittered in a swath of silver across the ocean. The young children enjoyed hanging from his tree height arms or playing games of tag that matched his reach and stride against their agility. The men would show him their kills for the day, competing against one another for acknowledgment of their prowess. And mothers would show him their newborn, sharing his sorrow as he studied the tiny detail and perfection of each new life.

Children ran panicky and screaming into camp a few hours after the dawn of a day of steel-gray skies.

The beach people had become increasingly reclusive during the dark, rainy days of late, but the excitement quickly spread. The men gathered their spears and moved down the beach at a trot. The women and children followed. Curious about the tones of anxiety and hostility in their voices, Jon followed. He fell behind until the group stopped a kilometer from the camp, gathering about in a semicircle at the foot of a short length of rock cliff.

The tribe stood silent and unmoving, staring at some pale object lying in the sand. As he approached, it looked to him to be a human body. He dismissed his initial impression, then reinstated it. He stopped outside the perimeter of the semicircle to peer over the heads of the beach people.

A tall, young woman lay on her back in the sand, her arms outstretched, one leg tucked beneath the calf of the other. High tide had washed sand over her feet. Jon could see no footprints in the sand. He glanced up the face of the cliff, estimating that she had fallen ten to fifteen meters. She couldn't have survived such a fall. She looked to have been civilized, her flesh tanned, but flawless, her features small and regular. A white gown was bunched about her shoulders.

The beach people murmured their disapproval as he pushed his way through the circle. He took a step forward and could feel the tangible swell of tension. They knew of this woman or her people and their reaction to her plight was a long way from that which he had received. Even in death they were frightened of her.

Instead of directly challenging their will, Jon walked in a slow circle about the body, gradually spiraling in closer. He took note of the expressions of loathing and disgust and sidelong glances of reluctant curiosity. Jon noticed a bad gash on the woman's right hip, but it hadn't occurred in the fall. Perhaps she had stumbled over the cliff during the night suffering the effects of the injury. As he neared, he could see many bruises marring the perfection of her skin.

A woman behind him cried out in anger. Jon turned and with a sweeping gesture, indicated that they all return to camp. Some of the men tightened their grips on their spears. Jon tensed, but managed to stare them down. When they turned to leave, Jon noticed that the woman who had cried out to him was one of the twin sisters. She herded a small child ahead of her. He couldn't help but notice that she was pregnant again.

When they were gone except for two young men backed into the shadows of the overhanging cliff, Jon knelt beside the body. Only then did he notice the slight movement of her breasts. He placed his hand on her chest, repelled by the coolness of her skin. But he could feel the beat of her heart.

Jon felt a surge of exhilaration. She lived!

He couldn't resist a selfish moment to gaze at her face and glance down the length of her body. Even by his old standards she was beautiful with thin, wide lips and large, widely spaced eyes. She had a broad forehead and sparse but long platinum hair. She could have passed as a colony woman anywhere except for her full-bodied build in relation to the willow-thin colony women. Jon knew Earth to be primitive without the least indication of civilization. His find excited him. He wanted desperately for this woman to live and to communicate with him.

With growing excitement, he inspected her arms and legs for broken bones. He could not be sure of spinal injuries, but if she had hurt herself that badly, there'd be nothing anyone could do for her. He tried to reason out a course of action, looking back along the stretch of beach and searching his memory for a secluded shelter he could use. He recalled a small cave halfway the distance to camp, a cave frequented by young, unmated couples. He decided to do them the disservice of confiscating it.

Jon looked at the two young men standing in the shade of the cliff wall. Curiosity had overpowered their fear of the woman. Jon gestured for the pair to approach. Both of them shook their heads vigorously, but only one of the young men dashed headlong down the beach without looking back. The second boy remained in place, oblivious to the absence of his companion. Jon recognized him, a particularly rebellious young man who displayed more than average intelligence among his peers.

Jon collected his thoughts. He could never intimidate the boy into helping. His hands brushed his utility belt in search of something relatively useless to use as a bribe. All he carried was his canteen. Under the circumstances, he had no choice. Already the boy had shifted his gaze from the magnificent body of the stranger to the canteen Jon unhooked from his belt. Jon held it out. The boy tensed, his eyes brightening with delight. He glanced nervously back toward camp, then hesitantly approached.

Jon drew the curve of the shoreline in the sand with his finger. He pointed out the location of the cave he had in mind. The boy nodded recognition, taking the canteen reverently with both hands. He clipped it onto a ragged hole in his skins.

Jon stood and gestured for the youth to pick up the unconscious body of the woman. The boy balked at making physical contact with what he thought of as a corpse. Jon took the boy's hand and slowly brought it down to the woman's shoulder. The boy spent a lost moment caressing the soft skin, captivated by her beauty, then glancing up at Jon in frightened embarrassment. Jon smiled and shrugged his lack of concern.

The young man slid his hands beneath the legs and shoulders of the woman, lifting her from the sand with such incredible ease that it startled Jon. Jon led the way back, but only for the first few meters. The boy easily outpaced him despite his burden, but patiently held back at times to allow the gangly, slow-moving alien to catch up. When they reached the cave, Jon ducked through the low overhang first and pointed out a dry spot in the sand. The boy slipped past him and lowered the woman to the ground. He nodded an anxious farewell to Jon and left without looking back.

Jon felt his heart hammering in his chest. If the woman died, the question of her origin would haunt him for the rest of his life. He had one more chance of obtaining a companion for his exile on Earth. He couldn't let this woman of such stunning beauty die.

CHAPTER THREE

Base Commander Isaac Harper sat behind his console desk with an expression of grim determination, his small dark eyes darting to each person that entered the room. He waited for the last of the group to seat themselves along the far wall. Project Coordinator Ida Moore glanced down the line of his subordinates, ensuring that they were all present. He gave a curt nod to Harper and sat down.

"Gentlemen," Harper said, the tone of his voice warning them of the documentary they were about to hear. "You're all aware of Luna Nation's policy toward Mother Earth. We have been its caretakers for five centuries. Even the Outer System Federation has allowed us economic compensation to monitor Earth's environmental security. To fail in that duty would be to have the fleets of every major colony in the system breathing down our necks.

"As you know, situations have developed upon the face of the planet. A potential for serious disruptions in relations with the outer worlds exists. We've informed the highest authorities on Luna of our findings. They are demanding two things of us. First, we are to gather as much information as possible of events transpiring on the surface and second, based upon our unique expertise, we are to formulate a policy to ensure that these events remain strictly confidential. The general populations of the space nations will never know of these events.

"There's not a man, woman, or child alive in the solar system who does not feel a deep nostalgia toward and a deep kinship with Mother Earth, a connection to our home world that is not often conscious, but powerfully influential upon our lives. On unconscious levels, we are just visitors in the open realm of space. We are colonists and explorers. We still have our roots in the ecology, the biosphere, and the environmental rhythms of Earth. Earth is visible in the skies of all the worlds of mankind. It remains a moral support for us all.

"We have psychologists and anthropologists who feel that it will be centuries and perhaps millennia before humanity becomes a child of the universe and gives up allegiance to a world that cannot support us. It's vital to recognize these two factors. We have deep emotional connections to our mother world but we cannot return. On a practical level, it's obvious that one hundred billion people couldn't possibly try to go back. On an even more practical level, most of us simply can no longer tolerate the physical conditions on Earth. But as long as Earth remains essentially an uninhabited paradise, humanity feels secure. Earth is a piece of real estate. It belongs to all of us and yet no one person holds claim to a single square foot of its surface. It's the sanctuary of our fellow creatures, the birds and fish and animals who are literally our Earth-kin.

"Please, emotionally grasp the validity of this fact. We are not yet secure in our new environment. If humanity or any part of humanity felt the security of Earth to be threatened, warfleets would circle Earth and men would destroy and die to defend what is, in reality, a deep psychic need.

"Assuming I've made my point, we're all aware of the presence of the Valthyn. We don't know who they are other than the fact that they're apparently a nontechnological human society. On the surface, they are primitives, but our only contact with them has been catastrophic. The Valthyn have power we do not understand and, because of this, we feel that they claim what is rightfully ours. The Valthyn know that humanity would try to destroy them if it knew of their existence. They know but they don't seem to care. It's as if they consider themselves capable of defending themselves and Earth from any harm that could befall them at the hands of a civilization that has always been expert in the art of wholesale destruction. And we can't be sure whether or not their confidence is misplaced."

Ida Moore glanced down the length of his grim-faced crew. They were all frightened as he felt frightened. They were all more or less aware of the facts already, but they had not as yet assembled them in quite the order of sequence as Harper's foreboding logic.

"We've assumed the Valthyn would never be much of a problem," Harper said. "They give no visible evidence of being a threat. We've never had any reason to believe that the space nations would ever learn of the Valthyn presence on Earth. It has been our discovery and our secret.

"Three years ago, a Jovan fighter pilot successfully entered Earth's atmosphere. He crash-landed uninjured. By careful use of his personal antibiotics and by a process of gradual adaptation to the environment while his life-support facilities aboard the escape capsule lasted, he managed to survive. He would have died of starvation, unable to function in the intense gravitational field, but was adopted by a tribe of primitives who fish and hunt along the Pacific coast of what was once an Earth nation called the

United States of America. Two days ago, this Jovan Federation fighter pilot encountered an injured Valthyn. By careful observation and analysis of his behavior, we are certain that the Valthyn is alive and will communicate with him."

A shock as tangible as an electric current rippled through the group. Moore exchanged ominous glances with those who looked his way. They knew he was in charge of the high-resolution photography of the project, suspecting that he had been the single individual to stumble across this new turn of events.

"Because of this development," Harper continued, "Luna Nation will declare the Earth regions as off-limits for further military engagements. We'll take no further risks with survivors crash-landing on Earth. As well, this observational outpost has been quarantined to ensure that no unauthorized information is released. All communication is restricted to official business and will be labeled ultrasecret.

"The absence of personal communication would appear suspicious. Therefore, it will appear to continue, but will be censored and rehearsed before open transmission. Any deviation from approved communications will result in the arrest and indefinite detention of friends and relatives on Luna, so adhere to established procedures carefully. In essence, we have a job to do and the more efficient we are at performing it, the sooner the situation will return to normal. Unfortunately, it will be frustrating work, gathering information and ensuring that none of it is released to unauthorized personnel. Are there any questions?"

One of Ida Moore's technicians stood. "From what I gather, sir, the Jovan fighter pilot is the only potential leak we have to be concerned about. The chances of his escaping Earth are zilch. Even if the Federation learned about the Valthyn through rumor, they dare not react. There are always stories drifting around of exotic societies of humans living on Earth."

"The Jovan's chances of surviving this long were zilch," Harper said. "The crisis exists as long as he lives."

"It still seems that we are overreacting to the situation," the technician said. "How can the Jovan possibly contact his own people to tell them about the Valthyn?"

"You're overlooking one minor point."

"Sir?"

"What if the Valthyn desire contact with off-world societies? Evidently, you don't believe what you've heard about the Valthyn."

"No, sir, I don't believe in witches. I believe the Valthyn are extremely dangerous for the reasons you've outlined, but I don't believe they are omnipotent or stupid."

"I don't like being oppressive, young man, but our job isn't to speculate or ask questions. Our job is to collect data and ensure that nobody else has reason to speculate or ask questions. Do I make myself clear? There's a considerable gravity well separating the Valthyn from the rest of humanity. It's our job to keep it an impenetrable barrier."

Jon wove a bed of soft grasses and an insulating cover for the unconscious woman. He built a small fire in a circle of stones, feeding it with twigs until larger logs dried and began burning. He removed the woman's white gown, studying the smooth texture and fine weave of the material. It wasn't synthetic material, but neither was it the work of primitives. Beyond that, he could do little for her. He touched water to her lips, but she didn't seem to be dehydrated. He considered injecting her with his antibiotics, deciding it could do little harm and possibly a great deal of good.

During the afternoon, it began to rain again. Jon dug

a shallow drainage ditch in front of the cave, then walked back to the camp to pick up his meager belongings. He wondered how the beach people might react to this turn of events. They stood around and watched, but did not interfere. To let them know he wasn't leaving permanently, he left his laser pistol behind on the altar.

He returned with his grass mattress, a gourd, a shell bowl, and a flat stick he used as a spoon. The cave had warmed considerably. The woman had not moved, her head tilted back slightly, her face as still as a sculpture made by an artist who knew of beauty, but not of human expression. The remaining chore was to return to camp before nightfall and try to beg food from the old, one-eyed woman. She would not refuse him, he suspected. She had adopted him as a son, caring for his mundane needs now, but probably recognizing that he would not be able to provide for her in return during her declining years. Even in this, his closest relationship with the beach people, he would fail.

But when he left in the late afternoon with a dense mist shrouding the beach, he found a platter of warm food and dry firewood waiting just outside the cave. A large gourd set on the sand in the open had already collected enough rain water to last the night.

Half the food was mashed into a paste for him, the other half a collection of warm dried meat and vegetables for the unconscious woman should she return to life. Which meant that the beach people would provide for the both of them even though they had been willing to allow her to die. They knew her, if not as an individual, then as a member of a tribe or a society they had encountered in the past. It made sense. If they were fearful enough to let her die, they'd be fearful enough to cater to her should she survive.

Jon sat with the unconscious woman for three

days, forced to care for her personal sanitation just as the old woman had cared for him during his period of convalescence. He felt guilty at having to be that intimate with a complete stranger, but nothing mattered in contrast to his need for companionship. He had a thousand questions to ask of her even if it took years to learn her language. If she chose to leave the beach, Jon was determined to follow.

Jon left the wound on her hip exposed to the air. It healed incredibly fast. The open wound closed without scarring despite the amount of scar tissue that should have formed over it.

She awoke on the sunny dawn of the third day, too weak to sit, but hungry and thirsty. Jon sat beside her and propped her up by her shoulders, spoon-feeding her fresh food and rain water. She smiled and acquiesced to his touch without concern, oblivious to her nudity. She bewildered Jon by showing no curiosity toward him or her surroundings. He had spend a considerable amount of time bracing himself for her reaction toward him. How could she take for granted the sight of a frail giant in a metallic blue-and-gold flight uniform?

He didn't try to speak to her. He hadn't uttered a complete sentence since his arrival on this world. But, then again, he had spent most of his life in isolation. He used language as a tool and kept it put away when not in use. Even his internal dialogue had all but faded away in the constant roar of the ocean.

Jon had his back turned to her when she spoke.

"I speak your language."

Jon didn't turn around immediately. How? How could a native of Earth speak a language used halfway across the solar system?

"How do you feel?" Jon turned to the woman, suddenly frightened by this unexpected turn of events.

"I feel well."

57

She spoke his language with an odd, lilting accent. She couldn't be native to Earth to have recognized his origin so quickly and with so little surprise.

"What happened?" he asked.

"I frightened a bear with newborn cubs in the night and fell from the cliff in the darkness."

"How do you come to speak the Jovan language? There's not supposed to be anyone living on Earth above the level of the beach people."

"Is it so terrible for someone to have made an error?" The woman smiled.

"Then you recognized me when you awoke."

She nodded. "I recognized you."

Jon returned the woman's smile, pushing aside the mystery of her sudden recovery. "I am Jon. I'm the only Jon on this world so I don't believe my full identification code will be necessary for an introduction."

"And I am Lisa of the Valthyn, the only Lisa of my people. Welcome to Earth, Jon of the outer worlds."

Lisa sat cross-legged on the sand floor of the cave, the small campfire dancing warm flames between them. She wore her white gown that the beach people had cleaned for Jon and returned to the cave. Outside, the white moonlight washed across the beach from a clear sky. The surf sounded calm and subdued this cool night. Earlier in the evening, it had stormed.

"Why won't you answer my questions?" Jon asked, breaking a silence that had lasted an uncomfortable hour.

Lisa looked directly at him, her light brown eyes flashing in the firelight. He should have suspected something amiss when her wound had healed so impossibly fast. Jon had never seen a human being so alive. She had frightened him from the moment she had awakened and his fear hadn't abated since.

58

"Jon, a question can be worded so that a reasonable answer is impossible. Your questions will be answered. I remember each and every one of them."

Jon could not hold her steady gaze. He looked out into the moonlight.

"I'm not what you expected," she said.

"You say your people have no technology and yet you know of the space nations. How?"

"If the beach people asked how you could talk to men on other worlds, how would you answer them?"

"I'm not sure they'd understand," Jon said.

"If I said that I have the same problems answering your questions, would you say that I deceive you?"

"I don't know what to think," Jon said. "I guess you're not what I expected."

"I would apologize if it would accomplish anything," Lisa said, her voice softening. "What is done cannot be undone. I am what I am. I can leave if you wish. Otherwise, you must try to understand what I say to you."

Jon glanced up at her, appalled by her benign aggression. "Will you be leaving?"

"Not without you. You must come with me."

"I must?" Jon said, startled. "What do you mean I must?"

Lisa flashed a brilliant smile. "I mean that the choice is yours. There are alternatives. But you must."

"I've been dependent upon the beach people," Jon said. "If I left with you, I'd be dependent upon you. I don't know anything about you or your people. I have to know more."

"I can provide as they have provided," Lisa said. "If it takes time for you to learn to trust me, we have the time."

Jon stood and went outside. He watched the moon descend to the ocean. It was almost as if she had been planted for him to find, as if their encounter had

59

been arranged. She had awakened whole and well, prepared to leave immediately—with him.

Jon glanced down the beach. He could see nothing of the beach people, only the light of the fires burning along the sand. It would be easy to turn his back on this enigmatic and frightening woman and return to his own cave. The entire episode felt like something taking place in a dream, overwhelming him with its incomprehensibility. Who was she? Who were her people? But he didn't want to hear any more of her vague answers to specific questions. For one tense moment, he would have started walking without looking back if she had spoken to him.

Something very strange was happening. As the minutes passed in silence, Jon felt some of his fear taken over by an old solemn sense of responsibility. He had never run from danger in his life and he wouldn't start now. A society existed on Earth that spoke the languages of the space nations. Even if for his own satisfaction only, he would find out as much about it as possible.

When he turned back to the cave, Lisa had pulled off her gown and had stretched out on her grass mat. Her hands were crossed behind her neck and she gazed up at the ceiling of rock as if lost in thought. Her physical beauty reached the heights of irresistibility. Even her effervescent manner would have appealed to him had it not been mired in so much unnecessary mystery. Watching her lying in the warm light of the fire and the colder light of the setting moon, Jon thought that she might be attempting to seduce him, encouraging him to take a first step toward dependency upon her. But even as he watched, she closed her eyes and fell asleep. The rise and fall of her breasts slowed to where he didn't feel it to be a deception.

Jon ducked back inside the cave. He lay down on his own mat fully dressed and watched Lisa sleep until the shaft of moonlight faded completely. The fire became glowing embers and all the liabilities of his exile faded with the light. She had said that she would not leave without him. Even in the darkness and the stillness of the night he took comfort in the presence of another living, aware human being near him. Tomorrow, he would press harder and find out who she was.

They walked along the water's edge, alone in a world of sea and sky. Lisa walked slightly ahead of him, a saunter in her walk, but with an expression of studied thought.

"Jon, if you encounter something new to your experience, you tend to interpret it in ordinary ways, try to force fit it into old frameworks of thinking. You ask who I am. You think if I supply a name and my activities in life and explanations for my behavior, your question will be answered. If I answered in that fashion, you would still believe that I avoided a honest and direct answer."

"I don't see the sense in incorporating a lot of esoteric philosophy in life," Jon said. "If you have something to tell me, just tell me. You know the kind of information I need to make personal decisions. Why do you disregard its importance to me?"

"Because the truth is of more importance to you. If it is time to begin answering your questions directly, then we shall begin with the Valthyn. We are human, Jon, but we have origins that will be difficult for you to understand. There are new concepts for you to learn in order to avoid a blindness that you cannot afford."

"I don't know what you're talking about," Jon said in an even tone of voice.

"The Valthyn have no biological or cultural history. We have no origin in time and space as you understand it. We are something new to your experience. Your questions are as difficult for me to answer as it was difficult for you to satisfy the curiosity of the beach people. You ignored the questions implied by their behavior. Why did they choose to care for you if not out of curiosity?"

"I couldn't communicate with them!"

"You made no effort, Jon. They would have asked you who you are and you would not have been able to give them the simple answer they anticipated. That is my problem. I do want to answer your questions. I want you to know who I am. But you have much to learn before you will understand my answers. So I refuse to give direct answers."

Lisa's chain of logic unsettled Jon. He remained silent, bracing himself for an explanation.

"We met in the most advantageous circumstances possible, Jon. You know me as a woman vulnerable to the same hazards in the world that you face. On that level, it is the truth. But if you continue to refuse to listen to what I say to you, you're risking considerable shock when it becomes clear to you that I am not what I seem to be or what you try to make of me. Jon, even a question is framed in anticipation of a specific answer."

Jon knew his anger to be born of fear. His common-sense perception of the world told him that she deceived him with fantasies, but another part of him knew something to be amiss.

"Jon, you are being stubborn. I'm not playing word games with you. I have no ulterior motives for parrying your questions as I have and I don't mean to sound vague and deceptive. I have been as direct and honest with you as is possible. I don't mean to insult you, but it is your ignorance that blinds you to the answers I have given to your questions, an ignorance that narrows your focus of perception to a kind of world I don't belong to."

Jon stopped, unable to proceed further. She spoke utter nonsense and yet she spoke a language she could not have learned on Earth. She spoke nonsense and yet she had returned from the brink of death bubbling with her aggressive fantasies of being something more than a barefoot primitive. Lisa stopped as well, her back to him. Water lapped at her bare feet. Her wind-blown gown outlined the curve of her tall slender body. She stood with an unconscious pride, her head tilted back as if watching the gulls wheeling overhead. But he could sense her looking inward, somehow observing his reaction to her.

"Jon, listen to what I say and observe. You entered this world as a choice of life over death. You chose to allow your life to intersect with the unknown. If you suffer insecurity, abide with me. You strained against the bonds of slavery and shattered them. If you are free now, it is a freedom that carries with it a responsibility. It is a freedom in a new world you will have to learn to understand. Learning can be an uncomfortable experience, Jon, but only when you resist."

Jon would not have been able to face her had she turned around. She continued to stand with her back to him. Her gown fluttered in the wind, then slowly fell to brush against the sand, the white cloth gracefully draped from the width of her hips.

But the wind had not died. It whipped Jon's hair, and capped waves of the ocean in white froth. The trees above the beach thrashed quietly in the wind and the gulls overhead hovered in place. Lisa stood in a zone of utter stillness.

Hackles rose along Jon's back. When Lisa turned slowly, Jon began backing away from her.

"Fear of the unknown is the most terrible of fears," she said, her voice soft and yet carrying against the wind. "Luna Nation knows well how you feel. When it occurs to you that Earth is inhabited by a force superior to the technology of your own people, you will begin to feel alienated from this world. And then you will feel anger. You could not at one time walk this world or breath its air, but you feel that it belongs to the space nations even more than it belongs to the simple people who still live upon its surface. And the Valthyn, Jon? What will we become now that you know of our existence? Will we be trespassers? Invaders? Enemies, Jon?"

Jon turned and began walking.

"I can see your thoughts, Jon. I can see what you feel and know how you will behave. I know why we have been brought together and I know where it must lead. To you, the abilities I will demonstrate will mean power, a tool to be used to control and manipulate for one's personal gain. It will be a while, Jon, before you understand."

Jon tried to walk faster to escape her soft voice that penetrated the wind and the distance so clearly. He strained against his long, slow stride.

"Jon?"

He slowed, her voice suddenly so soft, he stopped to hear her words.

"I would have died. You are all I have left in this life. Take what time you need. I'll be waiting."

Jon finally remembered that the change in season caused by the tilt in the Earth's axis brought on the cold and wet weather. This would be winter and he feared for the snow, wondering if the ocean would freeze and if the world would become uninhabitable. After all, Earth was in the grip of a new ice age. Glaciers had pushed down below what were once the northern boundaries of the United States.

Fog often shrouded the beach, especially in the early-morning hours. Lisa could be seen at times through the haze, standing like a phantom with her gown blowing in the wind. When she appeared, the beach people retreated to their caves. During the first night, one of the twin sisters came to his cave with a haunted, frightened expression. He knew the beach people had forced her to abandon her family to come to him, trying to appease the turmoil his unrest caused among the tribe. Jon sent her away.

Fear spread like a contagion through the tribe. They stationed guards outside his cave at night to awaken him whenever imaginary terrors lurked along the beach, hidden in the perpetual gloom. Feelings of sadness and longing emanated from the foggy shores to the north in the late evenings. Lisa waited for him, literally broadcasting her strange need of him.

Lisa claimed to be human. Jon believed her. The Isinti, a small colony orbiting just beyond the rings of Saturn, had proven for centuries that the human mind had a greater depth than society as a whole cared to explore. He remembered what he had read about so-called paranormal aspects of reality published by the Isinti and filed in the public data banks. He recalled mention of how man had always stumbled across evidence of the unknown aspects of both outer and the inner reality of the human psyche. Science leaped upon the physical evidence of the unknown to add to the power of science and technology, but man had shunned adding to the scope and depth of his understanding of human consciousness, as if trying to keep it within easily understood and controllable limits.

From the official perspective, only the irrational and emotionally disturbed sought for those nonexistent powers of the mind as a cheap shortcut to personal power. The culturally sane insisted that reality had no depth beyond the physical senses or instrumental extensions of them. But the Isinti scathingly accused such official points of view of being both wrong and repressive, redefining cultural sanity as a form of psychopathological behavior. In retaliation, orthodox scientific authorities standing behind and supported by the governments of the Outer System Federation had ostracized the colony of fifty million for centuries. The general public could easily have rejected the propaganda, but what the Isinti had discovered discouraged the rest of mankind from following in their wake, a definition of reality that shifted the burden of responsibility for human experience away from statistical theory and probability and on to the individual.

Some of Jon's fears would not fade in the light of reason. He'd be as helpless within Lisa's sphere of influence as the beach people among the space nations. The discovery of a society superior to the space nations in terms of both knowledge and power would be a cataclysmic event in history. If Luna Nation knew of the Valthyn presence, they were sitting on one of the most dangerous time bombs in history.

On a personal level, Jon did not believe Lisa to be evil, but facing her would be like facing a reflection of himself and having that reflection speak and reveal to him the fearful depths of his own psyche. Lisa would be seeing in him parts of himself that he had never known.

Telepathy? Psychokinesis? What were the limits of such powers?

More out of a growing and insatiable curiosity than any personal virtue of courage, Jon took out along the north shore in an early-morning fog, knowing she'd be waiting. They sat together on two flat rocks beneath the dark overhang of the cliffs. The surf pounded around them.

"What do want of me?" Jon demanded to know. "You said we were brought together for a purpose. What did you mean by that?"

"If I explained now, you would fear being used by me," Lisa said. "But consider this. Luna Nation has watched you from the day you first arrived on Earth. They know you have survived. They are considering destroying you."

Jon had assumed that he had been written off as dead. But he hadn't known of the Valthyn then. "You're saying that I'm involved regardless."

"Indirectly, yes. Your presence here has been a crisis from their perspective since your landing."

"Why would I be safe with you? A battle laser could as easily take out the both of us."

Lisa smiled. "There have been incidents in the past. Together, they would not harm us."

"Am I being used?" Jon asked.

"Yes," Lisa said. "If you choose to be used."

"I hang from my fingertips here," Jon said, nodding back toward camp. "I don't like the idea of letting go."

"If you remain, you will harm the beach people. You can handle events intruding upon their world from yours. They cannot."

That had already occurred to Jon. That consideration alone tipped the scales. "Where will we go?"

"I could show you more of this world than you can discover on your own," Lisa said.

Before the beach people emerged from their caves in the gray, predawn light, Jon returned to the camp and gathered together his laser pistol and battery pack, his antibiotics stored beneath his mattress, a gourd for collecting rain water and a flat shell for eating. He had no idea of how they'd survive together in the wilderness, trusting in his observation that Lisa had not suffered hunger or thirst during the days she had spent alone on the beach. Jon feared the unknown as much as any man and now found himself dependent upon it for survival.

Jon left his cave for the last time. He ducked beneath the overhang of the entrance and dropped lightly the meter to the ground, forgetting the hazard it had once posed to him. The beaches remained deserted—except for one person. She stood off to one side, a small and lonely human being.

Jon walked over to her, towering above the aging, one-eyed woman. She had looked so grotesque to him at one time. Now, he saw only a quiet and noble beauty in her crippled body. With tears in her one eye, she held a small flat stone and a sharp piece of rock in her gnarled hands. Jon knew what they were for.

He knelt in front of her, still reaching her height with his knees in the sand. She leaned against his right shoulder and used the flat stone and rock to cut a piece of his thin, colorless hair. She would tie the hair clipping onto a cord of animal gut and wear it around her neck. The beach people wore such trinkets in remembrance of the dead.

On impulse, Jon removed the small radiation badge still clipped to his collar. He took the hair clipping from the old woman and clamped the badge around it. Her hand shook as she took the badge from him. It would be something more than just a memento for the old woman. The legend of the giant from the stars who had lived among the beach people would not soon be forgotten. The old woman would be cared for by the tribe if only to keep her stories of him alive.

She turned and hobbled slowly away, not looking back. Jon walked the other way toward a new life.

Jon found walking to be the most impractical form of transportation imaginable. Lisa stood tall and slender by the standards of the beach people, but small and full-bodied walking alongside him. Fortunately, his long, slow pace evenly matched her shorter, quicker steps.

They walked north for the day and slept on the open beach with a small campfire between them. In the morning, panicky over his growing hunger and thirst, Jon followed the woman east into dry grasslands.

Before midmorning, Lisa found a snaking, narrow creek of clear water. With an incredible agility and an absolute knowledge of her environment, she wove a net of vine tendrils and caught five, small, silvery fish. Striking pieces of translucent white stone together, she started a fire and fed it dried twigs, then larger branches broken in even lengths. While the fire grew, she collected several kinds of fruit from nearby trees. She fried the fish on a flat stone and showed Jon how to pick the flesh from the delicate skeletons. He hadn't as yet tried a diet of solid food, but his stomach no longer objected. He ate more than he would once had thought possible, but even so, they'd be stopping three or four times a day for the large numbers of smaller meals he'd require. During the first two days of their eastward trek, his diet varied more than he could have imagined.

Lisa entangled Jon in a fascinating array of details of the life and the variety of terrain of this massive world. He followed Lisa in an awestruck daze, his senses bombarded by the broad spectrum of things to perceive in this never-ending panorama of life. They stopped to watch a spider build a web, a bird feed its nested young, a snake weave its way through the grass, and two dragonflies mating on a reed by the shore of a small pond. Lisa explained the life cycles of insects and birds, and had the uncanny ability to encounter coincidentally a wide variety of creatures that Jon considered dangerous. He saw cats of several kinds, wild dogs and goats scampering the sides of low rocky hills. Herbivores grazed in large numbers in the flat grasslands. She told him that much life had been eradicated by the Holocaust, but that life had sprung from hidden sources since then, mutating and evolving rapidly to fill every ecological niche that had existed before man dominated his world.

"It's a different world in some respects," Lisa said. "Earth is gearing itself for a new area of experimentation and life will proliferate. The Earth itself is alive and it knows that man has been nurtured, weaned, and has left the womb. New kinds of intelligence will develop."

"People still live here," Jon reminded her.

"The beach tribes, the mountain dwellers, and the plains hunters will grow in new ways. Technology will not be their focus as it was for the ancestors of the space nations. And yet civilizations will develop that will rival your own in knowledge and complexity."

"But you understand technology," Jon said.

"If you see ways in which technology could provide me with a better life, tell me of them."

Jon thought of conveniences of transportation, shelter, luxuries of food and drink, sanitation, and entertainment. But it would have made all that he now experienced unnecessary, bringing back an old, intimate problem to haunt him—what to do with his life. Here, asking the purpose of life didn't seem to be a relevant question. Waiting for long periods of time in a damaged fighter, drifting through the silent void helpless and trapped, it had been the most vital question he could ask of himself.

"Technology gave birth to a people who will inhabit the stars and live in places where natural lifeforms cannot," Lisa said. "That, in itself, is an enviable accomplishment. I am not saying that the effort is misguided. It is not. But it is just one focus. You cannot imagine the other forms that civilization can take. Now that you have been removed from your artificial environment and your old direction in life, you will be shown other ways of thinking and ways of living. One is not superior to another. All ways complement one another."

"This isn't just idle conversation," Jon said. "Why are you telling me all this?"

Lisa looked surprised. "What enters the mind of one man enters the mind of the race. What you learn on a conscious level your people will have access to on an unconscious level."

"Why bother with me? It's in your mind, the minds of your people. Why am I important?"

She glanced at him with an expression of concern. "I am not of your race. The Valthyn stand alone."

"Tell me of your people, then."

"Soon," she replied.

It rained in the distances, walls of dense gray fog draping from sun-edged clouds. They could walk through a landscape sparkling with freshly fallen rain, but the showers were always occurring elsewhere. Lisa walked unerringly to sources of food and water, zigzagging on a generally easterly direction. She would launch upon a dissertation of one kind or another in response to his unspoken curiosity, falling silent when his attention waned. The rapport between them intensified to where Jon couldn't tell at times where his thoughts ended and hers began.

They made love for the first time in the dawn of a morning before Jon had fully awakened, moving together with a perfect harmony of body and mind that Jon knew he'd never experience with anyone else. Even if he resented Lisa's dominance over his life, they shared their complementary physical needs with a deep, mutual affection. Afterward, they lay nude to a warm sunrise, sprawled out on a dense lawn of moss. Insects spiraled and danced in sunbeams slanting nearly horizontal through an early morning haze. During the night, thunder had rolled across the landscape. Toward the east, a ridge of blue mountains had risen above the horizon.

"You know me better than I know myself," Jon said. "But when we make love, you respond like any woman I've ever known."

"It will be the only real bond between us," Lisa said, gazing into the clear morning sky without expression. "I've never known myself in that way."

"Why? Is there something wrong with the men of your people?"

Lisa flashed him a tolerant smile tinged with humor. "There are no men among my people."

"Lisa, one way or another, you had to have had a father." Jon laughed, wondering if humanity had finally seen a turn about in the ancient war between the sexes.

"I had no father," Lisa said. "There are no men among the Valthyn, Jon. The first Valthy gave birth to a daughter by the process you call parthenogenesis. The child was a genetic copy of its mother. The Valthyn are women. We give birth to ourselves. At first, the process was spontaneous, but when we knew who we were, the choice of pregnancy became ours.

"We are a different expression of humanity, Jon. We are not born forgetting our origin and purpose in life. We are expressed in physical terms to accomplish something quite specific. Our own lives on Earth were finished long ago."

Lisa continued to stare into the morning sky. Jon rolled onto his side to face her. He tried to imagine a society of genetic copies identical to Lisa. "You've lived before," he said.

"Life is bounded by birth and death, barriers beyond which men have not explored. They should have been your first frontiers to conquer. Instead, they will be your last. That has been your decision."

"Words alone don't threaten me," Jon said. He felt a chill despite the warming sun, but didn't know how to express the deep-seated unease he felt.

"It's enough for you to believe that I am not a threat to you, Jon. The Valthyn are not a threat to your people or your way of life. We will seem to be for a while, but our enemy is mutual. If is fear and the terrible things people do to defend themselves against it."

CHAPTER FOUR

Commander Isaac Harper met Moore in the photo labs. Ida Moore had already taken steps to ensure the lab and adjacent offices would be empty. Nobody had dared question the reason for the 12-hour recreational passes he had handed out. In addition, two security guards were present, but waiting outside to make sure they wouldn't be disturbed.

Moore cleared off a table in the center of the room. From a folder, he withdrew a photograph and set it on the table. Commander Harper did not visibly react to the 20x30-centimeter color photo of a nude woman taken from a full frontal perspective. The graininess and distortion in the photograph offered him the only clue he needed to identify the subject and her relation to the camera. The photo had been taken from orbit. The woman lay on her back, gazing into the sky, seemingly to gaze directly into the camera over a 160 kilometers overhead.

"This is the Valthyn woman," Harper stated.

"I didn't intent to startle you, sir, but it's the clearest and most valuable picture we have of the woman."

"She's quite beautiful. Startle me more often."

Moore placed other photographs beside the first one. Several showed the woman and the Jovan engaged in sex. Others were of an apparent conversation between the two.

"These stills were taken from film," Moore explained. "I've made arrangements to show it to the staff, but you'd better hear what I have to say first."

"Why? What's the problem?"

Moore paced in front of the table, seldom taking his eyes from the photographs. "She speaks the man's language."

Harper stiffened, angered at having the implications of Moore's disclosures escape him so readily.

"That's difficult to believe," he said in a level tone. "The Valthyn have had no contact with the Jovian nations. They have no electronics, no means of eavesdropping on radio transmissions. Most of those are in high-speed code and altered for computer-synthesized speech. I know they're supposed to be telepathic, Moore, but I can't believe—"

"We can't afford that error, sir. Belief is irrelevant. She speaks the man's language. As you can see, she's lying on her back, looking into the sky as she speaks. Despite the atmospheric distortion, we have managed to read her lips quite clearly. She's telling this Jovan about herself and her people. We've eavesdropped and learned things we've never imagined possible. This is the most revealing information we've received so far on the Valthyn and the relationship between the Jovan and this particular woman."

"This is amazing material, Moore, but it's what we've been after since this project began."

"Sir, the Valthyn wasn't speaking to the Jovan alone."

Commander Harper sighed, searching with a quiet desperation for any other implication he might have missed, not at all prepared for another shock.

"Sir, she was looking directly into the camera," Moore said. "I'm convinced she was aware of the

74

surveillance."

Harper glanced again at the photos, feeling a sense of relief, but convinced that Moore had cracked under the pressure brought to bare for a solution to the Jovan-Valthyn contact by the Luna Nation government. The quarantine amounted to virtual imprisonment. The photographs were disturbing, and it did appear as if the woman gazed directly into the camera, but outright paranoia would make it impossible to solve the very real mysteries begging for understanding. Even the mystery of the woman speaking the Jovan tongue could be explained by a prior survivor that the Lunan observational satellites had missed.

"Moore, the satellite that took this picture is two meters in diameter. It was one hundred and sixty kilometers directly overhead traveling at twenty-seven thousand kilometers per hour. It wouldn't even have been visible at night and certainly wouldn't have been in daylight."

Moore rearranged the photographs, laying five of the series down the length of the table. They looked the same, but upon closer examination, Harper could see a progressive variation in perspective in each one. The nude woman did not move except for slightly different positions of her lips as she spoke to her Jovan lover.

"If you're trying to make a point, Moore, spell it out! I haven't the time to play games."

"Commander, the first photograph is the first clear image we obtained as the satellite approached from the northeast. The center photograph, the clearest one, was taken from directly overhead and the last one as the satellite passed into the southwestern skies. The woman is looking directly into the camera in each shot. Her gaze has been analyzed to have been accurate to within several hundredths of a degree. She knows the satellite is there and she's telling us that she's aware of our presence and our activities."

"She could not have known," Harper muttered.

"Sir, it's difficult enough to accept what we already know about them. The Valthyn can kill at a distance. And it doesn't take statistical analysis to verify that they're telepathic. They can communicate in that way as easily as we can talk to one another. We could have deduced that she'd be able to speak his language. But in our own minds, we've isolated them on the face of the Earth. We've assumed that distance provides the barrier of protection we need from these people. I don't think any barrier exists, Commander."

Harper had used fear of Valthyn omnipotence to overkill the seriousness of the matter in the minds of Luna Authority, using simple deduction as a tool for his own purposes. But the Valthyn hadn't caused any trouble since the last Earth-landing mission. Why now? His guts were knotted in anxiety. To think that he had actually felt guilty exaggerating the Valthyn menace to ensure that they'd remain hidden on Earth, out of sight and out of mind.

"There's more, Commander," Ida Moore said, waiting for the officer to return from a journey down the corridor of his own thought processes.

"I know there's more, Ida. You know as well as I what might happen if they deliberately expose themselves."

"It's not them, sir. It's us. I think Luna Authority will be frightened enough by this new development to order these two individuals destroyed by an orbital battle laser. If Luna Authority considers the threat extreme enough, I believe they'll go as far as considering at thermonuclear attack on Valthyn settlements."

Harper didn't want to hear any more conjecture and speculation, but he didn't quite manage the courage to stop the Project Coordinator from speaking.

"Those are irrational extremes, Moore," he said in a tight voice.

"Yes, but there are other things that these photographs imply. This kind of power is inhuman. The Isinti prove that clearly demonstrable psychic powers exist, but the Isinti are nerve-racking in comparison to the Valthyn. The Valthyn are terrifying. They're going to be accused of being nonhuman, alien invaders who've sneaked in under our noses and taken over the Earth without anyone noticing. Already I think the situation is heading toward a crisis of unprecedented proportion."

Commander Harper leaned against the table, his back to the photographs. "Moore, you've obviously had time to think things through. You know you've caught me off balance."

"I'm not taking advantage of you," Moore said quietly. "Sir, we have to anticipate that Luna Authority will think in terms of violence in trying to neutralize this threat despite our previous run-ins with the Valthyn. For our own safety, we have to move to stop this from happening. We need direct contact with these two people. The Valthyn woman relates well with the Jovan. She might speak with us as well if we approach her directly and honestly. The Valthyn are dangerous, but we have no evidence to feel that they are monsters or invaders. At any rate, we can't afford to continue guessing about this situation and having our wildest speculations proved too conservative to be of use."

"Moore, if you're thinking of a landing mission, it's forbidden. That's a matter of treaty among all the space nations these days."

"Then we'll have to cheat on it. We need to learn more about these two people. If the Jovan ever returns to the outer world settlements with what he has learned. . . ."

"That can never happen," Harper said, ashamed of

having to contradict his own previous statements.

"If the Valthyn want it to happen," Moore said, "it will happen. We need to know why."

Jon and Lisa walked northeast for three days. By the end of the third day, Jon discovered that he could keep pace with Lisa without tiring frequently. His long, slow stride amused the woman, but Lisa's purposeless, incessant activity no longer frustrated or irritated Jon. He began enjoying the walking and camping and sleeping in the open. He had never undertaken any physical activity without at least rationalizing some purpose for it. The habit died hard.

"Where are we going, Lisa?"

"We have no particular destination, Jon."

"It seemed that you had one in mind when we left the beach."

"I had to separate you from the beach people," Lisa said. "You would have returned to them to escape me."

"I thought you might take me to meet your people."

"That could have been, but no longer. The Valthyn have broken into small groups and are moving away from one another."

"Luna Nation?"

Lisa nodded. "They have considered attempting to destroy us. We have removed the temptation from the realm of possibility."

"How do you know what Luna Nation intends to do? It's a light in the night sky four hundred thousand kilometers from here. There are two billion people living on the moon."

"The Valthyn are like cells of a body. We each have our individual lives, but we each have a life in the body. The body as a whole knows the minds of the space nations."

"And the body assigned you to get from me

whatever it has in store for me? Is that the arrangement?"

Lisa laughed at Jon's stubborn suspicions. "As individuals, we are free. We are aware of the purpose of our lives. It belongs to us as individuals. We are not chess pieces to be moved by forces outside of ourselves."

"You almost died on the beach," Jon said. "You said yourself you did not understand what was happening. Weren't you being used?"

"I acquiesced to darkness, to isolation from the body. It was offered as a role and I accepted in trust. I learned that it was important that we met as we did."

"It was a trick, a deception."

"It was an offering and a demonstration."

"All right, suppose I accept all that at face value. What is the purpose of all of this? Explain it to me."

Lisa shook her head. "I'm learning not to take such big steps with you. You'll know—in time."

They reached a stand of trees in middle of the grasslands. A creek ran through the center of the low-lying area. An outcropping of shale standing twenty meters high provided an overhang among the trees that would provide shelter.

Many of the trees bore fruit. Fish streaked in silver flashes through the creek. Escorting him through the trees, Lisa pointed out the vegetation they could eat, varieties of berries, roots, leaves, and stems.

"The beach people eat meat," Jon said. "I haven't seen you kill anything. Is there a reason for that?"

"We have enough fish," Lisa said. "If we lacked higher-quality protein, I would use what we need."

"You seem to have a way with animals," Jon said, half joking. "You'd eat them if you had to?"

"Yes and they know it. Some would eat me if necessary. At least, they'd try. There is no real competition or parasitism in nature, Jon. Life stands upon its own shoulders to reach summits a species standing alone cannot reach. To eat the flesh of a fellow creature is to stand upon its shoulders in that respect, not to destroy him. Much is taken from the earth to build a body of flesh. It must be recycled whenever possible."

Jon had seen creatures dying in the jaws of predators. "They seem to protest being eaten," Jon said dryly. "Nothing jumps into the campfires in honor of the occasion."

"Just as you fought to survive?"

Jon nodded once in emphatic agreement, assuming he had made his point.

"What of the day and the hour and the moment you fail to survive?"

"If it involves being eaten, I don't think I'd appreciate being recycled."

"Then what about the moment after your death when you may have a different perspective on life?"

Jon sighed in exasperation. He should have expected something like that from her. "I'll be conscious and rational after I die? Without a brain?"

"Physical activities expressed by the body are mediated by the structure of the brain. Transphysical environments are somewhat different. But such things are not important for you to know now. All forms of life build their personal experience in multiples of lives. Realities are caused by intersections of individual lives. But objective reality is not so very objective."

Dusk fell. Jon sat on a log in front of a low fire. Lisa stood a short distance away, looking out into the night.

"I know the difference between facts of reality and beliefs about reality," she told him in response to his own thoughts. "I don't confuse the two."

She depressed him at times, a reaction to a low-keyed, chronic fear that gnawed at him. Lisa posed no personal threat to him: He feared only the things

80

she told him and the things she had yet to tell. He could have doubted her if he chose to do so, but he didn't have the courage. Birds would alight near her without fear. A squirrel might clatter down a tree to investigate her presence in its world. These same creatures would have kept their distance from him. Lisa lived within the same world as himself, but she lived within it in a different way.

Jon knuckled down to accepting what he had known in his youth. What he perceived gave him a valid picture of the world, but complete only in proportion to what he had invested in it in terms of experience and knowledge. It wasn't an unscientific point of view. In fact, he had learned of many things on his own that he had ignored as irrelevant or too esoteric to be applied to everyday life. Perhaps they weren't.

Later in the evening, too keyed up to sleep, he watched Lisa weaving their sleeping mattresses, an indication that they'd be staying in this place for a time.

"I never knew what freedom really meant until now," Jon said, noticing the extreme depths of his own introspection this night. "I was born to fill a quota, raised and educated to be a fighter pilot. I never questioned the state's right to do that."

"Do you now?"

"If this is freedom, yes."

"You've never thought about such things before," Lisa stated.

"I was just thinking a moment ago. When I was young, before flight training, I remember getting caught up in theoretical physics. I remember reading about some of the things you've talked about. Especially about how the brain structures reality to about the same degree that reality structures the brain. And how time and space are supposed to be data-structuring techniques of the brain rather than attributes of objective reality. I forgot about that. And I used to take such an interest in the Earth environment, almost as if that period of my life was a memory in reverse of what I'm experiencing now."

"It does work as you suspect," Lisa said. "All men create their futures as they suspect. But more directly, they choose their futures and create the present moment as a bridge to what they feel to be inevitable on a deep level."

"That's a different way of looking at life," Jon said.

"It's more than just a way of looking," Lisa explained. "I could tell you a story if you'd like, an analogy of the truth that wouldn't otherwise fit into words. I could show you what the world is like for me."

Jon gazed into the campfire. The flames fluttered about. Crickets chirped in the darkness beyond the circle of light. But Jon was aware only of Lisa's voice and of his own train of thought.

"A bedtime story," he said. "Just make sure it doesn't give me nightmares."

"Imagine for the sake of the story that the world isn't what it seems to be," Lisa said. "Imagine entities who don't live in time and space as we know it. Imagine that these entities create different kinds of realities within their minds, then express themselves within these realities in order to explore them from the inside, giving these expressions of themselves complete freedom so that they can creatively surprise themselves by discovering potentials on the inside that they could not have foreseen from the outside.

"In other words, imagine that the physical universe is just one idea in one vast unified mind that is broken down into an expanding pyramid of gestalts of consciousness. These entities then express themselves inside these ideas, and using the physical universe as one example, as things that are alive in space and time, from bacteria to the kinds of creatures that might build civilizations among the stars. Imagine that behind the scenes, all of time and space exist at once, but that the people who live inside must structure experience in different ways. In human terms, we live in time and space. In larger terms, the past and future are happening all at once.

"Just as perceiving a rainbow depends upon your perspective, the relationship between yourself, the sun and droplets of water in the air, so do fundamental, subnuclear interactions give rise to a spectrum of reality. There is a blending of parallel worlds and parallel realities. We are three-dimensional expressions of multidimensional entities that exist in a reality that extends far beyond our vision.

"It's not easy to put this into words, but let's say that most people explore their personal reality bit by bit, living in time and space, slowly awakening to greater potentials. But let's say that there are other people who have gone beyond this way of living and can see the many different directions mankind takes in many different probabilities. Let's say that these people can see the blind alleys of human endeavor and that it's possible and practical to try to salvage them by returning and making changes. Not that there could ever be an end or a point where you could say that everything is perfect and unchangeable. Because every action creates new potential and a new definition of perfection.

"Say that these people are called the Valthyn. They are of one mind, but express themselves as a multitude of people who are aware of their origin and aware of the nature of reality in terms other than what most people experience for their own reasons. They see a direction that is a dead-end for humanity, a tragedy in ordinary terms. And they intervene to change it, not because they are superior outsiders imposing their will upon others, but really a kind of future part of humanity that has already experienced the tragedy and returned to do part over again and change it as best they can from another perspective.

"Jon, in the history that you know, humanity almost destroyed itself. But it learned very little by the experience, the part that escaped destruction. The potential still exists, but this time on a much larger scale than before. If the Valthyn seek to prevent this destruction, it will seem that the Valthyn will bring upon humanity the very thing it seeks to prevent. Our presence will serve as a mirror through which mankind will project the very fears that will cause this destruction. But we hope the shock of this reflection and the recognition of what it represents will stop humanity and force it to bring into the open what humanity should have faced openly time and time again.

"In some probabilities, Jon, humanity destroyed itself and no longer resides in the physical universe. In others, it met the challenges it presented for itself and moved on to new and greater challenges. In this probability, a great new challenge will soon present itself, but the old ones haven't been adequately resolved. We're here to hasten the process, risking another Holocaust in order to prevent annihilation."

When she finished, Jon's world shrank back down to the familiar environment of darkness and crickets chirping in the night. Even the campfire had faded to embers.

"It's too much," he told her. He could barely make out the glitter of her eyes in the starlight. "When you physically do something that violates the world as its supposed to be, you frighten me. But words don't have that kind of impact."

"A part of your mind reaches out and leads the way, Jon. I didn't intend to transform your whole perspective on life all at once. For right now, consider whether the mundane world that you experience might not be

84

seen from another point of view. I've seen you pick a flower for me and consider it a rather sentimental act, an appreciation of the beauty of nature. But you were attracted to the colors intended to attract another tiny creature who lives in symbiosis with the flower and aids in its reproductive cycle while gathering sustenance from it. I felt the plant's version of shock and pain when you mutilated its sex organ.

"The flower was meant for the bee, Jon. You did not know your proper place in the world of flowers and bees. Don't tell me that your interpretation of the world is inviolate because by using the same easy words that I used to tell you my story, I can destroy the version of the world that you identify so strongly with."

Jon felt a chill. Lisa had never talked to him in such a manner.

"You told me in your thoughts that you were afraid of me because of the things I'd know about you that you keep hidden from yourself. But if you are ever to perceive a larger world, you'll have to see beyond your petty one. This includes petty emotions, petty guilt, petty fear, and petty anger.

"The first step in perceiving a larger world, Jon, is to become aware of your beliefs about the world that, in turn, define it for you. Look to your emotions and your behavior for the invisible beliefs you have about your world. When you see what you've always taken for granted as fact, these beliefs can be changed and replaced by beliefs that aren't so limiting. Too many of them are lies that give you a false sense of control and prediction in a universe you perceive as basically hostile toward your existence. And that's a foundation for a world that doesn't even have to exist."

She had nothing more to say to him. She lay her mat near the dying campfire and fell asleep within moments. Jon didn't know whether to cry out in rage or to burst into laughter.

"I'll be a son-of-a-bitch," he said quietly to the night. "I've got myself a real live mentor."

Jon awoke in the morning to find Lisa preparing breakfast, only mildly insulted to note that she had caught a different kind of fish to add variety to his diet.

"That monologue of yours last night," he said. "How often is that going to happen?"

She glanced up from her work and smiled. "Experience is the real teacher in life. It's more effective if you don't put up too much resistance to it. I just lowered your resistance a small amount."

"That's what it was for? Just to keep me off balance?"

She frowned, but with a note of levity. "And to sidestep a few psychological defenses. Or do you think I cut you down a size or two in order to make myself feel better?"

Jon sat facing her, the campfire between them. "No, but you did hurt my feelings."

"Hurt is where it all starts. Hurt gives birth to anger. Then you look around and find something to pin the anger onto, placing responsibility for what you feel onto someone or something else."

Jon sighed and decided to keep his mouth shut.

"Anger is a reaction to a threat of some kind," Lisa continued. "But fright, a physiological reaction, is the trigger for anger. That's not the key to our discussion. Fear is."

"Fear?"

"If a snake dropped out of the tree above you and brushed past your face as it fell, you would experience a physiological reaction called fright. The reaction would fade once the stimulus is removed. If you looked down at the snake and imagined him biting you or wrapping his body around your neck, you would experience fear. Fright is a bodily reaction and fear is a mental reaction. All psychological defenses are erected in defense against fear. If the process goes too far, a person is living within and reacting to an imaginary reality and has difficulty functioning in a world of innocent, clumsy snakes. Can you think of another example of fear feeding upon itself?"

Relieved at having the conversation turned away from himself, Jon tried to think of an example.

"Are you talking about the space nations? Is that why you used the analogy of a mirror? Their fears feeding upon themselves? I still don't understand how you intend pitting yourself against them. You have no idea of the power of their weapons or the size of their warfleets."

Lisa smiled. "Have you noticed that you've been away for so long, you group all the nations together. The Jovans are no longer your people. The Lunans are no longer your enemy."

"The space nations have societies that believe in brotherhood," Jon said in defense.

"Not really. They fear the consequence of war. No civilian populations have been harmed in recent centuries, but when the Holocaust is forgotten, mass destruction will return. The colonies learned nothing by the Holocaust. Only fear."

"And fear gives rise to new enemies and new wars."

"That is the cycle that must be broken."

Jon climbed to his feet, deciding to take a walk before breakfast. He hesitated and looked back at the woman.

"You're going to do this singlehandedly?"

"No," Lisa said. "You're going to help."

In the evening, they walked together along a twisting path following the creek. Lisa appeared to be at peace with the world. Jon's fears and uncertainties continued to rage within him.

"What did you mean when you said that humanity faces a great new challenge? What old one hasn't been resolved?"

"I use the word *challenge*," Lisa said. "You might use another word. But there are reasons for your experience, your problems, dilemmas, and crises in life. You gain by them when they are solved."

"Then the old challenge is war, people learning to live with one another. What would the new one be?" Jon asked the question in a conversational tone, but he didn't like the ominous sound of a crisis greater than war.

"It's too soon to go into that right away."

"All of the old crises are gone—famine, disease, pollution. But people have conducted one long war since the days they could swing a club and bash in their neighbor's skull. I can't see people putting an end to that kind of behavior."

Lisa smiled. "I misjudged you. I honestly believed you'd take my advice and curb your curiosity."

Jon didn't believe a word of it. She had baited his curiosity, curiosity based on an overwhelming anxiety.

"You keep piling everything up. How much more is there?"

"Just one more factor to add, Jon. How long has humanity sought for evidence of life beyond your solar system?"

Jon stopped, shock coursing through him like a physical blow. In a curiously detached fashion, Jon knew that he had reached the limits to his tolerance. Anything more would just slip on by him without effect.

"They're not too far in advance of man," Lisa said. "There will be a mass encounter very soon. What do you think the consequences will be?"

Jon felt suffocated by a sense of doom. The thought of alien contact triggered fantasies of widespread panic. Every warfleet in the system would be pooled into one vast armada sent out to confront the unknown. There would be no chance at all for a peaceful encounter.

"Your thoughts are foreboding, but the Valthyn will be the first aliens your people will think they have encountered. It should be a most educational experience. Perhaps the encounter with the true aliens will take a different route."

"Lisa, I need time to think."

She did not respond. When he looked around for her, she had gone.

She used him and yet she did not. She understood him so well, it took very little to move him down a path that might well be the only one left to him in life. But he couldn't imagine his future as having any connection with the incredible scenarios she outlined for him. He was shipwrecked and isolated on the face of a rather large planet. He could never escape.

And how could Lisa's people make any kind of contact with the space nations? They possessed no technology, no means of communication. Lisa didn't even wear shoes. It all seemed so farfetched. And as for the idea of alien contact, Jon could imagine it happening in a nightmarish way. It wouldn't be a good part of human history for it to happen within. Earth nations had once actively searched out evidence of extraterrestial civilizations, listening for radio signals from the stars and broadcasting primitive versions of what they felt such communication might be like. They had expected to go into space, to conquer and flourish.

It might have happened that way. But after the Holocaust, isolated in that last frontier, the space nations realized the full extent of their vulnerability. They pitted sheet metal and glass against an infinite vacuum and starfields spread across an all-encompassing, eternal night. The space nations could not pit their technology against that vastness nor against the kinds of creatures that could travel within it. Dreams had once been panoramic, heroic, and romantic, but reality fell far short when a man could spend his entire span of life laboring in a sweat-stained canister to collect bits and pieces of debris for their precious metallic content.

Jon returned to the camp, too depressed to cope further with his own thoughts. He refused to talk to Lisa, stretching out alongside the campfire in the winter evening. Lisa stood over him and smiled.

"It will be all right in the end," she said.

She gazed at him, his thoughts as well open to her.

"And I have nothing more to say, Jon. You have what you need to work with in the days to come."

"When will it start?" he asked.

"When you have almost forgotton the stress I have caused you. When you begin to realize how necessary it has been."

They kept each other warm during the night, and the day that followed passed in a serenity Jon had never before experienced with her. Others days passed and paradise began. They were the same day endlessly repeated and, yet, each unique.

At first, Jon made love to Lisa too often, too ferverently, afraid that the tranquility would end soon, knowing it couldn't last forever. But when he began to believe that perhaps it could last forever, he began basking in the glow of her being. At first, he could hardly believe that Lisa could revel in the same primitive sensuality that ordinary people hungered for. But there could be no deception in her cries of passion during the night beneath the shelter of the overhang or during the rains that fell during the day or in sunlight alongside the creek.

When life quieted, the past forgotten, Jon began noticing once again the sunsets and the sunrises, the stars at night and the silence of the grove in the mild winter afternoons. Lisa reflected a depth and a quality to existence that Jon would never have experienced on his own.

CHAPTER FIVE

Departmental Coordinators of the Earth-monitor surveillance satellite system, anthropological studies and their technological subdivisions met in the conference room adjacent to Commander Harper's office. Harper entered the crowded room last, moving with brisk precision and a disciplined smile of satisfaction on his thin lips. He took his position behind a podium facing the assembly with Coordinator Ida Moore seated to his left, showing equal relief in his posture if less an air of confidence.

"Almost four years have passed since the crash-landing of the Jovan Cobra pilot on Earth," Harper began. "The Valthyn have scattered across the face of the globe and are no longer of concern to Luna Authority. But the Valthyn woman of personal concern to us lives with the Jovan pilot at this time in an isolated region near the Sierra Mountains in North America. We believe the crisis has passed. Luna Authority agrees that perhaps we overreacted to the threat we perceived and the severity of our quarantine, although still in effect, has been considerably reduced.

"As you all know, prior to the Earth Treaty of 2489 A.D., Luna Nation conducted a series of three Earth-landing missions, the first only one hundred and fifty years after the Holocaust when civilization as we know it only consisted of a few colonies on Luna and in Earth orbit. Luna Nation as a political entity did not as yet exist. That first expedition ended in unmitigated disaster. Several hundred men died of microbiological exposure. The single launch vehicle never returned.

"The Second African Expedition landed two centuries later, the first valid, but feeble attempt to recolonize Earth. Of the twenty ships and two thousand men and women that landed, five ships and less than four hundred survivors returned.

"There are two versions of the Third Asian Expedition. Officially, it is listed as a scientific expedition. Five landers went down. One of the craft encountered bad weather and set down five kilometers from the designated landing area. It alone returned. That incident occurred thirty years ago. I was aboard that single surviving craft.

"The ultrasecret version of that mission is considerably more interesting. It was launched to investigate a rapidly expanding population of primitives consisting entirely of females. They possessed no visual evidence of a technology, but gave other evidence of an intelligent and knowledgeable society, one that could not have simply appeared spontaneously. For example, from orbiting surveillance satellites, we were not able to confirm a single death in almost a century. We watched these people carefully on a day-to-day basis for almost a century before risking public displeasure on a landing mission. We understood nothing of what we observed of these people.

"I went down as a coordinator in communications, twenty-two years old and on my first mission. We didn't land apart from the main group by accident. We acted as a relay and backup station for the main party and Mission Command. So, of course, I did not personally witness any of the events that transpired.

"The main party set down a few kilometers from a garden-quality village setting. One of the women we now know as the Valthyn approached the landing craft, apparently alone and of her own volition. She was stunned to unconsciousness and taken aboard one of the ships for a routine examination by our investigation teams. After a thorough physical examination that verified the Valthyn to be human, she was turned over to our anthropologists for questioning. She gave no evidence of being able to speak or understand Lunan, but gave clear evidence of a telepathic ability. She somehow confused and disoriented her interrogators and attempted to escape. Security personnel attempted to stop her. Their hand weapons exploded.

"A panic spread and others attempted to fire upon the woman as she left the ship, believing themselves to be under attack. Twenty men died including several key personnel necessary for the launching of the ships of the main party. None of them ever got off the ground. I never received any coherent communication from the survivors until their power failed two weeks later. We returned alone—just the ship I was on."

Harper's voice had fallen off. Moore glanced up at the Commander. His faint smile hadn't altered during his speech. The tone of his voice hadn't changed. But sweat standing out in beads began to run down his face. Still smiling, Harper wiped his face on the sleeve of his dress uniform and continued.

"We have always believed the Valthyn to be a potential threat to the security of Luna Nation," Harper said, the volume of his voice returning to normal. "Ultimately, they are a threat to all the space nations. But we have been discreet about revealing the Valthyn presence to the space nations. Their

95

reaction would undoubtedly be destructive and futile, in itself as much a threat to peace as the Valthyn themselves.

"But to be technically correct, no Valthyn has ever initiated hostilities against any space nation or its citizens. The Valthyn woman who singlehandedly destroyed the Third Asian Expedition may have felt herself to be defending her life against hostilities initiated by Luna Nation forces. That incident could easily have been the product of a complete lack of communication.

"Now we see a Jovan, a space-nation citizen, mating and communicating with a Valthyn over a considerable period of time, proof in itself that it is possible to communicate with the people. We now have the option of reinitiating contact with the Valthyn. To be more specific, with one Valthyn woman. Fully agreeing that under no circumstances can we risk further misunderstanding, Luna Authority has authorized a small expeditionary force to Earth's surface.

"Immediately after the Third Asian Expedition, we published a report of our findings. Perhaps the Outer World Federation suspected something amiss. Continuing resistance to further landing missions led to the Earth Treaty tacked on as an amendment to the Ganymede Convention's Wargame Rulings and the general Code of International Conduct that has kept the peace in the solar system for five centuries. By treaty, no space nation is allowed a surface landing on Earth.

"The space nations do not know of the Valthyn presence. They simply want Earth to remain neutral territory remaining in its natural state. We intend violating the letter of the treaty, but not the spirit in which it was agreed upon. We are certain that the space nations would approve of our actions if they understood the peculiar circumstances that we, as caretakers of Earth, must cope with. We are sure they would realize that we have their best interests at heart by assuming full responsibility for investigating this frightening and dangerous situation.

"In short, we intend sending a five-man expedition to the surface of the Earth to interview the Jovan pilot and the Valthyn woman. We intend our meeting to be on the friendliest of terms. We fully expect to be greeted with courtesy and curiosity on their part. Our latest technology enables us to effect a landing and a launch from the surface using a single, two-staged vehicle. Project Coordinator Ida Moore will act as Commander of this expedition. He speaks the Jovan language and is the best qualified to conduct the interview and minimize the chance of misinterpretation of our behavior.

"Now, you've heard rumors circulating on the base. Trust the facts. You'll all be provided with details as soon as this meeting is adjourned. You'll each have a role to play on this momentous occasion. Are there any questions?"

There were none.

Commander Harper remained standing behind the podium after the conference room had emptied. He had been left alone with more responsibility toward the upcoming mission than he cared to shoulder. The rumors had been circulated deliberately and every individual's reaction and opinion duly noted by a staff of political psychologists. Commander Harper knew in detail what he could expect of his men. He had said nothing that would trigger dissent. He had included every bit of information useful in neutralizing any anxiety toward violating the long-standing taboo of an Earth-landing mission. One of the most controversial issues centered on the transportation of a weapon to Earth. Therefore, only Commander Isaac Harper and Luna Authority knew that, for the first time since the Holocaust, a thermonuclear weapon would descend to the face of the Earth fully armed. Under certain conditions, it would be detonated.

The first men set foot on the moon in a craft similar in design to the Earth-landing vehicle developed by Luna Nation. A broad, flat base would take the brunt of friction during atmospheric entry. The ablative shields would then be blown aside to expose six massive, monatomic hydrogen engines to lower the craft to touchdown. Once on the surface, the descent stage would serve as a launch platform for the streamlined ascent vehicle carrying the five passengers. The Earth-lander had been constructed and assembled in Lunar orbit and towed to Earth orbit by tugs, docking briefly at the research satellite to pick up its crew.

Technology had long since reached the point where mechanical and electronic systems approached total reliability. But less than five minutes after separation from the research satellite, telemetry readings indicated a malfunction in the system designed to separate the two stages during launch from the surface. The tugs accelerated in pursuit of the malfunctioning craft, the mission abruptly aborted. Seconds later, an emergency backup system designed to free the manned ascent vehicle in the event of a malfunction of the main engines detonated explosive bolts, splitting the craft to its two components.

The tugs rendezvoused with the manned launch stage without incident. All eyes were on the descent stage nearing destructive atmospheric entry when the ten megaton thermonuclear warhead hidden aboard the craft detonated 220 kilometers above the Earth.

For security reasons, Luna Nation had never permitted the Jovans use of their own Earth-orbiting satellites, but it had never been able to prevent Jovan monitors from orbiting both Earth and Luna in 800,000-kilometer orbits. The tiny satellites were difficult to track down and those destroyed were constantly replaced by others spiraling down from the distant Jovan colonies. Fifteen such satellites detected the nuclear explosion in low Earth orbit. Instantly, signals to the outer worlds were on their long journey at the speed of light.

The night sky over the Pacific blossomed to daylight in a flood of white glare tinged with ultraviolet. Jon was awake and on his feet instantly, trailing a long, dark shadow as he ran for the plains beyond the grove to view the phenomenon. Long after the light died to tolerable brightness, the night sky danced and shimmered in a display of the aurora borealis such as the equatorial regions had never seen. Jon had witnessed fireworks of that nature many times before, but never from such a perspective. It impressed upon him the impact the space wars fought in the near-Earth regions must have had upon the inhabitants of Earth.

How many had died in that accident? Jon couldn't imagine it being deliberately in violation of Earth Treaty. Not that close in. But even an accident was difficult to imagine.

"I have your answer," Lisa said, startling him from close behind. "Men sought to return weapons to the face of the Earth. That is forbidden. No one was harmed, but men have died in the past and will again soon. Not because the Valthyn murder, but because the intent to murder can be turned back upon its source."

Shock washed over him. "So, that's the kind of power the Valthyn have. I take it our picnic is about over."

"Soon."

"And you have it all planned out," Jon said. "You had all the moves down pat from the beginning."

"You choose your own destiny, Jon. The Valthyn cannot determine it for you, nor theirs for that matter." She nodded toward the fading light.

"Then why do I have this nasty premonition that I'm not going to be enjoying myself? Is that a warning of what I've chosen for myself?"

"You choose the role you will play in future events. What you are feeling is the proximity of an event, not your role within it."

"That was one hell of an explosion." Jon said. "The outer system will be demanding an explanation as fast as it takes a transmission to travel there and back. There's going to be hell to pay."

Lisa tilted her head back to watch the colors washing across the night sky.

"Beautiful, isn't it?" Jon said. "I'll bet there aren't too many people up there in a position to enjoy the pretty colors. What were they trying to accomplish?"

"They were visitors, Jon. We would have welcomed them, but they had their smiles painted on crooked."

"And the Valthyn really did that? You have that kind of power?"

"That was only the release of power. Containing it is the true accomplishment. Even the trees can contain their power."

Jon sat down on the grass and looked up at the silhouette of the woman standing against the fading light.

"I've never had a teacher as pretty as you. But I still don't think I'll be earning passing grades. I think you're overestimating what I can handle."

"Things will fall into place of their own accord," Lisa said. "Besides, you excel in one subject, even if you are on the tall and boney side."

Jon grinned, allowing Lisa to sidetrack him from his depressing thoughts.

"Most of my sex education consisted of visits to the genetic labs and baby factories. I suppose I can take credit for passing your course."

"Male chauvinism slowly dies." Lisa laughed and turned back to camp, no more concerned about the catastrophic explosion than about the crickets resuming their mating calls in the darkness.

Coordinator Ida Moore re-entered the corridors of the research satellite in the midst of a mass evacuation. He pushed through the crowds toward Commander Harper's office. Already his personal orders were coming through corridor speakers following his progress. Usually he responded to the computer-synthesized voice following him around the station with unerring precision like an automoton. Ignoring the voice at times convinced him that he retained some semblance of free will.

He stormed into Harper's office. The Commander sat hunched over his console, his face twisted in pained concentration. He pecked at a half dozen keyboards within his reach.

"Call it off!" Moore demanded.

"We're evacuating by Luna Authority directive!"

"Tell Luna Authority they were damned lucky that warhead didn't go off beneath their fat asses! Cancel the evacuation! We're not in any danger!"

Harper hesitated, giving Moore his full attention. "I'd have to relay your recommendation through my own authority, Moore. I don't like sticking my neck out."

"I don't blame you! Luna Authority stuck their necks out and their heads just fell off! But that warhead could just as easily have gone off with us aboard or when it was docked with this station! Commander, you'd best recommend that Luna Authority keep their aces up their own sleeves from here on out and quit trying to slip them into our deck! They

101

almost killed us!"

Harper considered Moore's logic and gave in, keying in his transmission in his own personal shorthand. The computers translated and sent it off. They processed the reply on Harper's desk monitor less than a minute later.

"They accepted our recommendation," Harper said. "Odd, they reacted so quickly."

"Not so odd. They jumped on it. Call a staff meeting of departmental coordinators and let's organize ourselves. Luna Authority will need a few more recommendations when the Jovans launch a goddamned warfleet to investigate that incident."

Moore turned and walked from the office. It took a delayed moment for the audacity of his behavior to reach full consciousness. He had never talked to Harper like that before. Repercussions would come later, if ever, when Harper had more elbow room to play king of the mountain.

Moore returned to his quarters and stripped off his pressure suit. He dropped to his bunk and relaxed to let the excess adrenaline drain away. After a time, his heart slowed its hard fast beat. Fantasies of catastrophe became thoughts of the recommendations he'd be making to Harper in the near future. In an unofficial capacity, he had always been second-in-command on the 1,200-man research satellite. His rank had never reflected his status. Ranks meant a tightening of reins held by Luna Authority, a trip he had avoided with meticulous care.

When he stood to change back into his station uniform, the image of the spidery black man in the wall mirror startled himself. Accustomed to seeing skin color ranging from ivory white to deep tan, he seldom saw a person as midnight black as himself. Often, he had the same effect of startling newcomers to the station, but had learned to take their reaction in stride. Not that it had ever been a liability. In fact, it made life quite interesting, especially considering the women attracted to him because of his genetic uniqueness rather than in spite of it. He had been a part of an experiment conducted thirty years ago to introduce high levels of melanin into the skins of preborns by manipulating genetic codes. Skin cancers triggered by high levels of ultraviolet radiation had always been a nagging problem among the space colonies.

Men who had evolved in the equatorial regions of Earth had once had black skin for much the same reason. All of the natural races of Earth had blended genetically within the space nations long ago, but in an era of genetic experimentation, even larger numbers of variations in the theme of *Homo sapiens* had arisen during the last two centuries. Ida Moore had clear light-blue eyes. His hair was platinum, almost colorless, and his features were the standard product of aesthetic preference.

Ida Moore took notice of his physique, all seven and a half feet of it. No amount of genetic engineering had yet managed to reduce the size to which a person tended to grow in low-gravity fields. Jon, the Jovan fighter pilot on Earth, had a similar physique, but the Valthyn woman was closer to Earth stock, smaller and imposingly muscular.

Moore finally put his finger on what was bothering him. Some kind of racial memory might have been triggered by the photographs of the nude woman. Moore had found her to be astoundingly beautiful. He had never seen a woman so full-bodied. Did he envy the Jovan?

Moore lived closer to Earth than the populations of the space nations. Although he had viewed Earth only from outside its atmosphere, he could imagine better than most the color and beauty and the variety of sensory impact on the surface. He was angry. He had come so close to experiencing Earth firsthand, only

103

to be thwarted by stupidity, greed, and fear. Perhaps, on a subconscious level, he wanted to compete with the Jovan for the Valthyn woman, convinced that he'd have more to offer her in the way of education and intelligence. He grinned at the primitive level of his thought processes. Catching sight of his own nudity had triggered those associative levels of sexual desire focused on the Valthyn woman.

Moore donned his station uniform and ordered a meal consisting of concentrate and a hot beverage. It arrived by automated dumbwaiter moments later. He sat at his desk eating slowly, his eye on his personal viewscreen set above the desk. A computer constantly collated and assembled data on the various projects assigned the research satellite and presented a running commentary and update on the affairs of the base. Of immediate priority at the moment was, of course, the incident involving the aborted Earth-landing mission, the detonation of a thermonuclear device, and projections of the repercussions that would result. They tended to be more nightmarish in their extremes than even he had anticipated.

Perhaps in the end, the research satellite would be evacuated after all. The Jovan nations had already demanded an explanation of the unprecedented incident violating several standing treaties. And, already, Luna Authority had lied, claiming a damaged cruiser from the last space war had somehow blown her engines. Even as an anthropologist, Moore knew enough of engine design to recognize the weakness of the excuse. Moore had no doubt that the Jovans would be sending a fleet to the Earth–Luna vicinity to investigate those violations firsthand. Harper had been perfectly correct in feeling that Earth Treaty had been established because of the suspicions of the outer world nations that something was amiss on Earth. If Luna Nation continued to fumble the situation, there'd be hell to pay in a frightfully short period of time.

Moore had difficulty handling the tense atmosphere at the staff meeting. Commander Harper usually had little trouble coordinating the meetings, but as a military man, he was tending to encourage speculations on possible military confrontations with the Jovans.

"Perhaps we should let Luna Authority handle the Jovans," Moore suggested. "They're going to be relying on us for a continuing evaluation of the Valthyn menace and recommendations for an official course of action to try to limit Valthyn involvement in our affairs. We have enough to worry about in that area."

Harper stared at him with a blank expression. "Valthyn menace? Valthyn involvement in our affairs? Moore, what are you talking about?"

"The Jovans are going to be looking for the cause of that explosion. Who do you think was responsible? If the Jovans learn of the Valthyn, Luna Nation is in trouble. The outer-world nations will overrun us to get to the Valthyn."

"That's why we've been here all along," Harper said. "To prevent just such a thing from happening. But the Jovans know nothing of the Valthyn. The confrontation will still be a diplomatic and military issue to settle."

"Fine," Moore said. "In the meanwhile, may I suggest we finish what we started out to do. Contact with the Valthyn may still be the only solution to the problem. Perhaps they don't understand the difficult position Luna Nation is in or the effect their presence has on the space nations."

"Luna Authority will not authorize another Earth-landing mission," Harper stated. "That's out of the question."

"Strongly recommend that they do," Moore said. "One without a bomb in it this time."

Moore let the Commander and the other Coordinators bat the idea around. There were objections and comments, but no ideas to replace Moore's. And they all realized the necessity of taking direct and productive action to help neutralize the dilemma.

Moore knew the people he worked with quite well. Most were specialists in the lifestyles of primitive societies on Earth. They weren't the best qualified for integrating a backwoods, low-interest scientific study into problems that were arising and involving international diplomacy. Most of his associates were assuming the Valthyn to be primitives with some kind of supernatural powers. Moore knew too much of the Isinti to believe that psychics could be primitive. Moore had studied the diverging cultures and ways of life among the space nations as a minor in the Earth Studies University at Tycho and understood the difficulties of handling the complex conflicts of interest among the space nations. Considering the level of technology available for weaponry, only the wargame rules of the Ganymede Convention prevented another Holocaust. But the continuing success of the wargames depended upon respect for the rules. What would happen to the rules if a frightened population relied upon their warfleets to conduct a witch hunt?

"At any rate," Harper concluded, "Luna Authority accepted my recommendation that we call off the evacuation. I don't know what we can hope to gain by attempting another landing. We have no clear-cut strategy to work with, but I agree with Coordinator Moore that only direct contact with the Valthyn will provide us with the data we need to fill in some of this vacuum we're operating in. If we get a new descent stage for the Earth-lander, we'll disembark as soon as it arrives, using the same program as before.

"Dismissed."

Moore went directly to the communications room

where transmissions from the numerous monitoring satellites orbiting the globe were in a continual process of collation. The behavior and movement of target tribes, weather patterns, radiation samplings from the lingering effects of the Holocaust, the slow ingrowth of burnout areas and creeping desert perimeters—everything sorted and combined by computer to give each discipline not only information of special interest, but a course study of anything that might conceivably affect it.

Ocean studies, the most frustrated of the Earth studies, was headed by a young, platinum blonde named Naomi. She latched onto him as he crossed the room.

"Has anyone reapplied for our probes? Moore, do you know the status of our probes?"

"Maybe soon, Naomi. We have a second Earthlander mission going. It might break the ice."

"Life in the ocean is as vital to the health of the planet as any surface conditions, Moore. I have surface water temperature readings, current movement, whale and porpoise sightings, but my job here is a farce without dropping well-equipped probes into the oceans. What conceivable harm can it cause?"

"I don't know, Naomi. Take up a minor study in human psychology and you tell me what all the paranoia is all about."

"Can you imagine the effect that explosion had on ocean life in the Pacific?"

"I can imagine. Use it as leverage for your next application."

"I intend to!" She turned and stomped off as if a demonstration of anger for the benefit of the head of anthropological studies would have a positive impact on her own problems.

Moore sought out Hans Oliver, his computer operator. "Valthyn movement. Anything?"

The aging computer specialist consulted his

screens and gestured for Moore to have a look for himself. Moore could make no sense of the screens.

"Interpret that for me, Hans."

"Target subjects, forty-nine. Lost thirty-eight under cloud cover. Gained fourteen, but some are probably just nomads. We haven't seen enough movement to analyze behavioral patterns. They've thoroughly scattered over an area of many millions of square kilometers. I've observed several desert crossings that weren't humanly possible. And if they have any particular destination in mind, it's directly in their path. They never deviate from a perfect straight line."

"How about our Jovan and his girlfriend?"

"Enjoying an idyllic lifestyle. Sleep, sex, and food. That woman is a real spook, Moore."

"I'm sure she is, Hans."

"She petted a cougar yesterday. The herd animals wander around that stand of trees, but never through it. It rains just at night and all of the worst storms bypass the area. It's like they have a glass bowl over the area, but at least it makes for good observation."

"Do you have the computer alerted for unusual movements?"

"I know their patterns so well, the computer will scream bloody murder if they sneeze too often."

"Just keep them under priority observation and let me know if they move."

"Still planning on paying them a visit?" Hans grinned.

"We might take another crack at it."

"That'll be the event of the century. Taking another bomb with you?"

Moore frowned. "Is security that lax?"

"No, but Luna Authority is that obvious. Those people down there are spooks, Moore. I don't think they're human."

Moore started to turn away, not wanting to get into

that level of speculation with low-security personnel. "They're human, Hans."

"Wouldn't it be something if we've been invaded right under our noses? Is that what the Jovans are going to be screaming about, do you imagine? I mean, if they ever find out?"

Moore gave the man a stern look of disapproval.

Hans' smile faded. "Okay, boss, back to the grindstone."

CHAPTER SIX

"You're feeling anxious," Lisa said.

The sun had just risen above the distant mountains, glaring like a fusion rocket through twin peaks. That in itself gave a clue to the nature of his thoughts.

"Look around you," Lisa said. "The world is serene. It offers a new day for you to experience. And you brood."

"Why are we of so much interest to them?"

"When the Lunans discovered the Valthyn, they sent ships down to investigate. One of us met with them to offer a shortcut for what was to come, an explanation of how fear gives birth to monsters and how feelings of inadequacy give birth to tyrants. They did not understand, but they did learn that they are defenseless against their monsters and tyrants. Knowing how the rest of the solar system would react and trample them to get to us, they've been trying to hide us, at the same time trying to gain more information in order to neutralize us as a source of chronic anxiety. Soon, their greatest fears will be realized."

"It feels like everything's going to come to an end, like something dark and ominous approaching. I felt something like that once. Do I need to tell you about

"I can feel what you experience," Lisa said, "but it's not easy to make sense of the world through the mind of another person. Everyone's world is unique, not in the things that are perceived, but in the symbolism and the feelings assigned to things that are perceived."

"We were on a field expedition," Jon said. "We were studying the geology of a group of Trojan asteroids. I must have been about twelve-years-old at the time. We were on the face of this hunk of rock, maybe eighty kilometers in diameter, just massive enough to hold us down if we were careful walking. The others were a short distance away, but below the horizon."

"This ship approached. I saw the sun glint against the hull and my faceplate. I turned around and saw a thousand lights approaching, like a cluster of stars moving in to engulf everything. When I could see the outline of the hull blotting out the stars, I knew it was a cargo transport, but here I was just a little kid standing alone on a hunk of rock in the middle of nowhere. I never realized how big those things were. It had a broad, flat hull on the bottom. The nose passed overhead and blotted out the entire sky. It must have been ten kilometers long. I could even feel the gravitational perturbations as it passed. It kept coming and coming, passing overhead for what seemed like hours. I lost my sense of perspective. It felt like I was standing upside down on a rock falling from the sky toward a landscape of iron. I really thought we were all doomed."

"Would it help if I told you that there are no endings, just one constant beginning?"

"It might if it made any sense to me."

"If I said that you and I are only beginning despite the interpretations you might place on the things you will experience?"

Jon sat by the burned-out campfire, leaning back against a small boulder imbedded in the ground. Lisa sat beside him, her body in reassuring contact with his.

"Yeah, that helps."

"But it won't be easy."

"Nothing's ever easy. Nothing could be as easy as this. Earth's a paradise. That's a fact."

"It's only a matter of perspective," Lisa said. "People once took Earth for granted and yearned for the romance of space travel."

"They were fools. But I feel guilty about doing so much of nothing. I can justify all of this as a vacation I deserve for getting shot down, but I'm starting to feel trapped."

"Life is motion. There's nothing wrong with you."

"You know what I mean. I feel trapped by all those lights in the sky at night. There are people up there watching us. I'd rather be left alone. I could have made a life here with you."

"If you know with such certainty that you'll be leaving Earth soon, you're beginning to trust in a new way of knowing the world. What happened to that pragmatic intellect of yours?"

Jon slipped his arms around the woman. "Haven't heard a peep from it since I discovered what sex was all about."

Lisa caught up with him five miles from the grove. Jon walked toward the line of mountains across an increasingly arid terrain, not bothering to slow for the woman coming up from behind. She'd know his whereabouts, his mood and intentions. And she could easily outdistance him any day.

They walked together in silence for an hour. Lisa finally sighed, aware that they would not be returning to the grove. She could feel Jon's curiosity about the mountains and the tension that drove him to walk for the sake of dispelling some of it. The part of Lisa that lived on Jon's level of existence felt the fear and sadness that he felt. That part of her dreaded the coming night. When it did, several hours into the darkness lights came from behind them, a thousand moving stars in the heavens shining with a light intense enough to cast multiple, fuzzy shadows.

Jon saw the long shadows cast before him and turned, his eyes dilating with awe at the spectacle approaching from the horizon.

A thousand Jovan warships decelerated into Earth orbit. Despite the distance and the ocean of atmosphere, Jon knew that staring into those intense lights could damage the eyes. When the fusion engines flickered to darkness, they were still bright stars passing rapidly overhead. The shadows in the night faded, the fleet itself flickering out as the ships passed into Earth's shadow.

"It must be an exploratory fleet," Jon said. "By the size of some of those ships, they must have brought along a military escort."

Lisa could sense the size of those craft and the human life aboard them. Despite her knowing, it astounded her that the entire population of the Earth didn't equal ten percent of the life she could feel in those bits of metal and on the moon that glowed so bright with the lights of a full-blown civilization.

"This is how you felt," Lisa said.

"Makes you feel insignificant, doesn't it? Do you suppose we're still being watched?"

"Yes, by the same people in one of the large Lunan satellites."

"Is there any way to hide from them?"

"There's no reason to try," Lisa said. "If you're asking if I have the power to turn aside their technology, I do not. Only my larger self could do that, not the part of me that you know."

"You're actually admitting to a limitation?" Jon

gave her a bleak smile.

"I cannot transcend life and experience it at the same time. You'll learn of my limitations soon enough."

"That's a shame. I don't want those people interfering in our lives. They don't own me. I'm not a piece of property for them to dispose of at their leisure."

"You can't hide in the mountains, Jon."

Jon continued walking. They'd reach the foothills in a day or two. Perhaps they could find some rugged terrain that would protect them from a landing craft. The off-worlders wouldn't fare well if they were forced to land at a distance and pursue them on foot. Jon wanted nothing to do with them, aware that he and Lisa were becoming a focus of attention that would lead civilization to the brink of catastrophe.

Ida Moore watched history unfold on the viewscreen in his personal quarters. The Jovan fleet decelerated into Earth orbit only 1,400 kilometers above the research satellite. From the observation deck he had visited earlier, the fleet looked like a dense band of artificial satellites arching over the equatorial regions of the planet, a phenomenon Earth had never before seen in its multibillion-year history.

For the first time since the Holocaust, a warfleet violated the rules of the Ganymede Convention. No command ship existed among the fleet to end an armed conflict. Most of the craft appeared to be scientific in nature, a true exploratory caravan, but it included warcraft capable of unacceptable levels of devastation.

Moore listened to the communication between Luna Authority and the Supreme Commander of the Jovan fleet broadcast on an open channel.

"Luna Navigational Control," a heavily accented Jovan voice spoke, "we are assuming a fifteen hundred and sixty kilometer equatorial Earth orbit. We are on a peaceful mission."

Luna Authority responded instantly. "The spirit and the letter of the Ganymede Convention has been violated. Never in the history of the space nations has civilization faced such grave risk of irresponsible catastrophe."

"Earth Treaty has been violated," the Jovans countered. "Earth is sacred to all peoples. There is no value within and no material value without that exceeds the value of Earth's security. We pose no threat to Luna Nation. We wish to join forces with our comrades of Luna Nation to define and evaluate all potential threats to Earth's security."

"You must specify the nature of your suspicions," Luna Authority demanded. Moore breathed a sigh of relief. A nondefensive attitude, letting the Jovans bear the burden of rationalizing their behavior would be the best strategy. Luna Authority could afford no more errors of the kind that had triggered the crisis to begin with.

"You have not adequately explained the nature and purpose of the high-yield thermonuclear detonation at altitudes forbidden by Earth Treaty. The data released to us of your Earth monitor activities do not adequately explain the reason for an attempted, unauthorized Earth-landing."

Moore tensed. They had somehow known of the Earth-landing mission, possibly from their sophisticated satellite monitors. It took several moments for Luna Authority to respond.

"We are providing access to all data storage of all aspects of our Earth-monitor activities. We will assume a passive role for the duration of this unfortunate confrontation and assume responsibility for preventing a military confrontation that your behavior has put within the realm of statistical probability."

Moore relaxed, satisfied with Luna Authority's

strategy. Allowing the Jovans to link directly to governmental data storage was both a courageous and desperate move, removing the possibility of further deception. The Jovans wouldn't have access to speculation or suspicions of the nature of the Valthyn presence, but they would learn of their existence and the survival of the Jovan fighter pilot. Undoubtedly, they'd attempt a rescue mission if only to stall for more time in search of Luna Authority's motivation for violating Earth Treaty.

"In the spirit of cooperation, do you have recommendations to offer concerning rescue attempts of the fighter pilot, the Jovan citizen, Jon B–897Y?"

"Affirmative," Luna Authority responded. "It is imperative that you land unarmed. Do not attempt an armed Earth-landing."

Moore sympathized with Luna Authority's recommendation. It had to be made. But it led to the logical query.

"May we request the purpose of such a recommendation?"

"We have released all information relevant to our Earth-monitor activities. We have withheld no information relevant to our recommendation. We repeat. Do not attempt to land armed in any fashion."

Moore chuckled in the ensuing silence. In an indirect way, Luna Nation had spilled its guts, but wasn't about to help the Jovans organize the morass of information. Included in the data would be a detailed account of the Third Asian Expedition. Now, it would be up to the Jovans to draw the proper conclusions. Eventually, the Jovans would realize that what Luna Authority left unsaid on open communication channels was better left unsaid.

Moore studied the size and complexity of the Jovan fleet. To demonstrate their largely peaceful intent, the Jovans had brought along a personnel satellite, a rotating double wheel twice the size of the research

117

satellite. It had been towed hundreds of millions of kilometers by the tugs that were an essential component of any military or scientific fleet. But the very vulnerability of the space station testified to the Jovan intent of not initiating a conflict. They would stand to lose thousands of undefended, valuable lives should one occur.

During the intermittent periods of silence, an enormous amount of activity would be going on behind the scenes. Commander Harper's call verified the inevitable. The research satellite had been swept into the momentum of snowballing events.

"Moore?" Harper looked distraught and harassed. "We've received orders. The Jovans want to go down after their pilot. We've offered the use of our lander. Another descent stage is on its way. We leave at 0900 hours. You're in command of Luna personnel, but there'll be five Jovan military specialists cross-trained in essential scientific disciplines going along."

"Acknowledged, Commander. We'll be ready to leave at 0900."

"One complication, Moore. That damned Jovan and the Valthyn woman have been on the move. They've reached the base of the Sierra Mountains. You won't be able to confront them as you planned. It'll take ground transportation to reach them now."

"Are the Jovans going down disarmed?"

"They're hedging on that. Lunan personnel will not be armed. Is that clear?"

"Commander, if I had my way, we'd go down stark naked except for a pair of velvet gloves assigned each man."

Harper cut off his screen.

It had finally happened. The dream of a lifetime that Moore had spent his entire life suppressing as a possibility in the real world. Within ten hours, he'd step foot upon the face of a world he had studied all his life, a world as familiar to him as the Luna environment upon which he had been born and raised, but a world as alien as some strange planet on the far edge of the galaxy. He wouldn't be able to stand for very long against its gravity nor breathe its air. But in very real terms, he was going home.

CHAPTER SEVEN

The Earth-lander backed into the atmosphere, the ablative shields covering the descent engines glaring white-hot. The slender, manned vehicle shuddered, protected from the shock wave of entry in the broad shadow of the descent stage. Ida Moore tried to lie very still, his eyes closed, stunned by the noise and vibration.

The six engines of the descent stage ignited, blasting aside the ablative shields. The craft settled into an erratic vibration as the noise of the rockets gradually increased in intensity in denser atmosphere.

Moore finally opened his eyes and watched the unending descent through a small viewscreen mounted above his cocoon of webbing. He recognized nothing of the pattern of color and texture of the landscape below until he saw the ripple of the Sierras. The rate of descent slowed, slipping off to one side. Finally, individual trees could be seen. Dust obscured his vision as the pilot sought to pinpoint the touchdown target, a small, level meadow 2,000 meters above sea level.

Touchdown impact rippled through the craft. Hydraulic levelers whined and the ship sighed as it settled to rest. The engines died and the descent stage shut itself down, now little more than a launch platform for the slender needle of the rocket towering upon its foundation.

Moore continued to lie very still. It felt as if the ship continued to decelerate. The sensation of weight refused to leave him. He knew he suffered minor shock when he finally recognized the pressure to be his normal weight upon the face of the Earth. He could hardly move.

When he did move, he did so very carefully, recalling the briefing session just prior to departure. Any injury sustained at this stage of the game would have to be endured for the rest of the mission. He released his webbing, uprighted himself, and placed his feet upon the deck for the first time. In freefall, there had been no deck.

He oriented himself to the new ups and downs within the passenger cabin. There were moans of protest and nervous laughter from those around him. Moore finally stood and let go of any support. He wobbled, his tall, slender frame constantly threatening to buckle under the load. His muscles weren't up to the task of maintaining an erect posture under such monstrous forces.

"This is intolerable," one of the Lunans complained. "How are we supposed to function in this gravitational field?"

"Your jaw still functions," another replied.

"We've been warned that this would be an unsettling experience," a third party commented, his voice heavy with a Jovan accent. Moore recognized him as the psychologist in charge of helping to alleviate the confusion of their first encounter with Earth's gravity.

"If anyone is feeling clausophobic, it will soon pass. Sedation is available for those who require it. We've been given twenty-four hours to acclimatize ourselves before our duties commence. Use this time to get to know your body under these conditions. We can afford no accidents."

Moore watched Jovan and Lunan citizens helping one another, joking away their anxieties. If it weren't for the accents and the uniforms, there'd be no way to tell the two peoples apart. Only Moore with his black skin stood out as different. The other differences were little more than ideological and yet sufficient to have justified routine and wholesale slaughter in the silent battlefields of space.

Despite the physical handicap, within an hour the first of the ship's complement stepped foot upon the surface of the Earth. Moore watched from a viewscreen with a control to direct his view. The men wore pressure suits and helmets, and were fitted with a lightweight framework known as man-amplifiers, an artificial exoskeleton of metal tubing operated by hydraulics to multiply and support the weak gestures of muscles accustomed to low-gravity and freefall environments. Equipped with the amplifiers, the men moved about quite freely.

Moore fully sympathized with Jon, the nameless figure on his photographic plates for so long. He had something of a name now, Jon B–897Y. Jon had experienced his weight, stranded alone in this alien environment, and had survived. How many of those around him might duplicate such a feat of perseverance and inner strength of character? Not many. Not himself, most certainly.

Moore caught sight of a laser rifle. In a flood of shock, he sought out the Jovan Commander and found him still within the passenger compartment.

"They are low-powered weapons required for some degree of personal protection," the officer explained. "There are savages here and wild animals. We are vulnerable."

Moore sympathized with the logic, but the Jovan Commander behaved nervously at having to defend

123

himself. Not that Moore knew the extent of their personal risk outside the ship, but he did know that these men would use the weapons with practiced ease if ordered to do so.

"One weapon among the group should suffice," Moore suggested.

The Jovan officer stiffened to his full height, a difficult achievement under the circumstances.

"You know something about this mission that we should know to ensure its success, Coordinator Moore. Luna Authority has not seen fit to divulge this information to us. Will you?"

"I have my orders," Moore said. "You have what information you require to both fulfill the mission and to assure your men of their safe return. The lasers endanger your safety. There are harmless means of frightening off native wildlife."

"My superiors determined that we should be minimally armed."

Moore turned aside and moved to the back of the compartment, resuming his watch through the viewscreen. The Jovans had already established a security watch, placing an armed man on each high spot about the blasted terrain. Despite his reluctance, Moore gave his permission for his men to step outside for a look around. They would have no specific tasks to fulfill until tomorrow. The free time would provide them with the opportunity to familiarize themselves with the operation of the man-amplifiers. They'd all be using them.

The twenty-four-hour acclimatization period took into consideration the need to cope with the distraction of the alien planet: the uneven landscape, the colors of the bowl of the sky, the clouds and the birds passing so far overhead, the insect and the plant life, the feel of a wind shifting to and fro, the noises and echoes never heard in an airless environment. At the end of the day, Moore decided to go out himself and watch the sun go down. The viewscreen couldn't do justice to the colors.

Moore walked unaided twenty feet from the airlock after having been lowered to the ground by a hydraulic ramp. He selected a large, flat boulder and sat carefully, facing west with his back to the ship. The radio in his helmet sounded tinny. He would have liked to have removed his helmet to hear what the openness sounded like, to smell the air, and feel the breeze against his face. The ten pounds difference in air pressure could be tolerated in time, but not the biological contamination. Even if he survived like Jon had, sterilization procedures upon re-entering the ship would be brutal and wouldn't be tolerated by the unprotected human body.

"Incredible," a voice said. "People lived in this environment."

"They still do," someone challenged. "The human body evolved to function in this environment."

"Mine evolved elsewhere. Bodies in general do quite well without all this weight to carry around. I'll bet the air stinks."

Moore chuckled, unable to identify the two through the distortion of the radio, then eavesdropped on two Jovans on a private, but unrestricted channel.

"Lunans appear to be friendly. Their Earth-lander is quite impressive. I wonder what they have up their sleeves?"

"Trouble. Something has frightened them. Suggesting that we land unarmed indicates they are frightened by a power that they consider harmless unless provoked."

The two men were speaking in Jovan. Watching lips move through faceplates around him, Moore identified one of the men, but not the other.

"That fighter pilot—Jon. He survived this—adapted to it."

"Something helped him to survive."

"There are other people down here. That is common knowledge."

"But no society advanced enough to pose a threat to the Lunans. There is no technology."

"That warhead that detonated just above the atmosphere. The Lunans wanted it detonated down here. Who sabotaged it? Consider the Isinti. Something strange is going on down here."

So, piece by piece, the Jovans would put the pieces of the puzzle into order. It would be for the best in the end. The Jovans would learn for themselves and face the same dilemma and learn the same responsibilities. Or none of them would be returning to orbit.

Shawn Edwards, one of Moore's communications men, sat down beside him on the boulder. "Channel fifteen."

A restricted channel. Moore switched over on his arm-mounted keyboard, identified himself to the ship's computer. The conversation would be scrambled.

"Anything new?" Moore asked.

"The Jovans are sending down a ground-effect transporter in a glider. It should be here in the morning. Heard anything about that Jovan fighter pilot we're supposed to be rescuing?"

"He's still moving into the mountains," Moore said.

"They must have seen us land. That's means trouble."

"It means he doesn't want to go back. That pits five armed Jovans against one armed ex-fighter pilot and a Valthyn."

"The Commander wants a report from you. You promised him an hourly update."

Moore glanced at his watch. "Tell him I owe him three no-reports. I'll get around to him before I turn in."

Moore watched his sunset alone when Edwards left. Men began drifting back into the well-lighted

126

ship as night fell, but a few remained outside, setting up floodlights to monitor wildlife, checking for mutations that may have occurred and proliferated during man's absence from Earth.

Moore doubted if he'd be able to sleep, but returned to the ship and his hammock. Exhaustion enabled him to drop into a restless, dream-filled sleep. He awoke often, glancing each time at the glowing digital clock across the cabin, counting down the hours to their departure across the face of the Earth.

"They're coming for us."

"Do you still hope to avoid a confrontation?" Lisa asked.

"You tell me what's going to happen."

"Are you trying to capitalize on me for a change?" Lisa said with a sly smile. "You're beginning to take me seriously to some small degree."

Lisa could indeed have told Jon of the most likely probabilities waiting for him. Looking ahead, she felt the rift between the two parts of herself grow. She grieved for herself, but from another vantage point, observed with knowing compassion.

They camped near a violently churning river of whitewater cascading through a bed of broken, water-worn rocks winding down a slope heavily populated with spruce. Despite the futility of their trek, Jon enjoyed the wild beauty of this corner of the world. But he placed an increasing burden on Lisa at this higher altitude. Underbrush had thinned out considerably and wildlife had grown scarce. There would be little sustenance here.

"They'll try to use force to take me back, but I'm not all that defenseless."

"What about me?"

Jon tried to make out Lisa's expression. Night had fallen and a full moon filtered through the trees.

"They have never studied a Valthyn," Lisa said. "Which of us is the greater prize?"

"Would you go with them?"

"No."

"They have no right to our lives. I'll vaporize the parasites if I have to, even if I see them maneuvering us into a position to take us by force."

Lisa remained silent, gazing at him.

"You have nothing to say?" Jon asked of her.

She shook her head. "You have expressed how you feel. That stands valid regardless of what happens."

"I'm not sure just how defenseless you really are. I don't believe you need me for protection. I'm not sure I can even defend myself."

"A thought can be so fleeting," Lisa said. "It's easy to deflect an unpleasant thought and not give it the consideration it needs. Words fix reality in a special way. Some thoughts need to be put into words."

"I'm scared. That needs to be put into words. I've never trusted frightened people. They're unpredictable."

"You asked me to tell you if I knew what was going to happen. You haven't pressured me for an answer."

"I'm not sure I want to know."

"There will be valid reasons for whatever happens, Jon. It will be so easy for you to misinterpret the reasons for things that must be."

They spent the rest of the night huddled close to a small campfire, watching the eastern horizon for the dawn. The men who had landed on a pillar of flame would arrive from the east.

The glider entered atmosphere below the horizon and sprang into view from the glare of the rising sun. It soared over the Earth-lander, a silvery, delta-winged craft of unexpected beauty. The glider banked in a wide arc and set down haphazardly on a rocky slope downhill from the ship. Moore cringed as the terrain sheared off sections of the hull and ground the underbelly to wreckage. The craft would never fly again, but had only this one mission to fulfill.

The glider lay silent and ruined, leaning askew on one broken wing. The ten men of the Earth-landing party waited patiently for signs of life.

Sheets of metal suddenly sprang from the back of the glider, spiraling through the air and clanking against the rocky ground. From the wreckage emerged a square, flat object hovering in the air and kicking up dust from the ground. It gained a few more meters of altitude with a subdued roar, then dipped its nose and moved toward the group.

The ground effect transporter had been designed with utmost pragmatism. Thrusters beneath the hull supplemented the roaring fans, the perimeter of the craft was lined with windows, and its upper surface was littered with instrumentation serving dozens of hastily assembled experimental packages. Its engineers had taken advantage of the opportunity to take a first intensive look at this part of the world in five centuries.

Moore didn't like this turn of events. He had planned for a tentative contact with the Earth-bound Jovan and the Valthyn woman by himself and one other man. They would have been on foot, struggling unaided against the gravity field and unarmed against a surprisingly benevolent environment. Moore felt certain that such a strategy would have succeeded.

But the Jovan influence dominated. They were armed to a man, an unwieldy and unnecessarily forceful contact party. The Jovan Commander insisted that the weapons were harmless tools in possession of experts who had direct orders not to use them. Knowing how they blended civilian and military aspects of their lives so thoroughly, Moore knew better than to force the issue now.

They filed aboard the ground-effect transporter and took seats along the sides of the interior cabin. The pilot and his console occupied the center area of the cabin, relying on a panel of viewscreens for a 360-degree view. Obviously, the craft had been designed by a computer to fulfill specific performance parameters. It never ceased to amaze Moore how a computer could handle the use of technology in such a bizarre yet totally practical way, while cultural and aesthetic values creeped into designs created by the mind of man.

Moore felt isolated among lifeless machines. Even his comrades in their gleaming pressure suits and whining man-amplifiers laced about their bodies looked more like robots than men. The sun reflecting from faceplates kept Moore from identifying the flesh and blood within.

He felt a sense of impending disaster. This was not the right way to contact the Valthyn. They'd be intruders without a thought of courtesy or respect, reduced to the cold-blooded level of efficiency of the machines they had become. What would the Valthyn woman think of these invaders? Many men had died on the face of the Earth by the unseen hand of the Valthyn and under identical circumstances. Even if he emphatically disbelieved that a human being could have such power, he also had a vivid feeling of unknown forces at work and an ensuing fear of the unknown.

The Jovans were too blind to their own ignorance, too confident of their right to intrude on the life of one of their own and too self-assured by their weapons and a technology that had allowed them to dominate inhospitable worlds. Moore had the haunting suspicion that Luna Nation sacrificed the lives of its five men just to observe firsthand the effect of a confrontation between armed men and the mythical power of the Valthyn, that Commander Harper, caught be-

130

tween immovable and irresistible forces, had already written off the loss of five key personnel, that the universe at large watched and waited for the outcome of the sacrificial offerings. Cameras were recording. Lunan and Jovan forces circling overhead in orbit were observing.

Moore had never been a natural leader of men. He despised the military mentality that dominated the unfolding course of events. He remained in the background to observe from a distance. He had not lost control of his own people. He knew perfectly well how they'd behave and react to his subtle commands.

The ground-effect transporter rode on a cushion of air, but ascended to higher altitudes on its thrusters whenever necessary. They maintained a low altitude over a forest of conifers, then dipped back down along a sloping meadow of sparse grass and rocky terrain cut by a raging stream of water falling from the mountains. Guided to the site of the two Earth-bound humans by telemetry from orbit, the craft unerringly slid along the ground, then abruptly fell to the earth with a sigh. Overwhelming silence descended. Outside, less than fifty meters away, a man and a woman stood side by side and waited.

Moore recognized the pair immediately, the woman in her white gown flowing with the breeze, the Jovan in his blue-and-gold uniform. Jon held the laser pistol in his right hand, the self-restoring battery clamped to his wrist. Moore's photographs had been too grainy for accurate identification of the weapon, but it was as formidable as they had suspected.

The Jovans did not fear their own. They took for granted that this man would acquiesce to his rescue despite the evidence to the contrary. Performing with practiced discipline, they exited the craft and lined up before the transporter with their hands at their sides, a ritual Moore recognized as symbolic of a peaceful encounter. The Lunans disembarked and clustered in front of the ramp, talking among themselves on a single channel of their radios.

The Jovan Commander strolled forward with a deceptively casual gait, his man-amplifier whining to provide the power his own muscles lacked. He stopped ten meters from the couple.

"Jon B–897Y, I am Commander Iltuland of the Third Expeditionary Forces assigned to the Luna–Earth regions during recent maneuvers. One of our missions is the rescue of a fighter-pilot who has miraculously survived the native Earth environment. Apparently, we have succeeded."

The Commander smiled informally.

Jon returned a wane smile and nodded. "Sir."

The officer studied the Earth-woman with open curiosity.

"Sir," Jon responded. "This is Lisa of the Valthyn."

She stood surprisingly tall, formidable, and incredibly beautiful. Moore wondered with discomfort if she'd know his thoughts if she glanced his way. He felt he had transgressed in his fantasies. But she kept her gaze fixed unerringly on the Jovan officer.

The Jovan looked back to Jon and said casually, "You are hereby scheduled to attend a debriefing session on my flagship immediately upon our arrival. Are you prepared to disembark immediately?"

"No, sir."

Moore felt the weak-kneed sensation of sheer horror. He had foreseen this all along, but had suppressed its full significance, swept away from the beginning by the strong current of progressing events.

The Jovan Commander took the negative response in stride, it seemed, but his tight voice said otherwise. "I have given you your orders, Pilot Jon."

"Sir, it should be quite obvious to you that I have refused them."

The Jovan officer remained still for a moment, then

132

took one step backward. "Arrest procedures!"

Jon and the Valthyn stood alone to confront an approaching line of uniformed scientists turned soldiers. They moved in single file to minimize Jon's potential targets, but the Jovans were still operating by ritual. They did not expect violence, ignoring the weapon Jon carried so lightly in his right hand.

Jon raised the nose of the pistol and fired. The beam passed within a meter of the officer and struck ground ten meters short of the advancing file of men. The white-hot blast triggered all helmets to instant protective blackness. The explosion tore through the tranquil atmosphere in a blast of debris and heated air. Moore's helmet snapped back to transparency in time to see the Jovan Commander cartwheeling through the air. He struck the ground and lay writhing. The other four more-distant Jovans were on the ground, struggling in panic to regain their footing.

But Jon and the Valthyn stood unscathed. The woman's gown stirred in little more than a harmless breeze. Moore continued to inch back behind the transporter for cover. His four men scrambled back aboard.

One of the fallen Jovans swung his laser rifle around to fire. The weapon malfunctioned. The man vanished in a flickering of light intense enough to black out all faceplates for a second time. Radio static crackled loudly through Moore's helmet. The babble of voices grew to a crescendo of terror interspersed with the screams of the injured and the dying.

Moore reflexively brought his hands up to the side of his head to cover his ears. The metal framework of the man-amplifier clamped about his wrists struck the sides of his helmet. He heard a sharp crack and smelled something damp and alien, the odors of Earth seeping slowly and ominously into his air supply. Moore turned away from the scene of death.

He had broken his radio as well. Merciful silence descended.

The transporter ramp rose and slammed shut. The craft whined and rose drunkenly in a cloud of billowing dust, then leveled out and gained altitude. The thrusters sent four flaming pillars to scorch the earth. Moore braced himself against the blast of flame and air, his man-amplifier screaming in protest. He yelled once before the transporter vanished over the trees, his voice echoing uselessly inside his helmet.

Moore stood alone on the side of a shallow slope. Fifty meters away, the Jovan fighter pilot and the Valthyn woman stood among the five dead or dying Jovans. Two thousand kilometers above the Earth, a Jovan battleship received a prearranged distress signal from the dying Jovan Commander. The signal to launch the thermonuclear missile did reach the weapon. The rockets failed to ignite, but the warhead detonated prematurely.

The ship's hull ruptured, an eye-searing glare piercing the darkness from within and casting stark shadows of nearby warcraft into infinity. A microsecond later, several tons of the warcraft flared to incandescence in a fireball of star-core fury.

Daylight flickered brighter. Moore caught a momentary glimpse of twin shadows at his feet. He wondered if the atmosphere would block the worst of the radiation from the glare in the daylight sky, intuitively knowing what had happened.

Jon saw the lone, unarmed Lunan standing across the clearing. Moore stared back at him, his ears popping against the rising air pressure.

Lisa walked forward and knelt beside the fallen Jovan officer. The man could not rise, his man-amplifier damaged in the fall. He could barely hold his head against the gravity to make eye-to-eye contact with the spectre of beauty and death.

134

"You can never destroy your own reflection," she told him.

Ida Moore heard her words despite the distance. Sounds carried incredibly well in the dense atmosphere. And he saw the fallen officer reach for a holstered pistol.

Moore cried out in warning.

Jon pivoted.

"Lisa, watch out! What are you doing!"

"I cannot burden you now," she said. "We shall meet again, Jon."

Her voice echoed among the trees in the stillness, but no time remained to react. The Jovan officer's pistol did not clear his holster. His dying reflex squeezed the trigger.

Moore's helmet blackened against the glare. When he could see an instant later, nothing recognizably human remained on the carboned circle of earth. Jon spun around once in the force of the explosion and fell to the ground on his knees, blinded, temporarily or permanently, by the light.

Jon leveled his pistol toward the sound of approaching footsteps. Moore ignored him and knelt beside one of the dead scientist-warriors. Debris from one of the explosions had torn a hole in the man's chest, but the helmet looked to be undamaged.

Moore removed his own helmet, breathing Earth atmosphere at full pressure and slowly losing consciousness. He fitted the dead man's helmet over his head and tried to latch it to the couplings of his pressure suit. Even if he could undo the damage already done, the fittings weren't compatible.

"This is Coordinator Ida Moore," he said over the radio. "Someone, please respond."

A voice sounded, but it wasn't speaking to him. "Earth-lander, this is Mission Control. We have systems override. You will not launch until we authorize. Standby."

Then: "Coordinator Moore, what is happening?"

Moore glanced around the scene of smoldering, foul-smelling death. His eyes watered, his lungs congesting and heaving. The Jovan fighter pilot silently towered above him.

"There are two survivors." Moore choked on the words. "We need help."

"Coordinator Moore," a second faltering voice said. "This is the Earth-lander, Pilot Davi speaking. Who is the other survivor?"

"The Jovan. Jon. I've broken my helmet. . . ."

"Coordinator Moore, this is Mission Control. We are receiving conflicting reports from the transporter, but the Jovan fighter-pilot must be disarmed before we will order it back. The two of you can share the isolation provisions aboard the Earth-lander. Can you comply?"

Moore glanced up at the Jovan, unable to tell if the man was still rational. Moore took a deep breath to speak.

"They won't come back for us unless you're disarmed." Moore remembered to speak in the man's native language. "You can't stay down here by yourself."

Jon heard the Lunan speak to him from the depths of his own private hell. Anger burned like madness, a raging maelstrom held at bay by a hurt so intense, it alone had mercifully begun to numb him. Beyond the fading emotion, he approached a psychic emptiness drowning his will and his desire to live.

Jon forced himself to focus on the black-faced Lunan speaking to him in his own language. He still couldn't focus on what the stranger was saying, but he felt the man's suffering. An infinitesimal part of him pitied the Lunan even though he would have destroyed him at the least provocation.

What did he care if anyone survived? If the transporter returned, he'd destroy it as well. He'd destroy anyone wearing a Jovan uniform without a second thought. But the Lunan who had once been his enemy was no longer. That surprised him. But not wanting to cope with the off-worlders further, Jon turned and stepped around the smoldering craters. He began heading back down the mountain slope into open country.

Why had he ever expected to leave Earth? Had he given any thought to where he'd go? He had forgotton how repressive Jovan society could be. Not so long ago, he would have responded to a direct order without hesitation, by reflex even. But the Jovan Commander hadn't been dealing with a subordinate pawn and there'd be no going back now. Not ever. He had murdered and he'd be summarily executed for such a crime. Even his very survival on Earth would be carried in the books as a crime.

His long, slow strides took him toward bleak, featureless terrain. An hour later, he heard the air-rushing noises of the ground-effect vehicle returning to rescue the Lunan. Soon, it would be abandoned. The Earth-lander would launch and he'd be alone, too far away from the beach people to ever find his way back.

Lisa could not have planned for it to be this way. What had gone wrong?

CHAPTER EIGHT

Ida Moore regained consciousness, confused by the presence of Base Commander Isaac Harper standing over him.

"Where am I? What the hell's going on?"

Moore felt strange and disoriented. Before Harper could answer, Moore noticed the transparency separating the two of them. He could easily enough deduce that he had survived and had been returned to the research satellite. He had lost consciousness even before the transporter had rescued him.

"You're in Medical," Harper said. "Isolation. How do you feel?"

"Funny. What's happening?" He repeated his question for an entirely different set of information.

"We've been isolated by Jovan forces," Harper said. "They've ordered Lunan forces to maintain a one-hundred-thousand-kilometer clear zone. They've broadcast across the system a declaration of war, saying that Earth is held by aliens."

Moore tried to rise. The transparency turned out to be just a helmet. With considerable effort and a nauseating vertigo, he managed to sit on the edge of a hard white bunk. He wore a white biological contamination suit, the kind used in working in hazardous environments. In his case, it was to keep biological contamination in.

"You're a walking cauldron of disease, Moore." Harper's bluntness on a personal level contrasted sharply with his usual political ambiguity. "The doctors say you may not survive, depending on the kinds of microorganisms they're dealing with and the effectiveness of the antibiotics they have available."

Medical personnel stood in the background, looking on as if dealing with something not quite human.

"What's our status?" Moore asked.

"The Jovans have designated us as a liaison between them and Luna Authority. They're requesting information and suggestions on the nature of the Valthyn presence on Earth and how it might be neutralized."

"In other words, they want to know how to get some weapons down there."

"You speak Jovan, Moore. You know as much about the Valthyn as anyone. We need your help."

"Then tell everyone to go home. The Valthyn woman is dead. The fighter pilot is as good as dead. There's nothing more to be done."

"Do you believe the Valthyn can be ignored?"

"You can stop trying to kill them."

"Moore, we're on the brink of war. There are no command ships. It will be a real war like the Holocaust if it happens. We'll die here, Moore. We'll all die if we can't come up with some plan of action to satisfy the Jovans."

Moore stood. He felt dizzy, but not incapacitated. Nobody moved to stop him. It hurt to breath and his muscles ached. Otherwise, everything seemed to be working right.

"Am I free to leave Medical?"

One of the doctors stepped forward. "You'll be required to remain in the isolation suit at all times. You're attached to self-contained sanitation facilities.

The food and water tubes in your helmet are supplied from sealed containers. We'll be warned of any break in the seal. The entire station will be in danger if that happens. In the meanwhile, if you need any help, we'll be at your disposal."

"I'm being monitored?"

"The suit is supplied with a considerable variety of medication fed into your body by an intravenous needle in your leg. You won't feel it. Telemetry is transmitted to our computers, giving us a moment-by-moment update of your physical condition. Commands are sent back to a microcomputer to regulate medication. Everything is being done that can be done. For the time being, you're in fairly good shape."

Moore turned back to Harper. "I need some time to myself. I need to sleep and think things out."

"We need an immediate debriefing," Harper said. "You talked with the Jovan. I can't believe some of the stories I've been hearing."

"Believe them. And you don't need a debriefing right now. I didn't speak with the fighter pilot. If he dies or commits suicide, we'll never know what happened between him and the Valthyn woman."

"Moore, if you're suggesting going back down. . . ."

"Even if it's a one-way, one-man mission. The Jovans have fouled up worse than Luna Authority. We still haven't accomplished what we wanted."

"The Jovans have written off that fighter pilot as dead," Harper said. "He killed a superior officer. You know how they are."

"Then we're his only hope of survival now. And he may well be our only hope of preventing another Holocaust."

"Moore, if you're serious, I'll put in the recommendation. But we still need that debriefing."

"You'll have it when I decide whether or not I'm going to survive whatever it is I've got crawling

141

around inside me."

Moore returned alone to his quarters. Harper didn't try to stop him. Stretching out on his bunk, he tried to sleep, but doubted if it would be possible bound up inside the contamination suit. Evidently, Medical anticipated him. He slept profoundly for hours, awakening refreshed and alert. Tranquilizers, stimulants, pain depressants—he had a whole arsenal of drugs at his command. He felt the numb area on his upper thigh through the suit with his fingertips, not enjoying the thought of having his inner workings controlled by remote computer.

Moore rose and sat at the desk before the wall-screen for an update on what was happening in low Earth orbit. The newscasts on every channel told a horror story. It had started with a warhead detonating in a Lunan Earth-lander violating Earth Treaty. Then, the Jovan half of a cooperative Earth-landing mission had died, destroyed by a mysterious Jovan survivor and a woman suspected of being something other than what she appeared to be. A battleship, two cruisers, and five assorted smaller craft had inexplicably vanished in a thermonuclear fireball in Earth orbit. It took Moore a few minutes to analyze Jovan strategy.

Despite the wargames, the Jovans considered themselves invincible. And the Lunans were their only worthy opponent in the solar system. Having their own ships blown up in orbit by unknown forces, the Lunans were no longer transgressors. Therefore, the Lunans were incompetents and the Jovans had stepped in to confront a powerful and unknown enemy. Luna Nation was basically a civilian society possessing a military force. But the Jovans were first and foremost a military society. They needed a clearcut enemy to maintain their own sense of identity. Luna Nation had suppressed news of the Valthyn in order to prevent public panic throughout

the system. The Jovans weren't in the least concerned with the fears of civilian populations, only with
the unthinking mobilization against a new enemy
that they hadn't as yet bothered to evaluate.

Moore called down to his lab and asked for an
update on the Jovan. The man moved aimlessly
eastward at a slowing pace. They had no way of
knowing the things Moore most wanted to know—
how the man felt, what his intentions were, how he'd
react to a visitor.

Moore contacted Harper. "I'm ready to go back
down."

Harper looked anxious. "If the medication you're
receiving stops, Moore, you'll stop. Have you considered your physical condition?"

"I'll not lose communication with the diagnostic
computers except for a few moments during re-
entry. You can relay telemetry through whatever I use
as a lander."

"Moore, I haven't received word back from the
Jovans."

"Don't wait for it. Just ready something that'll get
me down to the surface. You can worry about
retrieving me later."

"Why, Moore? Your behavior is suicidal. That
environment hurt you. Why do you want to return to
it?"

Moore grinned. "I thought we both understood the
effect of the Earth environment on the human
psyche. I've worked my entire life from a vantage
point that gives me a perfect view of the tops of
people's heads. I've had a taste of that environment
and it suits me fine. And I don't want to sit up here
and watch that Jovan die. He has the answers to a
thousand questions that I could ask as fast as I can
talk. Someone has to go down and get that information while it's still available."

"You'd have to remain in the isolation suit under

143

medication," Harper said, his voice level, but a note of eagerness creeping into his tone. "We'd require constant voice communication, perhaps a miniature camera transmitting visual data. . . ."

"You work out the details, Commander. Let me know when you've organized something."

"We're working on it, Moore. I just didn't think you'd be in any physical condition to take it on. The Jovans are depending upon us to interrogate the fighter pilot. I think they're going to kill him when we finish."

Jon could not find food nor water. He couldn't find the streams and the ponds, the orchards or the edible vegetation. At the end of the second day, he decided the dehydration would claim him first. He sat on a rise overlooking a flat, dry landscape, not even bothering to seek shelter for the coming night. He'd watch another sunrise and sunset, but doubted if he'd be conscious the dawn of the third day.

He was awake during the early-morning hours when the meteor streaked from the horizon to almost directly overhead. But when the retros fired and three huge parachutes blossomed, he revised his original assumption with a vague smile. He had a visitor. He had a fairly good idea of who it would be.

The craft was little more than a canister. Naturally, they knew his position from orbit. They could have dropped it directly on top of him, but discreetly put it down a quarter kilometer distant. Jon had no difficulty identifying the Lunan with the black skin in his white suit and plastic helmet. If it had been a Jovan uniform, he would have fired on it.

Jon rose to meet the stranger. The Lunan wore no man-amplifier this time and moved very slowly. He'd be sick still, probably under medication and not suffering as much as he had. Jon stopped thirty meters from the Lunan, surprised that he still experienced a low-keyed loathing after ten years of hating Lunans.

"Is there water abroad the lander?" Jon asked.

"Help yourself," the Lunan said in accurate Jovan.

Ida Moore sat on an outcropping of rock and made himself as comfortable as possible, already satisfied that the Jovan would at least speak with him. Watching Jon head for the landing capsule, Moore noticed the weight and muscle the Jovian had acquired during his stay on Earth's surface. He felt crippled by comparison. When the man finally returned brushing beads of moisture from his face, he sat on the ground in a carefree, cross-legged position facing Moore.

"Who the hell are you?" Jon demanded to know.

"Coordinator Ida Moore of the Department of Anthropological Studies aboard the Lunan Earth Research Satellite. I've been in charge of keeping track of your progress ever since you crash-landed."

"That's been quite a while. I've known about you, I suppose. What's happening upstairs?"

"Insanity," Moore looked up at the band of light arcing across the clear sky toward the south.

"They equate power with their war machinery," Jon said. "They have a few surprises in store for them. I wish the hell I knew what was going on."

"They?"

Jon gave a vague gesture. "The Federation. The Alliance. All of them. I don't belong any more. Not even here." Jon glanced at the capsule. "But at least mine wasn't a deliberate choice. What are you trying to accomplish?"

"I don't know," Moore said. "Whatever it is, I'm not sure it's worth the effort."

Jon studied the Lunan, tempted at first to just abandon him and walk on alone. But the radio transmitter inside the capsule had been sabotaged, a panel removed, and circuit boards broken by hand. The Lunan wasn't an agent, not for his own people or the Jovans. He was here on his own for his own personal reasons. That impressed Jon.

"Why did you volunteer for a mission like this?" Jon asked. "What are you after?"

"I didn't volunteer," Moore said. "It was my idea from the beginning. I thought I could talk with you and the woman and learn enough to keep everyone from panicking. I finally managed to do it my own way, but I seem to be a bit late to accomplish anything useful."

Jon felt a deep despair and nodded in agreement with the Lunan. "If you had come alone in the beginning, Lisa would have spoken with you."

"Lisa?"

"I still don't understand what happened," Jon said, fighting the turmoil still tearing at his guts. "She couldn't have meant for that to happen, but I don't see how. . . ."

"Was she human?"

Jon glanced up sharply, then relaxed. "She said she was."

Moore knew better than to push too hard. If Jon would talk, he could afford to sit and listen. He could still feel the antibiotics working against the illness raging through his body. He felt lethargic and tired, content to sit in this one spot forever.

"Did you know that people were once wild?" Jon said unexpectedly.

"Wild?"

"Like the animals here. When they lived on Earth. Governments didn't have the technology or the organization to keep track of everybody. They couldn't tell where each person was at, what he might be doing or thinking or planning. They relied on propaganda for whatever control they could manage. There wasn't any real unity of society. They had to tolerate a great deal of autonomy, people who lived their own lives as they desired. Free people. Wild people."

"Lisa told you this?"

"She said that people should be free. She said that a government should reflect the autonomy of each citizen. Isn't that incredible?"

"I don't understand what you're trying to say."

"I've killed my own people. They thought they owned my life. Luna Nation would do the same. They would own me or destroy me."

"I see."

"Aren't you going to be getting around to asking me to return with you? Are they sending another ship down for us? But it wouldn't accomplish anything for me to defect."

"I don't think I was going to ask you to defect," Moore said. "I just don't want to see war break out. It would segment and scatter the space nations. It would be the start of a new dark ages. I just want to know about the Valthyn. If you have information that would prevent a war, I'd like to be able to relay it on open channels for everyone to hear."

Jon grinned. "You destroyed your radio."

"But I can signal for a lander. If I learn anything of value, I can return that information to them. I'm not even sure if I can go back."

"Nothing I could tell you would be of any use," Jon said. "The only information the space nations want about the Valthyn is how to destroy them. But if humanity can't live without violence, the Valthyn will see them destroyed. If you relay that to the space nations, they'll only see it as a threat."

"I don't understand."

Jon sighed, wondering if the Lunan would believe what he had to say, hoping he could word it accurately.

"There are one hundred billion people living in the solar system. Only eight billion are either Jovan or Lunan. The rest are aligned with one or the other.

147

Except for the two billion people living on Luna, there isn't a satellite-based settlement or an orbital colony with more than fifty million people on board. Everytime a new colony is established, a new subculture is born along with it.

"Lisa said that technology amplifies man's assets as well as his liabilities. The greatest liability is the way we've aligned ourselves between two superpowers, one in the outer system and the other in the inner system. A colony is said to align itself for the purposes of security, but the motivation is a feeling of insecurity.

"People won't let each other be free," Jon said with real feeling in his voice for the first time. "They keep trying to control each other in order to keep from feeling threatened by different ideologies and different ways of life. Lisa said that if people were strong and aggressive to begin with, they wouldn't feel threatened or use violence to defend their interests. That's what led to the Holocaust on Earth. Governments enslaved their populations and pitted the concentrated power of an entire nation against others who were also trying to get everyone to think and feel and behave the same way for the sake of their own feelings of insecurity. The same thing is happening now, but the next time we have a real war, there won't be anywhere to hide. There's no defense against the war technology we have today."

"The Valthyn can't change the way things are," Moore said. Jon had said nothing that he'd disagree with, but Moore had invested a secret hope and longing toward a Valthyn moral superiority, a new factor in human affairs that would ultimately change the human condition for the better. He didn't want to hear futile criticism and impossible ultimatums backed with the kind of power they had demonstrated.

Jon shrugged. "We have to change. Lisa said we'll

be in contact with extraterrestrials in the near future. She says that the encounter will be mutually disastrous. There have to be changes."

His mind in a sudden turmoil, Moore tried to think out that sudden turn of events. The discomfort he felt had little to do with the sickness within him.

"Lisa said that there are wild creatures who will attack their own reflection in a mirror. They'd exhaust or injure themselves trying to pit defense and aggression against their own image. So, the Valthyn have established themselves on the most touchy piece of real estate in the solar system. It belongs to them as much as it does to us, but they know how humanity will react toward them. You can imagine what's going to happen when the Jovans add to their fleet already in orbit. The Alliance won't tolerate it. The crisis will trigger another Holocaust. But the Valthyn hope that humanity will see what's happening and realize the depths of mindless destruction they're capable of. If their strategy works, we'll stop short of destroying ourselves and the encounter with the real aliens will take place in a different way."

"That's it?" Moore said. "Is that what's been happening?"

Jon looked at him with an expression of angered sarcasm. "Do you want more?"

"Who are the Valthyn?" Moore said in a brittle-but, level tone.

"That's a hard question to answer," Jon said. "I don't know if I could repeat her explanation."

"What do you want to do? You can't stay down here. I can call down a lander to take us to the research satellite."

Jon stared off into space. "If I live, I'll show those arrogant bastards what destruction is all about."

Jon's depth of vehemence startled Moore. He was allowed that small view of the blinding hatred contained within a relaxed, self-confident exterior. Moore

149

still felt it necessary to try to get Jon to the research satellite to repeat his story to others. There had to be a way to stop the inexorable trend of events taking place above the Earth. He couldn't personally afford to evaluate Jon's story himself. Others had to hear. They had to believe and understand the part of Jon's story that told of an obvious truth. The course of history could not be allowed to barrel unchecked toward another Holocaust.

Moore stood, disregarding the pain. He walked to the capsule and pressed a small disk on the instrument panel. The automatic signal would bring down a lander. It mattered little what might happen once they reached orbit. It mattered only that they leave Earth.

Jon did not try to stop the Lunan. It wasn't relevant what the man tried to accomplish. Jon was living one moment at a time, moving with the flow of time without bothering with the direction each passing second took him. When Moore returned, he slid down the smooth surface of the boulder and sat on the ground, using the rock as a backrest. He closed his eyes, breathing deep and heavy.

"You've been watching me for four years?" Jon said.

"It was an invasion of your privacy," Moore said. "I apologize."

"I never knew life could be like that. I wonder why Lisa let herself die."

Moore felt a tear form in one eye. "I envied you, you son-of-a-bitch. If I had known what was going to happen, I would have stopped it."

"I don't think you could have." Jon studied the Lunan with renewed curiosity. "Why is your skin black?"

Moore held his gloved hand out into the sunlight. "It's supposed to help prevent harmful exposure to the ultraviolet component of sunlight. It keeps me

150

healthy."

"Oh, yeah? How are you feeling?"

"Like shit."

Moore weakened as the day passed. He doubted if he'd survive the acceleration of the launch, half contemplating not bothering to return with the Jovan. If he were going to die, he'd as soon die on the face of the Earth.

In the gathering dusk, the two of them watched the pyrotechnics of the descent of a Jovan version of an Earth-lander. Typical of Jovan arrogance, it dropped vertically, its orbital velocity spent before it even struck atmosphere. It entered atmosphere with a sun-brilliant glare of friction and burning descent engines. Glowing ionization spread through the stratosphere. A wind churned across the landscape as if nature responded with nervous anxiety to the intruder burning its way to Earth. It set down a safe distance away in a roaring cloud of flame and debris.

"Why didn't they send you down in that to begin with?" Jon wanted to know."

"The Jovans said it was a useless mission, but that they'd volunteer the equipment if I could guarantee that you'd return with me."

"Do you really believe they'll allow us to dock at your research satellite?"

"I don't know," Moore said. He hadn't moved and his eyes were closed again.

Jon smiled, studying the squat, streamlined fuselage of the craft. It would function well within the atmosphere of Earth. After all, it had been designed to function well within the atmosphere of Jupiter. Jon hadn't seriously considered returning with the Lunan, but he gave the idea some thought.

"Why don't we take a walk and check out the ship?" Jon said.

Moore sighed. "I can't promise you won't regret that decision."

"No matter. I'll wager we don't make it anyway."

Moore carefully and painfully struggled to his feet. He looked at the ship and the way Jon smiled. "What are you planning?"

"I'm not quite sure yet," Jon said. "But I promise you an interesting time, Lunan."

Base Commander Isaac Harper was a soldier among scientists, but an administrator among soldiers. He possessed life-and-death power over 1,200 people under his command and he didn't know what to do with it. It had never occurred to him how often he depended on Coordinator Moore's advice in handling less-than-routine decisions. Now the Jovans had isolated the research satellite and he'd probably never see Ida Moore's black face again. They had worked well together for almost a decade. Not once had Moore ever suspected that his commanding officer was frightened of him, by both his physical appearance and his competence.

"They have launched," Harper told the swarthy face on the viewscreen, a council member of Luna Authority. "It's a Jovan vessel interfaced with our own navigational computers. I have verification that they will dock at this station as intended. We have the facilities to question the Jovan and to collate new data with what we have on hand."

"The Jovans are reluctant to cooperate," the councilman stated. "They may intervene."

"We are not a military outpost," Harper pleaded. "There's a Jovan battleship matching orbit with us. This whole damned satellite isn't as large as the antenna array that monster carries. We need their cooperation in this matter if we are to gain any useful information."

"Is Coordinator Moore in communication with you?"

"Coordinator Moore is not conscious. He is anesthetized and packaged in acceleration webbing and may not survive the G stresses regardless. He is contaminated, ill, and possibly dying. The Jovan has overridden automatic pilot and is handling the craft himself, but like I stated, his trajectory shows he intends docking with this station."

"Commander Harper, it's imperative that Moore docks safely and briefs us on any new information he has obtained. He has spoken with the Jovan fighter pilot and perhaps even with the Valthyn woman herself. There are Outer System Federation fleets moving sunward and Inner System Alliance fleets maneuvering to intercept. The entire system is mobilizing for war. We need information to assuage the fears of the Federation and we need it now."

Harper noticed a priority screen flashing for his attention.

"I have confirmation that the launch module has achieved orbit, your honor. I must attend to docking procedures right away."

The councilman nodded and the screen darkened. Attend docking procedures, indeed! What would an administrator of a bunch of traitorous anthropologists know of docking procedures? The only people within five million kilometers of Earth who knew what they were doing were those with their fingers on firing triggers itching to blow their computer-assigned targets to oblivion.

Harper answered the flashing screen.

"Harper, command post!"

"Navigation, sir! A Jovan cruiser is moving in on the launch module! The launch module has deviated from docking trajectory! Sir, they're not going to make it!"

Harper signaled an alert throughout the station. He switched to readouts showing him the horror unfolding a half orbit around the face of the planet. He watched the Jovan cruiser moving in to intercept the

153

launch module. The Jovan pilot in the module had taken evasive action, accelerating into a higher orbit. Already, tens upon tens of Cobra fighters launched from a nearby carrier were moving in to block any remaining avenues of escape.

"The fools!" Harper thundered in frightened anger. "The murderous fools!"

Jon appreciated the sophistication of the atmosphere-worthy spacecraft, a vehicle designed originally to skim deep into the atmosphere of Jupiter to retrieve weather balloons headed for trouble. The ship had an enormous reserve of power and more instrumentation than he could make use of. Tied in with the navigational computers of the Lunan satellite, Jon had the location and movement of every craft in Earth orbit available for his onboard computer. With that information on hand, he evaded the Jovan cruiser that moved in to intercept.

It felt good to be back in space. A whole part of his mind that had vegetated on Earth came to life again, the part of him that could reflexively interpret and respond to the symbolism of the data screens. His fingertips danced over the console keyboards. He could feel the ship responding to his subtle commands.

Jon took the launch vehicle high in its orbit. When other craft moved in to intercept, Jon rotated the ship and fired his main engines. He dived for Earth's horizon, skimming atmosphere at a velocity that had the life support systems screaming their own minor crisis. His thumb ached for a firing trigger. The sight of a laser bolt punching a hole through the guts of the clumsy warcraft blocking his trajectory would have felt better in that moment than a multiple orgasm. All of his old loyalties were dead. They had died in the arms of a woman his own people had murdered.

There were Cobra fighters on the screens now,

distant and fast moving, converging on computer projections of his trajectory. Moving at hyperorbital velocities, they decreased his option of trajectories still open to him. Larger Jovan craft, even several nonmilitary cargo vessels, were moving in to block him off.

"Earth launch vehicle, this is Lunan Earth Research Satellite requesting trajectory update. You are not on your prearranged trajectory. You are not on a docking trajectory."

Jon could barely understand the voice through the heavy accent. Talking with Moore, he had forgotten that Lunans didn't speak his tongue.

Jon could only respond in his own language. "I am engaged in a game of three-dimensional chess," he said, ignoring formalities. "I am somewhat outnumbered as you may have noticed. I have a Lunan citizen aboard. I request Lunan military support."

"We have no military forces in the area, Earth-launch vehicle. We suggest that you cease evasive action and surrender to Jovan authorities. Luna Authority requests that your behavior does not risk open hostilities between Jovan and Lunan forces."

"What about Coordinator Moore?"

"We request that Coordinator Moore be suited and ejected from your craft in compliance with a ballistic trajectory we are feeding your computers. We have a shuttle on standby for retrieval."

"Whose idea is this?" Jon said with mounting anger.

"Earth-launch vehicle, we have no alternative but to suggest that you surrender to Jovan forces if you are unable to dock with our research satellite."

"Do you suppose I have time to file a petition with the Systems Confederation for the charter of an independent nation, population one?"

"Earth-launch vehicle, we suggest. . . ."

"Up your scrawny ass, Lunan!"

Most of Jon's screens went dead, his link to the satellite computers terminated. That left him with his onboard systems, rendering him blind to anything below Earth's horizon. Radar showed several craft moving in the area, but his own computers weren't up to the task of providing trajectory probability intersections on more than one at a time. Jon estimated that he had less than five minutes in which to act before the first of the Cobras were within effective firing range. Even if they had no intentions of destroying him with the Lunan aboard, they could knock out his engines, burn off his external-antenna array, paralyze and blind him.

Jon unbuckled himself and swung around in the zero gravity to attend to Moore. The medical monitor aboard the ship had had no trouble interfacing itself with the microcomputer in Moore's isolation suit. It still showed normal readings, but just barely. Jon fingered a keyboard on the monitor, feeding Moore enough of a stimulant to bring him to full consciousness.

Moore's eyes flew open instantly. Jon waited for the Lunan to orient himself.

"Moore? Can you understand me?"

"Yes." His voice sounded vague.

"Your research satellite just ordered me to suit you up and dump you outside. They'll have a shuttle waiting to pick you up."

"It's vital. . . ." Moore sounded confused. "It's suicide . . ."

"You'll be safe," Jon said. "But I have the entire Jovan warfleet converging on me. I doubt if they intend to salvage this mission."

"But, you're too valuable. . . ."

"You'll be better off going EVA, Moore. You'll survive."

Moore's voice sharpened as the stimulant took full effect. "Do I have a choice?"

156

"Well, I don't have the time to throw you out bodily if that's what you mean."

"Do we have a chance if I stay?"

Jon nodded. "Sure. I have an idea."

"What can you do? Can you escape them?"

"We don't have time to go into that for now. It's your choice, friend, but it will be a blind decision."

"I'll stay."

"How are you feeling?"

"Recently deceased."

"If you do get killed, don't say I didn't warn you."

Moore felt keenly alert then, appreciative of Jovan medical technology for this moment of synthetic clarity.

"The Valthyn have an ace up their sleeve. You know that."

"That's close to a meaningless metaphor, but I know what it means. You might think differently if you knew what I had in mind."

Jon swung back around and buckled himself in.

"Jon, I won't survive high-G forces."

"Delta, five, five, alpha. You'll sleep through it all."

Moore hadn't felt so alive in weeks. He didn't want to return to the limbo of unconsciousness. But as Jon's fingers flew over the controls of the ship, Moore quickly keyed in his delta, five, five, alpha on the monitor and put himself back to sleep.

Jon had his eye on the big S-5 cargo transporter perfectly visible on his screens despite the 2,000 kilometers between them. The huge craft normally ran ten kilometers in length, powered by engines large enough to nudge a small moon from its orbit. Manned by a crew of three, it was a portable warehouse stocked with the supplies and equipment a long-term expeditionary force might require considerable distances from major bases and drydock facilities. There were several in Earth orbit surrounded by tens of their attendant tugs.

The transporters were a flattened hexagon in cross-section, hulled only with sheet metal for micrometeor protection and defended against larger debris by automated lasers. The S-5 in Jon's screen blocked his trajectory while the more mobile spacecraft were moving in to form a corridor down through which he'd have to pass. Jon checked most of his forward speed and drifted into the trap, apparently defenseless, outwitted and thoroughly cowed by the gauntlet of firepower through which he'd have to run in order to attempt escape. Jon didn't make his intentions obvious, keeping the S-5 off to one side of his screens as he approached. Already the shuttle bay of a cruiser had opened to receive his ship.

Computers would have known better than to allow warships to trap an enemy vessel between them. Jon would never have been able to make his move without ensuring that he'd not be fired on. But computers had never been programmed to utilize an entire warfleet to blockade a single, unarmed spacecraft. Men were at the controls of these vessels, eager, arrogant, and taking sadistic pleasure in outwitting a first-class fighter-pilot.

"Earth-launch vehicle, prepare for docking," the cruiser warned.

"Prepared for docking," Jon returned, putting all minds at ease.

Jon's attitude jets sent delicate tendrils of vapor circling about the ship. The cruiser assumed he had oriented himself for smooth docking, but Jon swung the ship to point directly at the monstrous S-5 in the distance. Only meters from the brightly lit docking bay of the cruiser, Jon fired full main rockets, the monatomic hydrogen propulsion units designed to lift the craft away from the gravity of the most massive planet in the solar system. Jon never intended remaining conscious against such inhuman acceleration. He had already programmed his computers to carry out his plan.

The tiny craft with the oversized engines vanished in a stream of flame. Computers aboard the warcraft canceled the commands to fire upon the fleeing vessel. Friendly craft were dangerously close to the line of fire. The S-5's meteor defense fired automatically against the oncoming intruder. As the small craft spun end for end, attitude thrusters, antennae, and other external paraphernalia on the hull of the ship melted to slag or exploded in bright gouts of flame. At the last possible instant, the engines fired one last time. The deceleration wasn't quite sufficient to completely check the small craft's forward momentum. Jon hadn't intended for it to be sufficient.

The launch vehicle tore through the hull of the fragile S-5. Hull plating, superstructure, support beams, and decking material sparked and sheared aside at the onslaught. Careening through partitions, rebounding from masses larger than the ship itself, the tiny craft plummeted its zigzagging course through a haze of wreckage and floating debris into the guts of the leviathan.

Jon regained consciousness long after the violence ended. Secure in the pressure suit provided by the launch vehicle and connected to onboard life support, he checked the cabin's air pressure and found it still intact. Moore's monitor read well into the green. The unconscious Lunan had hardly reacted to the abuse. Jon glanced at the panel's chronometer, estimating it would be another fifteen minutes before the Jovan cruiser docked with the S-5.

There'd be a hard vacuum beyond the fused hull of the ship. Jon switched over to air canisters and prepared to leave the craft. It had flown its last mission, but had performed flawlessly. Now, it was time to move and move quick before he lost the few precious minutes he had gained.

159

The outer hatch was fused solid. Jon bled off the cabin pressure and blew it. Through a sudden hole in the side of the cabin, Jon watched the hatch tumble, ricochet through floating debris and vanish into darkness. A glow from the emergency light within the cabin filtered outside, illuminating dust and debris ranging in size from grit to multitonnage cargo drifting about. The remainder of his journey would be a hazardous one.

Attaching a flexible phosphor belt from an equip-ment locker above his holster, Jon pulled himself through the hatch. In the dim light, he surveyed the surrealistic landscape of twisted and torn metal. The trajectory of the ruined ship showed as a black tunnel rapidly filling with expanding debris.

Broad folding doors along an undamaged wall were down and locked. A monorail tube would lie beyond. Automated haulers moved along the mono-rail to store or retrieve cargo in the holds. And the small hatch above the larger doors would be the emergency personnel tube. Picturing the layout of the S-5 in his mind, he oriented himself in relation to the manned control and living compartments for the three-man crew of the S-5. He'd have to hustle. Once Fleet Command organized a search team, they'd swarm over the S-5 and disassemble it piece by piece, if necessary, to get to him. They'd know full well the hazard a renegade fighter-pilot would pose at the controls of an S-5. Ida Moore would have to remain on ice for the time being. He suspected the Lunan wouldn't object in the lĕast.

Fleet Command had made a fatal error by moving an S-5 into position to blockade him. Jon's first job assignment at the age of seventeen had been aboard an S-5. He had operated the haulers on the mono-rails, moving cargo by remote control through the endless tunnels of the base warehouses to the huge loading and receiving bays. That had been just before his admission to the Ganymede Military Training Center, Fighter Pilot Division.

Jon picked small pieces of debris from about him and threw them behind him for reaction mass, moving slowly through the free-floating obstacles to the hatch of the emergency personnel tube. He opened the sliding hatch and slipped inside the claustrophobic space.

The tube snaked along the spine of the juggernaut. Old skills returned with a nostalgic swiftness. He brushed his fingertips against the tube walls, gaining momentum patiently, dragging his knees softly against the sides to keep his body aligned head-first. The phosphor belt provided a band of illumination that moved along with him. Every few meters, he encountered the rectangular gap of exit hatches to other cargo holds and a white identification number showing his location along the longitudinal axis of the S-5. At first, the recessed hatches passed by slowly, but he gained steady momentum until they shot past faster than he could count them. His fingers regained the snapping agility needed to propel him at respectable speeds. The emergency tubes were seldom used except by young stock clerks at play in man's most limitless enviroment of air and gravity free space. Who'd ever suspect that he'd be able to transverse the few kilometers to the main control room within minutes?

The tube led directly to the pressurized areas of the ship. Nearing the airlock, Jon dragged his feet to cut his forward momentum. There were no security arrangements to the airlocks. The crew of the S-5 wouldn't be expecting him. He'd simply drop in with a large laser pistol in his right hand and order the crew to make a few minor alterations in the ship's course.

Jon was about to hijack a very large spaceship. He thought perhaps his first destination would be Earth's moon.

161

CHAPTER NINE

Moore awoke to a low-frequency vibration rattling his teeth together. Two men were peering down at him with dispassionate gazes. He thought at first that the launch vehicle had been swallowed by the docking bay of a Jovan warship. The two men wore Jovan pressure suits. But enough was amiss to encourage him to withhold judgment on the situation while the men released the hammock strapping for him and switched his white contamination suit from internal life support to air canisters. The connectors, at least, were universal.

Moore's thigh ached. Sometime during launch or shortly after, telemetry from the research satellite to his suit had been stopped, the needle in his thigh withdrawn automatically. He wondered how long the marvelous Jovan stimulant would last, how soon the old aches and pains of biological contamination would return.

He rose and found himself still within the cabin of the launch vehicle and in a near-weightless environment. But the airlock had been blown and starless darkness lay beyond. Even as he looked, a large piece of wreckage tumbled past.

"What's going on?" he asked.

He was either on the wrong radio channel or the two men chose not to answer. A monitor light low on the inside of his helmet warned that a vacuum lay beyond his pressurized suit. The two men took up positions on either side of him and holding him under each arm, used small suit thrusters to leave the ship and move through an incomprehensible void of debris still tumbling about from some recent catastrophe. Looking back, Moore hardly recognized the launch vehicle. He understood in a flash of insight. Jon had rammed some large cargo vessel, literally embedding the ship somewhere within its hull. And the huge craft was under power. The wreckage was collecting itself into a vast heap against one side of a cavernous cargo hold.

The two Jovans maneuvered him through more orderly masses of cargo beyond the damage caused by the launch vehicle. An upward rolling door of huge proportions revealed a tunnel more than 50 meters in diameter beyond, vanishing into darkness in either direction. Moore had never seen the interior of a Jovan cargo transport before, but the setup was similar enough to Lunan transports for comparison.

Above a large diameter monorail running the length of the tunnel ran a smaller rail and a waiting personnel carrier connected to it. Fighting against the barely perceptible acceleration, the two Jovans maneuvered him into the open cockpit between them. Once they were belted down, one of the men took the carrier speeding down the endless dark tunnel.

The carrier finally slowed and nosed into an airlock. Inside, Moore found himself weightless in a circular drum rimmed with five hatches. One hatch opened, revealing a ladder leading downward to a deck at the bottom. The entire affair rotated slowly. Descending the ladder ahead of the two men, his weight gradually increased, courtesy of centrifugal force.

At the base of the ladder, Moore looked around the control cabin crowded with equipment. Jon was seated at a communications console. He still wore his pressure suit and helmet.

"What's up, sleeping beauty?" Jon said.

Jon gestured with his laser pistol for the two Jovans to join a third sullen crew member seated across the cabin.

"I'll be damned," Ida Moore said softly, his voice barely carrying beyond the dome of his helmet.

"At the present time, we are not as damned as the Jovans would like. We're quite safe and secure, in fact."

"How long will that last?"

"Indefinitely. These oversized babies vibrate quite a bit when under power. Inflight docking is a strict no-no. Neither can our friends fire on us. Who knows how many billions of credits worth of cargo we're dragging along with us."

Moore took a seat near Jon. He felt lightheaded, but nothing too severe seemed to be happening physiologically.

"Feeling better?" Jon said. "The sedation might have helped. You've been out for quite some time."

"I'm okay, Jon. Why are you still wearing your helmet?"

Jon nodded to the three crewmen. "That's why they're so well behaved. We've both got considerable populations of Earth's microbiology crawling around inside us. If we're not damaged, they won't get sick and die."

"I only have one other question," Moore said. "Where are we going?"

Jon grinned. Lately, his familiar grins were growing broader and more spontaneous.

"We're going home. Your home to be specific. I've had our friends here key in a close lunar orbit. We're

165

broadcasting navigational data on open channels so that both sides know our intentions. For various reasons, most of them financial, nobody will fire on us as long as we're a relatively passive influence in the area."

Moore couldn't believe that Jon had actually escaped his own people. He had expected to fall into the hands of the Jovan authorities, intending to plea with every bit of logic and commonsense at his command to save Jon's life and convince the Jovans of the hazards they faced.

"Why?" Moore said. "What are we going to do with this ship once we reach Luna?"

"Well, it's sanctuary for the time being. And there's a courier ship aboard. I've been going through inventory while you were sleeping. It's a long-range, fast little ship. Two passengers. There are ways of escaping in it and ensuring that we won't be tailed or blasted as we launch."

Moore nodded in agreement, but there was more to accomplish than just escaping with their lives.

"Can we talk about this?" he asked.

Jon shook his head with mock exasperation. "You still want to try to talk reason with my former compatriots? I don't think either side will listen, Ida Moore."

"We have to warn them. We're at the center of attention right now. But when this has blown over, we'll be too insignificant to listen to."

Jon gestured to the communication screen. "Be my guest."

Moore switched seats and faced a small console and a dark screen. He looked to Jon for help, suspecting that the Jovan had already talked with the authorities.

Jon reached over and switched on the screen. A face formed, a gaunt, angry face, regal in appearance, apparently startled by the intrusion.

"I am General Hester Alboran, Fifth Jovan Warfleet and the Third Expeditionary Force." The man had automatically spoken in Lunan. Moore hadn't yet adapted to the fact that he'd be instantly recognizable anywhere in the Earth–Luna vicinity. "You are Ida Moore, Coordinator, formerly assigned to the Lunan Earth Research Satellite. Do you wish to speak with me?"

"Yes. . . ."

"You may speak."

Moore gazed bewildered at the stoic, grim face seething with suppressed tension, at the same time displaying an iron-clad patience that Moore suspected would never grow thin.

"I have a warning," Moore said.

"From yourself?"

"From the Valthyn. Indirectly."

"Identify the term Valthyn."

Moore tensed, choosing his words more carefully. "The Valthyn are the agents who can destroy any weapon turned against them. That's the only definition important to you."

"And what is the nature of your warning?"

Moore glanced at Jon looking on with a vague smile. "You threaten your own destruction. You're fighting an invisible enemy. You know it's there, but you'll only destroy yourselves by trying to attack it. They act as a catalyst. You and Luna Nation won't be able to control the warfleets converging on Earth. There is great danger of war and the rules of the Ganymede Convention are forgotten."

"Why do these Valthyn intervene in our affairs?"

"They are putting an end to destruction as a way of life," Moore said, uncertain as how to continue without sounding wildly insane. He could see by the General's expression how little effect he was having.

"Coordinator Moore, I am not a stupid man. But your words are vague, inconcise, and useless to our data banks. You hint at occult forces of unlimited power directed against a military force you cannot accurately evaluate. I still await useful communication between us."

"That we can agree on," Moore said. "Who do you think you're up against?"

"An unauthorized, highly technological entity using Earth as a refuge against effective retaliation."

"Don't you see the trap you've entered?" Moore demanded with growing frustration. "The Valthyn are a lure and you've taken the bait. I told you they were just a catalyst. When you discover that you don't have anything tangible to fight, the whole system will be fighting among itself in self-defense! You've let the Valthyn destroy the balance of power that the wargames provided!"

General Alboran sneered. "An anthropologist speaks knowingly of military matters. An untutored civilian instructs Federation High Command. I have heard of your ghost stories of these mysterious Valthyn and their great psychic powers. I have heard stories of the invulnerability of these godlike Amazons until one brave Jovan officer destroyed one of these creatures with apparent ease. And it didn't take an unknown power to kill him. It took only a traitor who will soon suffer the consequence of his betrayal. Do not waste my time, anthropologist. Luna Authority has also disclaimed your citizenship in the name of international peace. You also shall die."

The screen went dead.

Moore looked to Jon with a stunned expression. Jon gave him a lopsided grin and shrugged.

"How do your noble ideals fare now, anthropologist?"

"What the hell are we supposed to do?"

"I'm not exactly graced with total illumination. Perhaps a bit of action is what we need—starting with our own personal survival."

Moore nodded emphatically. "You're doing fine. Just keep us in one piece and maybe put a little distance between us and that Alboran buddy of yours."

Jon laughed. "Don't be cowered by appearances. The General doesn't have the intuitional ability of a good fighter pilot. Just watch one of Jupiter's finest make a fool of him."

The lunar landscape passed slowly below, a land of craters and seas of dust and the geometric patterns of civilization overlaying them. Moore watched Tycho pass at each revolution. He could just make out the landing bays that led to the underground city, the place of his birth and unbringing. Nostalgia and guilt gnawed at him.

Public broadcasts were full of hysteria, paranoia, and hatred. They were equating him with monsters of the past—Hitler, Graver, and Bostworth of the slaughter of the colonists in 2023 A.D. And Jon became a fiend holding a civilization ransom, threatening to split the crust of the moon with a thermonuclear explosion of gigaton proportions.

Moore watched a view of the ominous bulk of the S-5 plowing through the star-dusted black sky, orbiting now at less than 80 kilometers above the heads of millions of innocent people. The TV crews were fantastically effective at setting the mood of terror. A dot of light would show among the backdrop of stars. It would swell and dominate the field, then rumble overhead, kilometers upon kilometers of metallic landscape thundering overhead. The sound effect embarrassed Moore. They were overdoing it a bit.

Within the S-5, the noise and low-frequency vibration did irritate Moore. The transporter was not under power, but Jon kept the thermonuclear furnaces burning to discourage Jovan or Lunan warcraft from firing upon the S-5 and splitting it up into wreckage. Extinguished, the six huge engines could be destroyed and rendered harmless. But burning, they were miniature stars straining against invisible magnetic bottles, six glaring fireballs lined in two neat rows just beyond the array of magnetic thrust plates lining the circumference of the rounded stern. Normally, a laser blast damaging the engines would shut them down in millionths of a second, but Jon had sabotaged those protective circuits. Now any damage destabilizing the circuitry or field magnets of the magnetic bottles and those miniature suns would expand into miniature supernovas and reduce the lunar surface below to molten slag. The Jovans wouldn't have held off on crippling or even destroying the S-5 for economic reasons if they had known of the extent of Jon's technical skills.

"Blackmail," Moore said. "Holding an entire innocent population hostage. We're going to go down in history as a pair of real bad fellows."

"Want to surrender?" Jon asked, distracted momentarily from his data screens.

"No, I think I prefer terrorism. Besides, the entire solar system is watching this happen. They're bound to wonder who we are and why we're doing this."

Jon didn't seem to be impressed. "The military is feeding the newsmedia lies."

"Yeah, but the lies are contradictory. They'll trip over their own stories. The public expects propaganda from the military. They'll dig for the truth. It might do some good in the end."

Jon tapped his fingers against the data screens. "There's too much to keep track of here. Eventually, they'll try boarding us, dropping troopers somewhere along the hull. They'll burn through and work their way forward. These S-5s don't have much in the way of a security system."

"Since you've anticipated that strategy. . . ."

"We'll be leaving soon," Jon finished.

Moore glanced over at the three crewmen cooperatively monitoring the ship's dangerously low orbit. Jon ignored them. He had holstered his pistol.

"How are you going to work it?" Moore asked.

"I have the emergency shutdown circuits bypassed We're already sitting inside a very large bomb. And I could collapse the magnetic bottles that would detonate it. All I have to do is rig a transmitter aboard the courier to generate a signal and program the magnetic bottles here to collapse if the signal is interrupted. The courier is serviced, fueled, and ready to launch. We can be safely away before they can analyze and duplicate the signal or board the ship and repair the damage."

"You're that good with computers?"

Jon gave him a smug grin. "A fighter-pilot has lots of spare time to kill. Hobbies are essential to sanity. Mine was computer programming and electronics, the game variety where you try to outwit programming parameters, then cover your trail when you get more out of it then it was intended to provide. Cheating, in other words."

"Then there's just a small matter of a destination left to consider."

Jon's grin broadened. "And where do you suppose that would be?"

With a ripple of gooseflesh, Moore knew the answer, but approached it with caution. "What range does the courier have?"

"With a single, high-efficiency fusion engine and a multikilogram, metallic hydrogen fuel supply? Would you like to try to Alpha Centauri?"

Moore shook his head. "No, you're thinking of Saturn. The Isinti colony."

Jon nodded, abruptly dead serious. "If that place isn't an orbiting insane asylum, they might know of the Valthyn. They might know something of the aliens

171

Lisa mentioned."

"They may not want anything to do with us," Moore suggested.

"We're running blind, Lunan. I don't know what else to do."

"Lisa never offered any suggestions?"

"Lisa told me that things would fall into place as they happened. I had no idea this would be happening. Since it all started, I've never been able to see beyond the tip of my nose."

Moore looked around the cramped control cabin. "There's nothing more we can do here."

"You realize that finally?"

"I've always known how incompetent Luna Authority could be. I never knew how arrogantly your people behaved. I can't believe this is really happening."

"It's going to be be an Armageddon," Jon said. "A sloppy one." He sighed, a hint of the depression that had slowly befallen him as the bitterness over Lisa's death passed. "Lisa did a lot of her dirty work where it isn't visible." He tapped his head with a finger. "In here, down deep."

Jon nodded to the three S–5 crewmembers. "I was like them. I was told what to do. I performed. I reaped whatever rewards were bestowed upon me. I believed what they told me and I did my best. But I still don't understand how they manage to manipulate people with such banality? How did they get so good at shoving across such nonsense? I feel like I've been color blind all my life. Not blind, but just never trained to see color. Now, I can see and I wonder why I didn't notice before. Those three are intelligent people. They're nice guys. I guess they move when their strings are pulled because they don't know any better."

"It's the same with us," Moore said. "We've always taken pride in not having as oppressive a society as the Federation. There's more elbow room for independence, just no opportunity to abuse it. I've been free to do what I've been told to do."

"I had Lisa rattle me loose from the crap I've been swallowing," Jon said. "Who rattled your cage?"

"Not who. What. Earth dominates our skies. I've spent my life studying it. I suppose while you were playing games with your computers, I had my own share of spare time to kill. Nobody has much use for an anthropologist these days. Just watching the primitives living on Earth for a decade or two was enough to lead me to suspect that the rest of humanity isn't quite sane. What did you think of the tribe you lived with for so long?"

Jon nodded in recognition of the point Moore was trying to make.

"They weren't primitives. They were real people, maybe the only kind that count."

Ida Moore felt secure in the cramped, but luxurious, cabin of the courier. Two days out from the Earth–Luna system, they were little more than a speck of ballistic metal speeding through interplanetary space near the orbit of Mars. The courier had been designed for the rapid and comfortable transportation of VIPs through the system. Jon sat at the controls for hours on end, monitoring the movement of military craft moving in from the outer system. Moore sat beside him in a large, soft acceleration couch facing the long-range communications station, listening to the flood of panic overwhelm the Alliance.

Jon suddenly reached over and switched the screens to a magnified view of Earth.

"Look what's happening."

Sparkling light encircled the equator of Earth.

"What—" Then panic flooded through Moore, a solid sheet of ice-cold horror. "Oh, my God!"

Each bit of light would be a thermonuclear explosion. Simultaneous static overrode the public broadcasts on the screens and their audio components sounding in his earphones.

"Don't panic," Jon warned. "The solar system's a big place. Chances are, they'll be able to stop it before it spreads too far. Keep track of the public broadcasts and give me an idea of what's happening."

It took Moore hours to piece together what had happened. The Jovan fleet surrounding Earth had turned their battle lasers toward the face of the Earth. Nobody knew the source of the attack that had destroyed the warfleet, but Luna Nation had attacked the remaining Jovan forces in the vicinity, expecting to clear the area of any threat to civilian populations. They failed. A single, surviving battleship had inflicted heavy damage upon Lunan surface installations.

The chain reaction of violence shifted to the Martian orbital and surface colonies ambushing Jovan reinforcements. Moore watched the colonies obliterated by other fleets moving in from the outerworld nations, the face of Mars itself rearranged by high-speed, thermonuclear missiles.

"Jon, they won't stop," Moore said with an edge to his voice.

Nobody had ever suspected that illegal Lunan missiles lay dormant and undetected in a Trojan orbit near Jupiter. Jon tensed, but remained silent at news of the missile attacks upon Jovan city-fortresses orbiting the major satellites and the planet itself.

After the major attacks and counterattacks, the momentum of aggression died, unsupported by the level of fanaticism it would have required to destroy the largest civilian populations. When the first wave of fighting ended, the Federation and the Alliance both held their hand, waiting for the next move to be made. Horrified by the destruction wrought by sheer blind reflex, the two major powers called a truce to investigate the incident in Earth orbit that had triggered unthinking paranoia.

Moore had studied his history well. Eighty percent of the solar system remained undamaged by the first major war since the Holocaust that had all but depopulated Earth. But the remaining twenty percent represented twenty billion lives, millions at a time decimated by fusion warheads burning through the silicate cones, metal hulls, and electronmagnetic shielding that separated man and the warmth and atmosphere he needed from the cold airlessness of space.

Man had lived with the star-flame of hydrogen fusion too long to fear it in the same way as man had on Earth. On Earth, the skies had seethed with multicolored platforms of towering, churning radioactivity spelling death for millions of horrified survivors days, months, and even years later. But in space, fusion warheads flashed clear, bright, and quick. Men, women, and children were unscathed or they vanished in the hard light that left no horror stories to tell, no suffering, pain, or lingering death to endure. A civilization without the family unit it had once known left little psychological damage behind. People were numbers added or subtracted from statistics. Destruction became automated reconstruction. There were no bodies to stumble upon, no funerals or memories of death to ponder.

Moore sensed that the general public had no idea of what had caused the sudden vicious conflict spreading like a plague through the system. When it ended, Earth remained unscathed and humanity breathed a sigh of relief, too intimidated to ask questions that would only be answered by lies.

Jon helped Moore set up an electronically enhanced image of Earth on the main viewscreen. Uncountable tons of wreckage orbited the Earth. A constant stream of meteors brightened the night skies. The darkened moon smoldered, its surface installations reduced to glowing slag. The basic strategy of the Lunans had always been to play the underdog, knowing their concentrated population center to be too vulnerable for the kind of arrogance the Jovans could afford to display. But in the end, the missiles that rained upon Jovan strongholds caught them entirely off guard. Retaliation had been surprisingly futile. Both the Martians and the Lunans had their strongholds dug deep within the face of their tiny, rich worlds.

Moore wondered if the beach people thought of Jon while the fire raged in their skies. Jon felt suddenly cut off from his own past. Phenomedon, the city-fortress of his birth, had been destroyed.

A computer analyzing a radar echo determined the data to be a priority item, triggered the critical hazard alarm and transferred the information to a screen in a form Jon had preprogrammed.

Jon recognized the object as a missile, his fear translated as a sudden cold alertness. He had the computer backtrack the trajectory of the missile to its source.

"Probably a computer launch," he told Moore. "One of the automated weapons platforms in Martian orbit."

A star burned on the tail of the missile. "Hydrogen fusion. They're reserved for major targets."

"Us?" Moore said.

"I doubt it. Probably the platform has lost communication link with the Alliance. It's just exhausting its remaining missiles at convenient targets as a measure of desperation."

"Can we outrun it?" Moore asked with growing anxiety.

"No way."

"Outmaneuver it?"

Jon looked disgusted. "Of course not."

"Then what? The lasers?"

"It would take an hour for the lasers to burn through the shields those things carry. A courier is not exactly a warcraft."

"Then what?" Moore wanted to know with a quiet desperation.

"Estimated time to proximity detonation, eight minutes. Get strapped down."

Jon accelerated the courier, curving away from the incoming missile, scanning deep into the vacuum ahead for any signs of debris. They were entering the asteroid belt, but locating a piece of rock larger than the courier would be a thousand-to-one shot.

"What are you trying to do?" Moore said.

"Find something to duck behind. The missile will disarm if it loses its target. I read four minutes to detonation." Jon pointed to a glowing chronometer. "Count it down every half minute or so for me."

With the alarm silenced, Moore had no emotional grasp of their predicament to sustain his panic. The two of them sat side by side in the darkened cabin, the console blinking its language of color to Jon, the panorama of the galaxy a tapestry of diamond dust on black velvet spread across the forward screens.

"Three minutes, thirty seconds," Moore said.

Moore fought against the hard pressure of acceleration. The stars were reading a significant doppler shift into the ultraviolet, even if the color shift didn't register to the naked eye.

"Three minutes," Moore said. "Find anything?"

"I think so. We'll have to take another few Gs, Moore. It might be a bit uncomfortable for you."

The acceleration slammed Moore into the couch. He opened his mouth to cry out in alarm, but his lungs wouldn't expel air. Approaching blackness felt like death itself. He regained consciousness, nauseous and lightheaded, without realizing that he had

177

lost it.

"I've cut the main drive," Jon informed him. "I've got a little friend dead center behind us."

Moore flipped on a rear viewscreen, drawing a grin from Jon. Nothing moved in the field of stars.

"Thirty seconds," he said, wondering where he had lost two minutes.

"It'll be close," Jon said, tapping a keyboard at odd moments with the forefinger of his right hand, guiding the ship now with only the attitude thrusters. "If it doesn't work, we'll never know it."

Moore had little more than a rough idea of the demands Jon was placing on the navigational computer of the courier in trying to duck into the radar shadow of a piece of rock already hundreds of kilometers behind them. He felt detached from reality. A vague anxiety was the best he could manage facing imminent death. Only the most superficial layers of his intellect told him that he was within thirty seconds of being vaporized so quickly, a pain impulse wouldn't even begin its journey to his brain.

Moore closed his eyes and waited. When the tension became unbearable, he opened his eyes and glanced into the rear screens, half expecting to see a fireball the intensity of a thermonuclear explosion bearing down from behind.

"Dead yet?" Jon asked.

"I don't think so. What's happening?"

"It'll overtake us in a moment. Brace yourself."

"Jon, for what? What the hell's happening?"

The courier's engine cut in, pushing Moore hard into his couch. After a moment, it eased and vanished.

"Look out the port side," Jon said.

Moore glanced at the viewscreen. There were only stars. Then something black and wedge-shaped nosed into the starfield. It was the missile, its thrust

178

plates still glowing white hot.

"That's what chased us?"

"An old Jarson model five." Jon moved the ship in closer and cut in a spotlight. "At the speed we're moving, it'll be out of the solar system in a few days. There must be thousands of these things fanning out across the galaxy. Can you imagine what life out there must think of us when they run across one of these things?"

"Are they dangerous?"

"It won't detonate accidentally. If it fails to obliterate its assigned target, it goes quite dead."

"Well, thanks for the commentary. Can we be on our way now? Aren't we a bit off our course?"

"Too far off," Jon admitted. "I've got to go EVA and salvage what's left of its fuel supply. That was an expensive ride and it'll be just as expensive to put things right."

Moore watched Jon suit up and collect the tools he'd require from a well-equipped locker. Jon was an inordinately intelligent jack-of-all-trades and master of just as many, a true technologist in every sense of the word. Moore felt small in comparison to him.

"Don't go away while I'm gone," Jon said.

"No, of course not. You might need me to count down a few more seconds the next time we get chased by something nasty."

"I'm not tired," Moore said. "I don't need a nap right now. And I don't normally sleep for a year and a half at a time. Six hours a day, period, is plenty."

"It might get a bit monotonous twiddling your thumbs for a year and a half, Moore. We're only a week from the orbit of Saturn, but we've been thirty degrees off course for the past few million kilometers or so. We don't have the fuel to set things straight in a reasonable amount of time. It's more economical to decelerate into an eccentric solar orbit that will

179

intersect Saturn."

"A year and a half from now."

"So? Pleasant dreams."

"Like hell!" Moore said. "I don't like the idea of a computer turning me off and on like a goddamned light bulb!"

"It doesn't shut you off. You shut yourself off when your body temperature drops below a certain point. The antifreeze solution keeps your body cells from being damaged by ice crystals. When you thaw out, the computer retriggers enough of the bioelectrical current in the brain to get things working again."

"Sounds simple."

"It's a complex biomechanical system not without its hazards, an emergency system I've used four or five times in the past ten years."

"Four or five times? Fighter damage?"

"Sure. I'm a decade younger than my chronological age. You don't age very fast when you're a deactivated quasi-solid at near absolute zero."

"I wouldn't imagine so."

"Are you game?"

Moore looked at Jon and sighed. "I'd just as soon sit back and enjoy the scenery."

Jon programmed the computers and released control of the ship. They took turns changing into special pressure suits connected to the courier's life support system. The emergency system designed to keep a body alive or in suspended animation during emergencies ranging from shipwreck to a coronary initiated suspension procedures by inserting a hypodermic needle into Moore's leg. He reacted with sudden anger at having so much of his personal welfare removed from his direct control, but took what satisfaction he could in seeing Jon wince. The sedative took effect within fractions of a second.

"Okay?" Jon asked before losing consciousness.

"It's good, but I'm beginning to feel like a piece of excess baggage."

180

CHAPTER TEN

Saturn hung unmoving against the stars, a three-dimensional masterpiece of dusky, swirled color with its impossible system of rings sprawling razor-edged about its equators in concentric, shaded bands. There were lights in the sky about the massive world, white lights too bright to be stars, too small to be natural satellites.

"Saturn, area population, five billion," Jon said. "The Isinti colony occupies a city orbiting the outer edge of the ring system. There are maybe fifty cities in or near the rings themselves. It's quiet. There's no background chatter on the radio."

"What's been happening during the past year and a half?" Moore asked. "They might fire on us."

Jon shook his head, most of his attention on the screens giving him a second-by-second update of their entrance into Saturn's system of orbiting colonies and satellites. He had little hard information to work with on the location of the Isinti colony.

"The people out here aren't as tightly organized as the Jovans," Jon said, talking as if he no longer identified himself as a Jovan. "I don't think they suffered any missile damage. They're a bit neutral politically, even if they are aligned with the Federation for its economic advantages."

Moore noticed the diminished size and brilliance of the sun. He knew the outer worlds to be poor in heavy elements. "What economic advantages could there be in this neck of the woods?"

"They're specialists in the manufacture of metallic hydrogen. Metallic and monatomic hydrogen provides most of the fuel used in propulsion technology for the entire system. I doubt if we'll see much in the way of hostility, but there are colonies out here who refuse to respond to even emergency beacons, people who haven't had voice-to-voice contact with civilization for over a century. God only knows what's happening to them. Genetic engineering, philosophy, culture—a society can go a long way by itself in a span of a few centuries."

"And the Isinti?"

"They haven't isolated themselves. They've been isolated by an almost superstitious fear of the unknown. They're the first people to live entirely in a gravity-free environment. And you know what's been said about that."

Moore had heard the conjecture. The human body had been designed by eons of evolution to function within a gravitational field. Regardless of what had become of the Isinti, it was generally accepted that no Isinti would ever again function within or even survive within a gravitational field. The Isinti, unlike the rest of humanity living in space, had utterly and irrevocably cut their bonds with man's biological heritage. For the remaining span of their existence, they would survive only by their skills in providing an artificial environment in the hard vacuum of space.

"Have you tried radio contact yet?" Moore asked.

"I've been trying for the past half hour. I'm picking up a dim beacon. It's within the known area of the settlement, but there's no ID tag on it."

"What happens if we fail?"

Jon didn't bother asking what kind of failure he had

in mind. "We're near the top of the sun's gravity well. We can spiral down and make any port within the system without trouble. What's the problem?"

"We need somewhere to hang our helmets without being summarily executed, imprisoned, or exiled," Moore said. "I hope like hell someone's home."

"Strange, how silent the radio spectrum is," Jon said. "I knew these people were a long way from being sociable, but this is ridiculous. It's more like a blackout. Everything I'm receiving is low-frequency, low-power signals that wouldn't carry halfway across the system."

"What's Jupiter sounding like?" Moore asked on impulse.

Jon gave him a startled look. He swung the long-range, directional antenna around. "They're silent! All the way through the system!"

"Luna Nation?"

Jon spent another moment adjusting the antenna. "Everything, Moore! The whole system's dead!"

Moore shivered with the hollow fear of his personal doom. A year and a half had passed, but only on the digital readout of a clock. A century might have passed or the end of civilization 10,000 years from the age he had known. His imagination could squirm down the narrowest corridors of speculation, but he knew the sleepers aboard the courier couldn't keep a man alive indefinitely. Neither could the instruments have malfunctioned and then mysteriously corrected themslves.

Jon swung his cameras sunward and tied them in with the computer to track down the spectrum of fusion burns of space traffic. In an instant he had his answer—normal to slightly heavy traffic, much of it the colder burns of heavy-cargo caravans, probably automated ore carriers sliding down through the solar system from the asteroid belt.

"Everything looks normal. Something odd is going on."

"War?" Moore asked.

"The torch of a warcraft stands out. What I'm seeing is heavy industrial traffic."

Moore's gooseflesh intensified. "The Valthyn?"

Jon shook his head. "A radio blackout? Heavy industry?"

"Jon, the aliens you said Lisa mentioned! Imminent contact with aliens! What if. . . ."

Jon shoved himself back in his seat. "That's it. Damn, what a nightmare!"

"Can we go back now?"

"Back to what? Can you guarantee the Alliance and the Federation learned something from the war? Moore, if there are aliens nearby, I'd hate to think of how the space nations are reacting. Who do you suppose started it all?"

"You did," Moore said. "And I suppose I get one small silver star for aiding and abetting. Didn't Lisa give you any idea of what to expect—?"

"You keep going back to that with monotonous regularity, Moore. Trying to make practical sense of what Lisa told me is like trying to interpret a bad dream. I didn't pay all that close attention to what she told me. I liked it on Earth and I sure the hell never expected to get kicked off the face of the planet."

The computer called for Jon's attention with a rhythmic beeping. "Radar contact with something big," he said. "The beacon was what we were after. It's directional, leading us in."

Moore forced his attention back to matters at hand. "That sounds like a welcome mat of sorts."

Jon magnified the view on the forward screens. An object rushed into view, an image of a disk cupped on both sides by ruddy glowing domes. The colony was an incredible divergence from any torus or cylindrical shape that Moore had ever seen.

"Size?" Moore asked.

"Really big. A hundred kilometers in diameter. Thirty through the domes. The domes are silicates, emitting in the infrared, but I don't know why."

Jon turned the ship end for end and began final deceleration. Without radar guidance, he tried to locate the docking bays visually. The disk sandwiched between the domes appeared to be of a flat-black, rough textured material, infinitely detailed with the paraphernalia of enviromental maintenance, but missing most of the familiar evidence of an industrialized, thriving community.

A low-priority warning warbled through the cabin. Jon shut it off. Various sections of the space city were emitting a haze. As the haze spread and approached, radar isolated individual components of it.

"We have ships coming out to greet us," Jon said. "Entire fleets of them. They're tiny, not more than one-man craft."

Jon cut the engines and began drifting into whatever kind of reception awaited them. The screens showed the small craft to be dart-shaped objects, moving without visible means of propulsion.

"It must be the general population," Moore said.

"They're emitting nothing on the radio spectrum. There's no evidence of gaseous emissions. Look at the way they handle."

Jon gave Moore a quick, ominous glance. It was unsettling to watch the formation envelope the ship and form an open corridor down through which they drifted.

"Beautifully organized," Moore said.

"Weird. I've never seen anything like it."

Moore riveted his attention on the approaching city. The edge of the disk began swelling in the screens to reveal an ever-expanding detail of the manmade world. Few lights shone from the city itself.

185

Finally, against an expanse of bright metal, Moore caught a glance of the tiny craft silhouetted on reflected starlight.

"We're at thirty kilometers and closing," Jon said.

Like fish in a strange sea, the multitudes of silent craft narrowed the shortening corridor, guiding the courier toward a wall of blackness. At ten kilometers, an opening dilated like the iris of an eye and light shone forth.

Jon guided the ship in on attitude thrusters. "It looks like a conventional docking bay."

Moore watched the screens carefully. The dart-shaped Isinti craft moved in formations, swooping and shifting in a disconcerting way that reminded him of freefall ballet, as if they moved to silent music and a spontaneous, but highly organized choreography.

"Do you see how they move?" Moore said, awed by the spectacle.

"There has to be some form of communication between them. They shift and move instantaneously. I hate to say what I'm thinking."

"All of the rumors can't be fantasy," Moore said. "I wonder why they don't communicate with us."

"They have," Jon replied. "When you stop to think about it, we've received all the direction we've need-ed for docking. A bit unconventional, maybe."

The docking bay loomed closer, filling the entire forward screen. Moore could make out individual lights lining the bay doors and the multilayered interior with their familiar nose-in docking ports that would seal to pressurized compartments beyond. But the bay, large enough to accommodate several hundred craft, was empty, devoid of a single ship other than the tiny courier nosing into the light of the gaping metallic cavern.

"The ships!" Jon yelled. "Look at the ships!"

Thousands swooped in arcs and formed a graceful

186

single file, diving and weaving in a complex double helix, then vanishing off to one side of the docking bay, entering the city by another route.

A stroboscope identified the docking portal assigned to the courier. With the last clang of physical contact and a green light on the control panel signifying a pressure seal, their long voyage had ended.

They both remained seated, put off by the unpredictability of their hosts.

"Let's say we meet with them, exchange cordialities," Moore said. "Then they'll ask us what we want. What do we tell them?"

"I got us here," Jon said. "A division of labor is supposed to be the best way to work things. So you do the talking."

"Gee, thanks."

Moore unbuckled himself and stood. "You said something about this being a zero-gravity environment."

Jon freed himself from his pilot's couch and tested the gravity field with a few kneebends. "It feels like one-quarter G. I think we'd better just take things at face value and ask questions when we have the opportunity."

Jon opened the airlock in the side of the cabin. A catwalk transversed a ten-foot space to an airlock. They both wore their pressure suits, but vented to outside atmosphere. The Isinti would be well aware of the risks of biological contamination.

The lighting was shifted toward the ultraviolet slightly, the air thin and cool. An abyss stretched on all sides of them, broken by hundreds of other catwalks spanning the short distance between the inner and outer bulkheads of the rear wall of the docking bay. Slipping through the second airlock, they stepped into a corridor. It led them to a room, the

187

interior of a flattened spheroid. There were two seats near the center of the chamber facing a viewscreen suspended in midair, flickering blue-and-white static.

"By the reception we got outside," Jon said, "I was expecting large crowds, fanfare. I think we're in quarantine."

Moore continuously forgot about their exposure to Earth's biosphere and the hazard it posed to the space colonies. He had forgotton about his fading illness.

"Be seated," a voice instructed in Jovan. It didn't sound like a mechanical reproduction, but it seemed to be emitted from the air around them.

"That's not telepathy," Jon said, seating himself in response to the instruction. Moore sat beside him and removed his helmet.

"We know of your identity and your purpose in visiting our city," the voice said. "We know of your past experience that is relevant to your journey here. And we know of the Valthyn."

The voice sounded normal, well-modulated masculine in accent-free Jovian.

"You know more than we know," Jon said. "I would like to speak with you face to face if possible."

"We know also of the Neighbors who would meet with men. They are curious and disturbed by the presence of an intelligence of these worlds so close to their own. For eons we have been neighbors, evolving in different ways to eventually awaken and discover one another. Tentative contact has already been made. Both species await the reaction of the other."

Jon stood. "I would like to talk with you face to face."

"Initial contact must be made by men capable of handling an alien reality, but men representative of the multitudes of humanity. So do the Neighbors

188

realize how initial contact must be made. They await beyond the last world of Sol."

"Is this a recording?" Jon said, speaking in a softer tone. In the silence, he sat back down.

"If the two of you acquiesce to the roles you must play, you will return to Earth. Two Valthyn will accompany you to the outer limits of the solar system where the Neighbors await the meeting between species."

Jon looked to Moore in angered confusion. Moore mocked a nonchalant attitude, letting Jon do the reacting for the both of them.

"Your roles will encompass more than you imagine," the voice continued. "You will be an embassy sent by a part of man's psyche unknown to humanity, ambassadors for a peace and growth that can belong to the human race. You will stand between fear and annihilation and as men, you may succeed or you may fail."

Silence.

"Is that it?" Moore said.

"Did you catch it all?" Jon had been afraid of receiving cryptic instructions of the kind Lisa had given him. But he understood what they were to do, even if he had no idea of how it might be accomplished.

"I caught it," Moore said. "I think."

"Of course you did," Jon said, his voice sounding level and calm. "We're supposed to go back to Earth, pick up two Valthyn somewhere and take a short trip to the edge of solar system. That's only about a tenth of a light-year out."

Jon stood and began pacing the width of the chamber. Moore hadn't noticed the depth of Jon's anxiety.

"We're mere men, my Lunan buddy! Tools of gods of few words and lots of action. What the hell. It's been fun hasn't it? Beats eavesdropping on Earth from a spinning tin can, doesn't it? And we've completely missed getting our asses blown apart by hordes of raving maniacs, haven't we?"

Jon hadn't intended blowing off steam quite so blatantly. He saw his own pain reflected in Moore's astonished expression. Again, he began pacing, shifting his focus back to more immediate matters.

"Do you know that the Valthyn all look alike? Parthenogenic twins. They all look like Lisa. I don't know if I can take that."

Minutes passed in silence.

"Maybe we're supposed to go back to the ship," Moore said.

"What for? Without fuel or provisions, the courier is just a life raft. It would take years in suspended animation to spiral down on a ballistic trajectory."

Jon glanced at the open door behind them. In response to an unspoken thought, he started back to the ship. Moore followed.

It wasn't the same ship. The courier was gone, another craft taking its place. The control console was twice the size, three seats lined before a wide viewscreen. Six passenger seats rimmed a broad cabin. Jon walked around the compartment once, then opened a hatch in the rear bulkhead, and slipped inside. He reappeared with a shocked expression.

"It's a Transtar Model Ten. I've never seen one before."

Jon slipped into the pilot's couch and lifted an extension console that unfolded from overhead. He thumbed switches and watched the craft come slowly to life. Data screens rippled with instructive graphics. Jon sat transfixed for a moment, then nodded in recognition.

"And I suppose you can pilot a Transtar Model Ten as easily as a Cobra fighter or an S-5 transporter or a courier."

"A damned idiot can pilot a Transtar Model Ten," Jon said, unaware of Moore's depressed sarcasm. "The computer is smarter than I am. But it's a handful. You have no idea of what this thing can do."

"No idea," Moore said.

Jon turned to him, his eyes bright. "It's the only civilian craft in production that can outrun and outgun a Jovian CB fighter. It isn't armored, of course, but it's agile. The navigational computer has an evasion mode that would drive a cruiser to distraction. This will get us back to Earth."

"All the way down? To the surface and back?" Moore knew enough about astronautics to doubt if the Transtar carried the massive monatomic engines necessary for atmospheric use. Fusion engines could operate only in a vacuum. Igniting one in atmosphere would be an identical procedure to detonating a fusion warhead.

"No, of course not," Jon said. "We'll worry about getting down to the surface when we get there."

"That's all there is to it? Back to Earth for more answers?"

"More answers? I didn't know we had any as yet. What else is there to do?"

Despite Moore's reluctance to be carted around the solar system by a renegade fighter pilot, he felt a definite elation at the thought of returning to the Earth–Luna regions. How badly had the moon been hit? How many had died? How had industry, and commerce fared since the mindless plague of war? Luna Nation was the only home he had ever known. He hadn't enjoyed a secure or comfortable moment free of anxiety since leaving it. It even hurt his jaw at times to speak in the unfamiliar language of Jon's heritage. He tried to gain a balance of emotion by realizing that Jon was in the same position as himself. The both of them were reacting in anger and depression at being thrown from side to side by the

191

enormous influx of events intruding upon their personal lives. And Jon had lost Lisa. Even Moore had lost nothing in comparison with that.

"We stand between fear and annihilation," Moore said aloud. "I think we're both in shock and don't know it yet. We're going to go stark raving mad when all this starts to catch up with us."

Something dawned on Moore, the source of his growing irritation with Jon.

"What am I here for? What's my role in all of this?"

Jon gave him a weak smile. "Why knock the imposition? The Isinti just promised you a Valthyn all your very own. They're quite friendly. You'll like them. She'll explain things to you, like the true nature of reality and the significance of life and death. Eventually, she'll decide you don't need her anymore."

"All right," Moore said. "I give up." He glanced at the open airlock. "I'd like to go back and try to get a few questions answered."

"Sure, if you think it will accomplish anything."

"It would take ten years of my salary to buy transportation out here on my own. I'm an anthropologist, Jon. This is an opportunity of a lifetime. I can't let it pass without trying."

Jon gestured for him to lead the way. They returned to the flattened, spherical chamber and reseated themselves.

"Go ahead and say something," Jon urged.

"I think they know," Moore replied with quiet confidence.

The voice spoke.

"Man explored his psychological and physical environments. He populated the face of one world, then many others. With industrialization, man specialized in his labors. Complex lifeforms are based on cells that specialize in the tasks they perform in the body. The lifeform becomes flexible in its sphere of activity. So man became flexible and enlarged his sphere of activity through specialization of function as you know it to be.

"Specialization requires communication and co-ordination, just as the specialized organs of the body require coordination for the whole to function. But man is an organism that lives on higher levels than individual man recognizes. Humanity has a psyche, a mind that exists on a level of reality far above the comprehension of the individual.

"The Valthyn are an expression of that gestalt consciousness, a unique response to the need for adjustment and change in the body of the race. The mind of humanity intercedes in its own behalf, much like a man who has never questioned the contents of his own consciousness. He learns that it is his beliefs and ideas and focus in life that provide him with his sense of identity and determines how he relates to the world, even the experiences that seem to occur by random coincidence. Such a man might need to search out and correct deep-seated conflicts and replace them with alternate beliefs in order to end suffering and experience life in a more satsifying manner.

"Mankind is to meet a counterpart of itself, another species that perceives reality in a different way. The meeting will trigger man's fear of the unknown. On this momentous occasion, that fear must be con-sciously recognized and not allowed to trigger habit-ual or reflexive and unthinking behavior. The Valthyn will ensure that mankind will not be blind to the consequences of such behavior. Alternate patterns of behavior are to be explored."

The screen before them danced with white snow on a dark-blue background. Suddenly, the screen came to life. A white line drawing of a naked male figure on a dark background appeared.

"The form of the human body evolved to function

193

in the Earth environment. The Isinti live within the psyche of *Homo sapiens,* but our bodies live in new environments. Consciousness must expand to fill previously unconscious roles.

"Many changes are necessary for a human body to function in a zero-gravity field and utilize inherent advantages fully, most involving body chemistry, internal structure, and functioning of the organs, especially the cardiovascular system. Certain structural modifications were deemed advantageous. First, a smaller overall size."

The line drawing shrank to half its former size, but the head remained the same, giving the line drawing a childlike appearance with the facial features occupying the lower third of the skull.

"Next, the elimination of body rigidity and excess muscular development."

The body thinned down considerably, the arms long and curved with an apparently flexible bone structure, but with proportionately oversized hands and long, slender fingers.

"The legs, designed primarily for support and locomotion upon a two-dimensional plane within a gravity field, can be entirely redesigned."

The drawing changed again. Now, the legs extended perpendicular from the torso, parallel to outstretched arms, the entire pelvis changed. The feet became another pair of hands complete with five long and slender fingers.

"These changes are on a genetic level. We give live birth to children like ourselves. You have requested to speak with me in person. You are curious and fascinated, but shocked and uncomfortable as well. We seem to have destroyed our natural beauty and denied our human heritage. A deep level of your mind protests that which we have committed upon ourselves, a biological prejudice that cannot be countered by intellectual rationalization. You do not

194

wish to meet me in person. I would not appear to be human to you."

"Why are we experiencing a gravitational field?" Jon asked.

"Mass warps the fabric of space and time, giving rise to what is defined as gravity. We can provide the same effect without the mass. It is, as you suspect, provided for your comfort by a form of telekinesis. The line drawing does not exist upon the screen. It exists in your minds. We place it there and maintain it as a visual aid of the kind you would take for granted. Many aspects of what you perceive within our sphere of influence are not as they seem. Why should not a telepathic voice be at least as vivid as an audio hallucination? We anticipate and neutralize adverse reaction when we desire. We appease your sensitivities. Or we foster revulsion and fear to form a barrier of security between the Isinti and the rest of humanity, between man as he is and man as he will be."

"As he will be?" Moore said, secretly insisting that he was too fascinated by what he had experienced to feel any prejudice or animosity toward these awesome people.

"Man lets go of old securities only as rapidly as he gains confidence in new knowledge and discoveries. Interior changes precede exterior changes. Our descendants will never walk the face of a world, but the world we have gained will support us long after the sun has reddened and the Earth lies buried beneath the snow of its own atmosphere. Others will follow us in the centuries to come, either through volition or through unthinking adaption. Man is not defined by the shape of his body. In words which inevitably reflect cultural prejudice, we cannot define man for you at all. Your concepts of humanity do not include the Valthyn. They would not include us for long. We, however, include and honor you."

Moore thought he detected a note of humor in that,

195

but a trace of rising anger blocked that evidence of the Isinti's essentially human nature.

"Why did so many innocent people have to die to accomplish what you said was necessary?"

"Jon will soon know of life and death. Look to him for your answers. When you encounter something new to your experience that conflicts with the way you think the world should be, it can be said that new experience is conflicting with old ideas that must die and be replaced. You say that people are not ideas and that their death is more real. You would be surprised to know what people are, their origins and destinations in terms other than physical ones. Search for understanding rather than justification. I will not defend reality against your injuries."

Moore looked to Jon, suspecting he had just been put down. Jon grinned.

"It's like talking into a cavern and getting confused by your own echo. Ask a question and instead of an answer, you end up with a thousand more questions."

"I have a thousand questions," Moore said. "I don't know where to begin."

"I shall resolve the dilemma for you," the Isinti said. "I shall not answer any more of your questions."

Jon stood before Moore could react.

"Let's go," he said. "Talking gives me too much time to think. I'm starting to fidget."

The cabin darkened, the control console alive with light. The colors were mere entertainment to Moore, but to Jon they represented a vast sum of information upon which to draw as he needed.

Jon backed the ship into open space a safe distance from the Isinti colony, swung it around and ignited the fusion engines. There were two of them. Moore felt the familiar thud of the thermonuclear fireballs forming in their magnetic bottles.

"We're off and running," Jon said. "I'll hold Luna

normal acceleration, but this ship is capable of some really wild rides." He nodded to the coffinlike boxes lying alongside each of their couches. "Those are liquid acceleration tanks. We can maintain several hundred Gs on automatic using them. They're not very comfortable, though. Feels too much like drowning."

"Why would we have to use them?"

"We could have outrun that missile with these tanks. Apparently the Valthyn and the Isinti aren't our guardian angels. There's something about our free will that's very important in all this despite the support we have. We can fail, Moore, We can be killed."

"In other words, we still have your former compatriots to deal with."

"And yours."

"So, it's back to fun and games."

Jon grinned. "Quite so."

Moore sighed. "Hell, I suppose if you're enjoying yourself you'll do a better job of getting us through this alive."

"Disgusting, isn't it?"

A day passed in relative silence under constant acceleration. Moore tried to relax, but worried about the enormous velocity they were building up on their sunward journey.

"You have no idea of the range of these sensors," Jon said. "Radar, spectrographs, mass detectors, wide-band radiation spectrum receivers, automatic correlation and interpretation of incoming data, automatic reaction and defense systems tied into navigational and weapon systems. We won't be taken by surprise, that's for sure."

"You mean nobody can sneak up from behind and punch a hole through us?"

Jon laughed. "This ship could detect the faster

photon component of a dense proton beam, throw up the electromagnetic shields, take evasive action, and begin electronic countermeasures before I'd have time to react to a warning signal."

"I'll take your word for it. What brought up that bit of unsolicited information to begin with?"

"We're approaching Jupiter's orbit. Jupiter isn't in the area, but there's an overlapping string of defense satellites along the ecliptic in its orbit."

Moore didn't like the way Jon studied his incomprehensible data screens with such worried intent.

"What does that mean?"

"It means they've seen us."

Moore felt his guts knotting up. "We never had problems on the way out. Why are you getting us in trouble now?"

"They ignore small ships. We're bigger than small and faster than slow and we sure the hell haven't filed a flight plan with the Defense Network. Keep in mind that the Transtar used to be illegal as hell. They still make the military nervous."

"What's the chance of having problems with those defense satellites?"

"Let's say forty percent. We're bound to gain a certain notoriety re-entering the inner system. We're moving rather fast."

"You're not going out of your way to avoid trouble," Moore said. "Is that what you're trying to say? You miss the wargames?"

"It won't serve any purpose to sneak into Earth orbit undetected. We need to know how the Federation and the Alliance are going to react to us if we expect to con them out of an Earth-lander. Keep in mind that we don't know anything about the aliens or how the system has reacted. Some of those defense satellites are of recent construction. There's bound to be a critical priority military alert going on throughout the system. We didn't have to contend with that on the

198

way out."

Moore settled back and tried to relax. He wouldn't have time for a nervous breakdown on the way in. They were approaching the legal and rational speed limit within the solar system. No ship could legally travel so fast as to make it impossible for others to detect, react, and avoid a potential collision, no matter how remote the possibility. After a nap and a few exercises on the rear bulkhead that the equivalent of Luna normal gravity determined to be the deck while under acceleration, Moore returned to his seat and took a renewed interest in their progress.

"Things still looking quiet?"

"Yes. Very quiet."

"How is our forty percent holding up?"

"It just increased to one hundred percent. Computer has just given me a torch trajectory of a fusion burn behind us. It's moving in for intercept."

"Something nasty again?"

"Even nastier. These have men in them."

CHAPTER ELEVEN

Jon identified their adversary as a small carrier. They'd soon be demanding identification and flight authorization. Jon had neither. He had no idea of whether or not the Transtar had been registered, but if it was, it wasn't transmitting its authorization code. The outer system crawled with wide varieties of small spacecraft. An unwritten law stated that fusion engines below a certain energy level were ignored by traffic control. The Transtar carried two bright Mag-5 units that would have done justice to a small freighter.

The incoming carrier blossomed into a flurry of smaller fusion burns, launching its squadron of Cobras. Jon felt no extreme concern for the moment, but he did have a major decision to make soon. If he intended to try to talk with the authorities, they'd expect him to cut his engines. Otherwise, he'd escape only by using the liquid acceleration tanks and letting the Transtar do its inhuman best to outrun and outmaneuver the fighters.

"Unidentified Transtar," a slow, sonorous voice sounded. "This is the voice of the Outer System Defense League. You are hereby ordered to cease acceleration. Acknowledge."

Moore squirmed in his seat. "Sounds like they mean business."

"It's a computer-synthesized voice. It's supposed to sound like someone who eats iron-nickel meteoroids for breakfast." Jon grinned. "Do we run or talk?"

"Whichever involves the least physical discomfort."

"Have you read the instructions for using the tanks?"

Moore glanced around the darkened cabin. "I've read the instructions for everything this ship has going for it."

Only a military pilot could have noticed that the fighters were not deployed in the usual attack mode. Jon knew better than to consider it a tactical error. Something odd was happening and Jon decided to capitalize on whatever was holding them back. The twin thermonuclear fireballs fixed in the vacuum behind the smooth stern of the Transtar swelled to twice their normal diameters. For the moment, the clusters of thrust plates arranged around the stern of the ship glowed white-hot just keeping the two miniature stars at bay, but prepared at any instant to transfer the sudden thrust of the engines should Jon choose to unleash their fury. The Jovan carrier could not have misunderstood his intentions of defying its order.

"Unidentified Transtar, we request secure interrogation."

Jon breathed a sigh of relief. He shut the engines down. The fusion torches dwindled and died, the thrust plates fading to cherry red.

"What are you doing?" Moore wanted to know in a tight voice.

"Secure interrogation means we talk."

Secure interrogation meant that the Cobras wouldn't fire on him if he agreed to open communications, a procedure guaranteed by military law.

Without the provision, too many unauthorized vessels would have preferred taking their chances with whatever evasive tactics they had at their disposal. The Outer System's criminal codes were incredibly complex and detailed. Few independent colonists managed to comply with even a fraction of them. Conversely, Jovan authorities seldom intended enforcing the bulk of minor transgressions. Secure interrogation was less an unconditional surrender than a direct order and had evolved as a compromise for everyone.

Moore felt queasy in the sudden freefall. By Jon's behavior, he understood that some kind of safe compromise had been reached. The low-keyed crisis surprised him. It had been drummed into him since birth that Jovans were reptilian fanatics. By contrast, Jon tended to be cold, but only on a professional level. And the Jovan military forces didn't seem to be any more vicious than their Lunan counterparts.

"I'm getting a request for visual." Jon nodded to a screen to the left of the console. A familiar face appeared, features chiseled from granite, black hair streaked with silver gray.

"Jon. Ida Moore," General Hester Alboran said in greeting.

Jon visibly tensed. "Sir."

General Alboran studied Ida Moore for a moment, then looked back to Jon. "Apparently, you are on a course between Saturn and Earth. Is it safe to assume you have visited the Isinti colony?"

"Yes, sir," Jon said, noticing the three-second gap in the General's response. That meant the General wasn't aboard the nearby carrier. The carrier relayed transmission from elsewhere.

"May I ask the purpose of your visit to the Isinti colony and your return to the Earth–Luna region?"

Moore expected Jon to do the talking, but Jon sighed in exasperation and shook his head. The

203

General turned to Ida Moore for his answers. Moore felt the same intense stirrings of emotion that had paralyzed Jon, but they needed the man's cooperation. Moore took whatever consolation he could in the fact that General Alboran hadn't succeeded in killing them. And he had been vindicated. His warnings had been more imminently critical then even he had imagined.

"We obtained information on Earth vital to the security of the human race," Moore said. "Nobody would listen to what we had to say at the time. The Isinti colony seemed to be the only sanctuary possible for us at the time. We've been instructed to return to Earth where we are to be contacted by someone who will help us make some practical use of that information. When we reach Earth, we're going to require the use of an Earth-lander."

Eyes blinked. The General's expression remained inviolate.

"Do you speak of the Valthyn? Does this information relate to the detection of alien spacecraft orbiting on the outer regions of the solar system?"

Moore had questions of his own to ask. He suppressed his excitement, knowing for certain now that the aliens were a reality that the whole system knew about.

"That's what this has been about from the beginning. The Valthyn have been trying to ensure that man's first contact with the aliens is peaceful. It wouldn't have been if you hadn't been forced to deal with the Valthyn first."

"You never mentioned aliens during our first confrontation," General Alboran stated.

"I told you what I thought I could get you to believe! I came off sounding like a complete fool!"

"I request that you board the carrier and submit to further interrogation," General Alboran said in a hard and level voice.

204

Jon looked up. "Go to hell!"

A glimmer of anger and frustration crossed the General's face. In the next moment, it smoothed over to a persistent stoicism.

"It would be better if you allow us to depart in peace," Moore said quietly in the gathering silence.

General Alboran nodded. "We shall escort you to the Earth–Luna region."

Jon cocked his head in surprise. "What about the Lunans?"

"All military forces have merged under common command," the General said. "For the past year, delegates from every major nation in the system have been holding military, scientific, and diplomatic conferences that shall determine how we must react to the presence of the alien task force."

"What's been happening, General?" Jon said in a tone that took Moore by surprise.

"They must have know about us for some time," the General said. "They must have known we'd eventually meet and decided it would be in their best interest to initiate contact under controlled circumstances. The size of that fleet must have taxed the resources of an extensive civilization. We believe that if we react to their presence with any form of violence, they will destroy us."

Moore could hardly believe the attitude of defeatism coming from the Jovan. "Why is it necessary to perceive this event as a threat?" he asked. "This could be the greatest thing that has ever happened to the human race!"

General Alboran raised his bushy eyebrows in surprise. "Your naive enthusiasm would be tempered with caution if you could see the size of that fleet."

Moore didn't bother to counter the General's opinion. He could see in the General something of the fear the entire system must have been experiencing in that moment. Nothing in the history of the species could approach the significance of imminent contact with aliens from the stars. The stress was unimaginable.

"If you react to their presence with passive curiosity, they may intend initiating friendly communication," Moore said finally.

"That may be, but is not necessarily true," the General responded. "You claim that both the Valthyn and the Isinti are aware of the alien presence. What is your relationship to these groups?"

Jon spoke. "Pawns."

By the General's expression, Moore could almost see the situation from his perspective. One probable thought was clear, the question of how two such miserably low-ranking human beings could be so intimately involved in a crisis of such magnitude affecting every man, woman, and child in the system. The Valthyn and the Isinti were holding the General back from an accurate assessment of the situation. They were two unknown factors in a complex equation.

"Who are the Valthyn?" General Alboran said. He had no choice but to continue to try to understand.

Jon accepted the challenge of trying to explain. "They are people from the future, people from another time and space. But they are still barefoot and have no technology. You should already know about the Isinti, but you've ignored them for too long. It won't accomplish anything for you to continue to question us about the Valthyn, the Isinti, or our relationship with them. Nothing I can say about them is really accurate. You can communicate with them yourself. You've always had that option open to you."

"We can provide the Earth-lander you require. The equipment is in our inventory in the region. May we escort you?"

"Of course," Jon said. "We have no reason to resist."

"When the carrier has matched your course, you may resume your original navigational strategy. Other vessels of the First Confederation Warfleet will join you in due time."

"I don't trust them," Ida Moore decided.

Earth loomed in the viewscreens, magnified several hundred times, but approaching rapidly. They were in the deceleration stage of their journey. When the engines cut off, they'd be in a perfect, 200-kilometer orbit about Earth.

Jon disagreed. The Jovans were acting out of character, but then again, their characteristic behavior had caused them a few problems lately.

"We have what we need for the time being," he told Moore.

Although anxious for the trip to end, Moore wasn't looking forward to the discomfort of an Earth landing.

"We must have set some kind of record getting here. How's our fuel holding out?"

Jon suppressed laughter. Moore had been growing increasingly sensitive during the last two days.

"We haven't set much of a record, but we're in trouble if we get billed for the fuel we've used. It's not easy turning hydrogen into a metal, but it makes for one hell of a long-lasting fuel supply. I'd say we have more than half of our original supply."

"What's going to happen when we land?"

"I don't know," Jon said. "I'm more concerned about where. I assume we won't be setting down on the Arctic or Antarctic ice caps or in an ocean. That leaves about two major land masses to consider."

Jon noticed that the debris had been cleared from orbit. His radar showed a clean sweep ahead. For Moore's benefit, he put a magnified view of the moon on the forward screens. Moore felt his flesh crawl at the evidence of new cratering obliterating old and familiar landmarks. And yet, public broadcasts

207

crowded the radio spectrum, mostly public-information documentaries on details of new phases of construction in progress, some of it reconstruction, some involving shipyard construction of new warships in the drydock facilities of the solar-orbiting factories.

"Both sides survived," Jon said. "They're even working together. It was a tragedy, Moore, but they're too blind to face what happened."

Moore gained some perspective of their incredible velocity and rate of deceleration as the Transtar backed into Earth orbit with both engines blazing. The globe ballooned in their screens and came to a dead halt in the same instant the engines stopped. And they had been decelerating at that same rate for days on end.

In the forward screens, a sizable Jovan fleet backed into the same general orbit, their fusion engines gleaming like silver-white stars. Jon had not tried to maintain communication with any of them.

"We're home free," Jon said. "The Transtar has just shut itself down for a nap."

Earth stretched below, a convex plain of deep blue, glaring white and landscapes of green, yellow, and rusty browns. No world in the solar system could match it for sheer beauty.

"Would you believe I'm homesick for that ball of mud?" Jon said. "I've spent the best years of my life down there."

"It frightens me," Moore said. "I still find it hard to believe we can survive down there."

"Wait until you see what it has in store for you this time."

Jon said it knowing the same applied to himself. Facing another Valthyn would be facing Lisa's death once again. Another Valthyn would be a physical duplicate of Lisa. Jon resented having to comply with the only direction he had left in his life. Another

208

Valthyn could never take Lisa's place.

"Transtar, this is the Cruiser Io transmitting navigational data on channel eighty-six. We are to rendezvous and to place the Earth-lander vehicle in close orbit. You are to remain passive and secure until we have achieved a ten-kilometer encounter. You may then dock with the vehicle at your discretion."

"Acknowledged," Jon responded.

"It's too easy," Moore said.

"Have you noticed the Lunan ships further out?"

Moore could read the screens well enough to notice the blips hovering at nonorbital velocities several thousand kilometers out.

"They're playing some kind of game with us," Moore said. "What are they up to?"

"We'll get down to the surface without interference."

"Have you seen anything of the research satellite?"

"I've seen a few communication relay satellites. That's about all."

It was hard for Moore to imagine Commander Harper dead and the satellite destroyed. He had never been particularly close to anyone aboard the station, but he had lived and worked with the 1,200 of them for many years. He couldn't grasp the deaths of even that small group of people. It would be like facing the death of a large part of his own life.

A black, oblong, Jovan warcraft angled down in a burst of glare. On the magnified viewscreen, Moore watched the squat, streamlined Earth-lander emerge from a lighted bay, a toy in comparison with the deadly cruiser. When the larger ship accelerated and shot out of view, Jon moved the Transtar in for a closer view, circling once to line up the airlocks before allowing the computers to perform the docking procedure without a perceptible impact. Moore heard machinery latching in place, then silence.

"They gave us the same model J-retriever we used to escape with the first time," Jon said. "The one we buried in the S-5. It must be all they have in inventory to do the job. I'll have to check it over pretty carefully to make sure they haven't sabotaged or bugged it in some way. I don't think they like the thought of us launching in a craft with engines of that level of power. We could give them a run for their money the second time around as well. You realize, don't you, Moore, that they won't make their move until we're on our way back up with the two Valthyn?"

"That assumes we get down and find what we're looking for."

"Insignificant details."

Transferring to the Earth-lander, Jon buckled in and brought the ship to life, giving Moore enough time to get settled in before separating from the Transtar. He let go of the sophisticated spacecraft with a twinge of concern and regret. He had never piloted anything as responsive as the Transtar. There weren't a thousand individuals in the system wealthy enough to own one outright, but that particular ship felt like personal property to him. Under the circumstances, Jon doubted if the Jovans would bother messing with it. Even if they tried boarding it for any reason, they'd have their hands full coping with the onboard security systems. Jon had participated in his share of caravan raids in search of contraband within the asteroid belt. Over the years, he had caught onto a great deal of the elusive maneuvers and strategies of the independents and miners in their never-ending struggle to hide their drugs, women, illegal fuel supplies, and black-market cargo from the government. In memory of that long-gone phase of his life, he had programmed the Transtar to respond only to his voice pattern and an old miner's code phrase that associated Jupiter, a gas giant, with divine flatulence.

"Shall we be on our way?" Jon said with a grin to the anxious Lunan.

Moore shrugged.

"Stand down, Cruiser Io," Jon transmitted. "You should be on green status and enjoying the good life until we return. Our ETA is whenever we happen to arrive."

Jon fired the retros. Cutting their orbital velocity, the Earth-lander began dropping, the blunt nose of the craft glowing in the dawn on Earth's horizon.

"Jon, damn it! You didn't give the least consideration to where we're going to land!"

"What's the difference? The Valthyn are masters of coincidence. Coincidentally, everything goes the way they had it planned from the beginning."

"Eventually, you're liable to take a little too much for granted," Moore warned.

Jon ignored the edge in Moore's voice. "We live in a fraction of a second of time we call the present. The past is just memory and the future, speculation. According to our own physicists, though, time as we perceive it doesn't exist. The future and the past all exist simultaneously."

"What does that have to do with pushing buttons at random?"

"What's theory for us is direct experience for the Valthyn. So spoke Lisa. She didn't even give a damn about dying. Everything she ever told me implies more than I'll ever be able to put together for myself. But one implication I trust—they'll know where we'll land and they'll be there waiting for us."

Moore felt a cold chill. He couldn't accept the impossible. Nor could he doubt it any longer. He hung in a web of indecision and helplessness as he had from the first moment he had seen Jon standing next to a strikingly beautiful, otherwise ordinary-looking human being.

"I'm going in hard," Jon said. "You'll feel two jolts, one when the engines ignite for descent and the other when we touch down. As far as I can determine right now, it looks like we'll be going down somewhere in the northern Atlantic Ocean."

The dark cramped cabin, the pressing weight building up, and the rising level of noise tore at Moore's nerves. He'd be helpless again when they set down, a burden to Jon and useless to himself. He kept his eyes on the viewscreens, watching the high-altitude landscape of clouds move slowly by. He could see through them at times to a land ravished by burnout regions and charred deserts that wouldn't see life again for another 2,000 years. Deceleration made it hard to breath after the engines fired. The jolt of touchdown panicked him, sparkles of blackness warning of imminent blackout. But he held on and focused a return of awareness of the luxury of silence.

Jon moved with difficulty, unstrapping himself and reaching out over the controls to turn on the cameras that would give them a close view of the surrounding terrain. Moore surprised himself. Knowing what to expect made it easier to adjust to his impossible weight. It hadn't been so long since he had visited this world after all.

The Earth-lander towered on a grassy plain, testament to Earth that man and his power still reigned supreme in the same glory and strife it had once known. Its nose gleamed, implacable against a blue, cloud-swept sky. The wind could blow the dust and bow the grasses, but no force that nature could summon would disturb the resting power of that visiting artifact.

Two women stood on the plain a short distance from the rocket, one to the east and the other to the south, their white gowns billowing in the wind, their faces lifted to the unseen cameras that watched. One waited a little more than 500 meters away, the other, the one to the south, stood a half kilometer away.

"You take the closest one," Jon said, the tone of his voice harsh and tension-ridden. "I can walk to the other one easier. They want to talk with us, separate and alone."

Too frightened to protest, Moore felt trapped in a fantasy turned reality. Jon could accept this impossible occurrence and had, in fact, anticipated it with total confidence. Fear, hurt, and bitterness emanated from the Jovan, but below it all, a stoic calm that underlay the conflict. Jon would weather the storm of his emotions and regain his equilibrium. Moore felt that he did not have that tenaciousness of spirit. He did not have the unassailable confidence of the Jovan fighter pilot, nor his aggressiveness and determination.

They rode the elevator down to the airlock. The whirring of the hydraulics rasped on their nerves in the confined space. Jon patted a transceiver hooked on his belt alongside the ever-present laser pistol. Moore also carried a small radio on his belt.

"We'll be in communication, but reserve it for emergencies. We'll meet back here at the ship to discuss our plans for launch."

Moore nodded agreement and Jon opened the outer lock.

The sun shone brilliantly through the widening opening in the hull. A breeze ruffled Moore's hair and he closed his eyes and breathed deeply of air smelling faintly of all the things it had ever kept alive in its billions of years of existence.

They stood 100 meters above the landscape. The hydraulic ramp that would lower them to the ground unfolded from the hull beneath the airlock. They stepped onto the platform. It moved down the length of the hull on tracks, swinging out and down past the still glowing engines to the scorched ground. They stepped from the ramp and moved away from withering heat.

Without a word to Moore, Jon began walking to the south. Moore watched his slow, ponderous stride for a moment, a sense of desolation closing in on him. Alienated from Jon by the Valthyn waiting for him in the distance, he felt fear descending like a tangible halo of something engulfing and permeating him. He thought of returning to the security of the control cabin, letting Jon handle anything that had to be done on the surface of this overwhelming world, but instead, he walked around the base of the rocket and stopped when she came into view.

She stood only a short distance away. It took a conscious effort to stand against the gravity, to keep from buckling and folding into a ruined mass of broken bones and torn ligaments. Still, he moved toward her, entranced by her strange beauty. One side of her gown clung to her body and revealed a curved figure that spoke of the muscular system the Earth-born required. She stood a foot shorter than his own height, but probably weighed considerably more. Moore had always thought of surface-bound primitives as being unattractively stocky, but the Valthyn did not have that effect on him. Had the outline of a perfect female body been burned into the mind of man for so long that he'd respond to it instinctively despite cultural prejudice? Or was it just this particular woman, a twin of the bright-eyed beauty in the photographs and the way she stood so strong and confident with her bare feet planted firmly on the ground? Moore could sense patience in her unmoving, statuesque figure, but not arrogance. He could sense passivity, but when he looked down upon her, he did so in the physical sense only.

"Ida Moore," she said, her voice clear and soft, speaking his native language. "I have known of you.

You were a consciousness in the skies thinking thoughts of error and confusion. You held us in fear, but not in hatred."

Moore didn't know how to answer. She was something more than human, but she aroused something within him, a longing for more than just a feel of her body in his hands.

"Do you speak?" she asked with a brilliant smile.

"As soon as I know what to say." But he was still too frightened to return her smile.

"You are the man with a thousand questions. Remember?"

"Jon has told me a lot about you. About Lisa."

"Yes," she said. "Jon has related to you his nut-and-bolt collection of organized facts. And you envy his concise and specific nature. You do not know that he envies your powers of synthesis and creativity."

She spoke just as Jon had warned she would speak.

"We're different," Moore said. "But Jon and I complement each other in some ways. Do you know why? Why am I involved in all of this?"

"You have involved yourself, haven't you? Are you not here of your own volition or do you suppose the events that have led to this moment to be more than just coincidental?"

Moore felt a shiver of fear. He tried to divert the train of her conversation.

"What is your name?"

"I've given it some thought," she said. "I've decided upon Dora."

She gazed at him with a level expression. It took Moore a moment for its significance to dawn on him.

"Pandora. Of course."

"I cannot promise that our relationship will always be comfortable. I am certain, however, that you will find it very interesting."

Moore felt a sinking sensation of anxious depression.

"I've heard that before somewhere. I think I'm in real trouble now."

Jon had grown from childhood without ever having looked back. He had no conscious memory of feeling small and insecure in a world too big to comprehend. He identified completely with adult logic and causality and took them to be absolutes, the only structure to life that could or had ever mattered. Lisa had destroyed some of his belief in a logical world of cause and effect. Now, he could barely stand the hurt of seeing a reflection of Lisa again, forgetting that he had reverted to the kind of world that she had worked to tear down for him.

A strong association took him back many decades. He remembered the dark barracks as a child after a day of having been pushed too hard and too fast by unfeeling people who impatiently strived to make him one of them. A day had come when he had determined that he would never cry again. But now, there were tears in his eyes. He blinked them away while looking down upon a ghost who smiled. Again, he made a commitment to himself. He would never for an instant confuse this woman for the one he had loved, cherished, and watched die.

"You are not Lisa," he said.

"I am not Lisa. Lisa is dead. Is that what you want to hear from me?"

"It doesn't matter what you say. I have to say it."

"You've disowned your emotions for so long, you've forgotton how to manage them, Jon."

"Don't make it any harder than it has to be," he told her. "I don't have anywhere else to go. I'm here to do whatever has to be done."

She smiled as Lisa would have smiled. They would all smile in the same way. Each time, the hurt would be so intense, his throat would ache to hold back the

216

pain.

"You are here because you want to be here," the woman said. "You have the courage to face me because you know that we are important. You have the courage to face anything this universe has to offer because you respect that which lies outside of yourself. But you have disowned too much of that which lies within."

She reached out and touched his arm. Jon tensed, not knowing how long he could tolerate her touch, not knowing what would happen if his control broke.

"You have learned no compassion," she said. "Without knowing compassion, you can never apply it to yourself. I'll teach you compassion. I'll show you compassion so that you'll never doubt its existence again or ever withhold it from yourself."

She pulled her gown over her head and stood naked before him, defiantly, her feet slightly spread, her hands on the curve of her broad hips. Lisa would have done the same to make her point, to throw him off guard.

"I told you once that we are human. I told you that we differ only in knowing ourselves in ways different from the way you know yourself. Jon, I told you that the Valthyn are of one mind. I had to explain in a language structured by the same assumptions and beliefs about reality that I tried to alter, but I had hoped that you would recognize the contradictions and resolve them by looking within yourself to the place where my world functions. You were stopped, Jon, by hurt and anger, but you can't avoid hurt by turning away from it. You can only stop growing until you decide to resolve the hurt and move through it."

I don't know what you're trying to tell me!" Jon roared in sudden anger. "You're not Lisa! I saw Lisa die!"

"You saw a human body die, but minds do not die! I told you that a body is an expression in physical

217

reality of something that does not even live in time and space! I told you that the Valthyn is a single entity expressed in a multitude of bodies!

"Jon, Lisa could not have died as long as one Valthyn lives. I have no name except that which you might use for your own convenience. I am Lisa. We are all Lisa if that is what you choose to call us. I am the same person. I remember you and me as vividly as I remember the thousands of other people that I am. I am Dora speaking with Ida Moore. We are not just conscious of one another, Jon, *we are the same person.* If a thousand of us die and a thousand more are born, we are still one individual.

"Jon, I never experienced your feelings toward death. I never intended for you to suffer so. I lived only to nurture you for the time when you would depart Earth, but I intended to be here to greet you upon your return. You misunderstood what happened, but as I told you, Jon, experience is the best teacher."

Jon stood shaking, unable to speak. Lisa smiled.

"If you think I am a traumatic person to get to know, wait until you meet those who are not human."

CHAPTER TWELVE

They sat around a campfire in the night, the blunt nose of the Earth-lander silhouetted against the stars. Moore sat self-consciously alongside Dora, watching Jon and the second Valthyn with a gnawing anxiety. Something strange had happened between the two of them. Jon called her Lisa, but not without a haunted resistance. He had a bewildered expression on his face and avoided talking to or even looking at Dora.

Moore took note of the fact that Dora and Lisa never spoke to one another. They moved and spoke in an odd kind of synchronization, speaking in turns sometimes, as if sharing the same thoughts. They moved around one another with an impossible grace, as if invisible to one another and yet instinctively knowing of the presence of the other. Moore waited to catch Jon alone to question him about the parthenogenic twins, but the opportunity never arose. Jon refused to leave Lisa's side. Dora never left his.

Moore had talked alone with Dora for most of the afternoon. He could not fathom her interest in him. She questioned him incessantly about his life, his personal past, his beliefs and ideas about the things that were happening. Her questions were too pertinent and penetrating to have originated in any kind of mind that Moore had ever known.

Jon grew increasingly restless. "When do we leave?" He had asked the question several times since the four of them had gathered around the campfire to talk.

"We have further information that you must know to ensure the success of our mission," Lisa told him.

"Such as?"

"The Jovans and the Lunans have formed an alliance to meet the common threat of what they feel to be an alien invasion. They believe the Valthyn to be a part of that invasion. They believe you and Ida Moore to be unwitting agents for alien powers. But they do not know how to form a strategy of defense.

"Helpless against the unknown, they have projected their worst fears upon it, believing that this alien power can influence the human mind. They have sought advice from the Isinti since your landing, but the Isinti discovered that the Alliance will hear only that which it wishes to hear. Therefore, the Alliance also believes the Isinti to be a part of the alien conspiracy."

"They're paranoid," Moore said quietly.

Dora said to him, "There has never been a time in Earth's history that the human race could have remained unshaken by contact with alien lifeforms."

"There has always been other life observing the Earth," Lisa continued. "There have always been individuals aware of their existence, always a contact or a liaison between human and alien minds somewhere upon the Earth, one studying the other, but never on the level of direct confrontation."

"Call man paranoid if you will," Dora said from beside him. "We have succeeded in demonstrating to man the extent of his paranoia. He recognizes his own self-destructiveness and holds his hand at this time. He does not assemble his warfleet to do battle with the aliens, but waits and watches for the truth to emerge and considers what to do with the fear that drives him. Remember, we are not dealing with an enemy, but with ourselves."

"Why do we have to be the ones to meet with the aliens?" Jon asked.

"The aliens are better qualified to know man than man is to know the aliens. Therefore, you will serve as specimens and examples upon which the aliens will build an understanding of what it requires to communicate with humanity. We mediate for humanity and buffer the initial incompatibilities."

Lisa smiled. "You must act."

"But we can guide," Dora finished. "The Valthyn will follow, but decisions made by men will determine the course of future events. We cannot intervene in those decisions, nor alter the consequences of them."

"If what you say is true," Jon said, "the Alliance will try to take us prisoner when we launch. They're not going to be making the same mistakes twice. I won't be able to evade them once we achieve orbit."

"The Isinti anticipated these events," Lisa said. "Your Transtar, Jon, is a Transtar in appearance only. It is of Isinti technology."

"I thought the Isinti lagged in technological innovation." Jon wanted to withdraw the comment as soon as he made it, remembering their firsthand experience with the Isinti colony.

"Technology is a tool, not an end in itself," Lisa said. "The Isinti possess more knowledge than is necessary to utilize."

"Do I get a rundown on what I have to work with?"

Lisa shrugged. "We have no idea of the technicalities involved. You have the background, the training, and the need to explore its potentials."

"We are not omniscient nor omnipotent," Dora said in the same tone of voice.

"We're not primitive enough to bore you?" Jon

asked of Dora in deliberate violation of the tacit pairing between the four of them.

"No," Dora said, startling Jon. "Not at all."

When their talk ended late in the night, Jon and Lisa wandered off away from the ship. They were a physical mismatch, but Moore could sense the unsettling, strong rapport between the two of them. Jon loved the woman, but something strange had occurred. She could not be Lisa.

"She is Lisa," Dora said.

Moore spun around, all but panicked by the idea that she could intrude upon his thoughts so easily.

"I saw her die," Moore said.

"You saw a body die. It is enough that Jon believes that Lisa still lives. You resent their strong bonding after empathizing with the pain he has felt for so long."

"I saw her die," Moore said.

"You resent Jon's trust."

"Why should I distrust you?"

"Because you believe that we are superior and that we could easily deceive you for some unknown reason. You have warned Jon that his open trust will eventually be misplaced. You have invested much hope for the future in our intervention in human affairs, but your fear of the unknown in this case takes the form of distrust."

Moore tried to stem the flow of his emotions, to stop the fear from overwhelming him. But she could see into his thoughts, know his feelings, and he tried to block. . . .

"You feel guilt because you desire me. Your culture debases sex, divorces it from the kind of interpersonal dependency you call love in the name of individual freedom. Even in your youth you recognized that your society works to substitute personal relationships with a psychologically engineered loyalty and dependency on the social structure of the state that supplies intimacy as a right and seeks appreciation for its response to individual need.

"You questioned the rationality and morality of the state and freed your life for potentials you would not have otherwise realized, but that kind of alienation breeds fear. Fear of disclosure and of reprisal. You know personal integrity, but you do not have the level of self-esteem necessary to really believe that you could be right and your society wrong."

It felt like falling through blackness, panic-stricken and horrified, awaiting final impact of destruction—and then awakening to discover the fall to be a safe, secure freefall. Dora had not meant to harm him.

He looked into a very beautiful face. Her eyes reflected starlight. She shared his thoughts and fed them back to him in a moment of brilliant revelation of his own being.

"You fell in love with me in a photograph and in your fantasies. There is no harm in that. Your fear of me will be gone when you know me as Jon knows Lisa."

"What can Jon know of Lisa? What could I ever know of you?"

Dora knelt and selected a pebble from the ground. She handed it to him.

"Your senses are limited, Ida Moore. You would not recognize the pebble if you could perceive it as I do. Yet your perception of the pebble is a comfortable part of your world. And your world is a part of yourself. That is how it should be and that is how Jon knows Lisa. That is how you will know me."

"I've got a computer link!" Jon cried out over the loudspeaker from the control cabin of the Earthlander. "One hundred percent interface with the Transtar!"

Intolerably anxious to leave, Jon had stalled for

hours, formulating plans to cope with the Alliance forces waiting for them in Earth orbit.

Moore and the two Valthyn joined Jon aboard the ship. Jon pulled up the ramp behind them and sealed the airlock.

"What are you talking about?" Moore wanted to know.

"It's illegal for civilian passenger craft to have remote navigational capacity. There were some problems with piracy and some obscene military tactics during the early days of the wargames—like taking control of a civilian passenger and running it through an enemy military formation. But the Isinti Transtar has it."

"What does it mean for us?" Moore asked, already feeling better about the upcoming launch.

"It means that I can program the Transtar by maser to function on automatic pilot. We can appear to launch at random and require a full orbit to dock with the Transtar. While the Alliance is waiting to spring their trap, we can launch directly away from Earth while we're on the far side of the planet. The Transtar will launch pilotless right from under their noses. By the time they calculate a rendezvous between the two ships, they won't be able to catch us without one hell of a chase."

Jon turned to Lisa standing behind him. "I need to know the location of the alien fleet."

"Just beyond the orbit of the eleventh world at two hundred degrees."

Jon stared at her. "Those must be the most concise navigational coordinates I've ever encountered. You're talking about a distance of several light months and an area of intersteller space the volume of the entire solar system."

Lisa shrugged and smiled. "Nothing further is required."

"We don't have the fuel or the supplies to search

for a dust mote in that volume of space. It would take years."

"Not a dust mote, Jon. The alien task force consists of tens of millions of individual craft."

Jon continued to gaze at her.

"Why do you think the Alliance has panicked so badly? Haven't you bothered to consider what it would take to prevent the Jovan–Lunan alliance from launching a military task force of its own to investigate a single or small number of alien craft? Its size, Jon, is overwhelming."

Jon turned back to his controls as if studying them for the answer to a dilemma beyond manageable proportions.

"It would be a highly visible target, even from here," Jon said.

"Does that solve the problem?" Moore asked.

Jon gave him a look of subdued fury. "All that remains is for us to get away from Earth in one piece and run a gauntlet of every military base in the solar system. And we're talking about a journey of about two years."

"I see."

"I don't see how we can do it," Jon continued. "The Transtar is armed, but the equipment looks conventional to me. Nothing impressive enough to take on a fleet of battleships."

Jon looked to Lisa with a level expression. "Let's think this over a bit more carefully. A short walk around the world will give us enough time. How do you cross an ocean?"

Lisa smiled, but didn't otherwise respond. Moore noticed that Dora kept her eyes on him, observing with the same cool detachment.

"We'll launch and make our initial escape from the Alliance," Jon said. "We'll assume the Transtar is somehow equipped to enable us to survive a two-year journey and cope with a blockade."

"We're launching blind, then," Moore said.

"So? Didn't I hear a few protests about landing blind?

"Yes. Want to hear a few more?"

Moore took for granted he'd loose conciousness during the launch. He'd be pulling far more Gs than he could tolerate. He awakened long after the incredible noise had been left far behind and gave a shuddering sigh of relief, thankful that the acceleration couch was effective enough to prevent damage to his frail physique. The sky had blackened and the stars glimmered through the ports. In the freedom of freefall, he and Jon were home once again, sharing the void with the machines that all but shared their souls. Lisa and Dora watched the viewscreens with wide-eyed wonder, needing to share nothing in words between one another.

"We came up directly beneath the Transtar. In thirty minutes, we'll be on the other side of the world coming in for docking. We'll accelerate on automatic."

"On automatic?" Moore said.

"Sorry, buddy. We'll all black out temporarily. We'll have high-speed warcraft on our tails and we need as much leeway as possible for docking and transfer. I think I can arrange to blow these main engines after we transfer aboard the Transtar to cover our tracks for a few minutes."

"They can still get us with missiles," Moore said with reluctance, knowing Jon hadn't overlooked the possibility.

"They won't try to destroy us until they've lost all opportunity to capture us alive."

"Can we outrun them?" Moore said, glancing at the two acceleration tanks. But there were four of them now.

"No. We'll have one rammed right up our engines."

226

Moore waited for someone to say something encouraging. Minutes passed in silence.

"Ignition in ten seconds," Jon said finally. He didn't bother counting them down.

Moore didn't stand a chance of fighting the pressure shoving him into oblivion. He regained consciousness with sharp pains in his joints and a headache that felt like a skull fracture.

"We have our Transtar pulling up from behind," Jon was saying.

In the merciful weightlessness, Moore twisted in agony. Dora reached over and placed a hand on the side of his neck. Inexplicably, the pain faded.

Jon removed a side panel from the console. He pulled loose a circuit board and picked a component loose with his fingernail.

"That freezes a fuel valve in full-open position." He unstrapped himself and sought out an access panel on the rear bulkhead, sabotaging another circuit. "And that breaks feedback circuits from the valve."

Jon pulled his way back into his couch. "I'm setting in a delayed ignition. When it happens, the monatomic fuel supply blows."

"That won't be a nuclear explosion," Moore said.

"No, but the debris from the ship will act as interference for a time. They'll lose us on their radar."

Moore and the women watched through the ports for the approach of the Transtar. It moved in smooth and fast, mating with the Earth-launch vehicle with a slight lurch.

"I'm pressurizing the Transtar to Earth normal. We're all comfortable with that."

Jon and Moore both worked to help the two women through the mated airlocks. Their gowns billowed about their bodies, their long hair wavering about their heads. Two pairs of slender legs kicked about and Moore tried desperately to suppress an emerging thought, the opportunities freefall offered

227

for—sex.

Dora laughed aloud without looking his way.

"You two tie your hair back with something," Jon said to the women. "There are coveralls in the equipment lockers that should fit reasonably well."

Lisa and Dora somersaulted into the Transtar, laughing in delight at the new experience. Once Jon and Moore had helped them into their couches, Moore took a seat beside Jon, aware, at least, that Jon valued his companionship. Jon's fingers danced momentarily over the keyboards. With a gentle lurch, the Transtar moved.

"We'll accelerate at one-half gravity," Jon informed them. "If we haven't the weaponry to defend ourselves now, there's no sense in even trying to outrun trouble."

"Hasn't the Alliance tried to communicate with us?" Moore asked.

Jon grinned. "From the moment we left orbit. They've been politely inquiring as to our reasons for departing in such a hasty manner. Engine ignition for the Earth-lander in three minutes."

The Transtar's smooth fusion engines provided little distraction in the way of noise or vibration.

"We have a cruiser coming up from behind on heavy burn," Jon said. "If we get a few missiles to contend with, that'll be their source."

Moore tried to calculate in his head how far they'd travel in three minutes at one-half gravity acceleration.

"I'm tracking two missiles coming in like something very mean and hungry."

Moore began to panic. A stroke of genius on Jon's part had saved their lives the last time and he didn't expect to see an outside chance save them a second time. He knew how deadly those wedge-shaped missiles were now. Jon had told him a story of a colony in the asteroid belt that executed condemned criminals by sealing them in the nosecones of outmoded Jarls and launching them into interstellar space. The acceleration, Jon said, flattened a human body against the rear bulkhead of the nosecone to a thickness of a film of moisture.

The viewscreens and the ports blackened out.

"What was that!" Moore cried out.

"Ignition in the Earth-lander," Jon said. "The engines blew. Both missiles were still on the other side. They've just shut down."

"What if they launch more?" Moore said.

"They just did. Two more."

"What are you going to do?" Moore said too loudly, frightened by even the odd quality of terror rising in his voice. Some part of him could still observe his own behavior with a dispassionate calm.

"We have less than two minutes to penetrate their armor with whatever we have aboard as weaponry." He folded over a section of the control console and put his eyes to two, shielded oculars.

"Talk about quality. I've got two bright and stable targets already locked in. But it's nothing but a conventional, high-powered laser. It won't come close . . ."

"Try it, Jon," Lisa urged.

They heard a whine of the laser turrets swinging around on the belly of the Transtar. Jon pressed the firing button. The cabin blacked out.

"What the hell was that for?" Jon mumbled, overriding the protective filters.

The cabin glared to a blinding, silver-white light. Moore jammed his hands to his eyes, desperate to block out the sudden pain. Both women cried out in shock and alarm. That more than the intensity of the explosion frightened Jon. Even the Valthyn hadn't known.

Shocked by the impossible power of the laser, Jon knew he had blinded himself and perhaps doomed them all by underestimating the Isinti. The second target should have remained locked in. He waited a few seconds for the interference to fade, then pressed the firing button again. This time, he left the filters in place, but had no way of telling if the second target had been hit.

When the four of them regained their eyesight, the stars shone through the ports and on the viewscreen, the universe undisturbed by man's violence.

Jon put the technical blueprints of the Transtar on the screens. "I can't figure out what it might have been."

He felt cold fingers of shock moving down his spine. The prints were indecipherable.

"It packed more of a wallop than you figured," Moore suggested, trying to cover over the panic that had embarrassed him so badly.

Jon shook his head. "This ship is not a Transtar. It just looks like one. Nothing a ship this size could carry should have stopped those missiles."

"How does a Cobra avoid them?" Moore asked quietly.

"They're expensive," Jon said, "not worth a small, unimportant target. Only another missile can take them out."

Moore stayed quiet, knowing he couldn't contribute a useful idea. Jon glanced back at Lisa.

"Antineutrons. It couldn't have been anything else. Protons can be deflected by electromagnetic shielding. A dense neutron beam can't be stopped except by massive shielding, but they're difficult to focus into a dense enough beam. An antineutron beam can't be stopped by anything."

Moore had heard of exotic, lethal new weapons in various stages of development. Antimatter weapons wouldn't just revolutionize warfare. They would render warfare in space as devastating as full-scale thermonuclear warfare on the face of the Earth.

230

CHAPTER THIRTEEN

Jon took a consensus of opinion on what time of the day or night it felt like, and programmed the ship's interior lighting to correspond. Day had lost its real meaning in an eternal night where the sun burned forever. The cabin lights were dim and Lisa and Dora slept in hammocks in the rear of the cabin.

For a time, Jon gazed at the stars through the forward screens. An odd, unsettling fear continued to gnaw at him. The Isinti possessed a weapon that could conquer every nation in the solar system without a shot being fired. And they had entrusted it to him. The Transtar was now as much of a threat to the Alliance as the alien fleet waiting outside the solar system. They'd have radioed ahead by now. A reception committee would be set up somewhere just outside the inner system. Beyond that, they had a long, long journey ahead of them.

Moore stayed awake, glancing often back at the women. Jon finally noticed his preoccupation with the two.

"I wonder how interchangeable they are," Jon said. "There wouldn't be much variety in switching partners."

Moore squirmed in his seat. Jon noticed his

reaction and grinned.

"Or are you planning for a purely platonic relationship?"

"The time and the circumstances aren't right for anything more than that."

"You mean having Dora breathing down your neck doesn't have any effect on your adrenaline level? Or is there some other reason why you're too nervous to sleep?"

Moore turned his head aside and pretended to nap, the console lights forming patterns of color behind his closed eyelids.

"You can't hide your feelings from them, Moore."

"No, but I'd still have some trouble expressing them."

"Do you think I do a better job of that?" Jon said.

Moore looked back at Jon, curiosity getting the best of him. "I've heard stories about Jovan fighter-pilots. I know most of it was just propaganda. . . ."

"Keep going."

Moore looked away again, turning vague. "Things about returning to port after a battle."

"Like rape on the public thoroughfares?"

Moore nodded. "Just about that crude."

Jon looked surprised. "Sounds like we're supposed to be real barbarians. We must have had one hell of a reputation among your people."

"You did. How much truth was there in stories like that?"

"Truth? Sex was furnished by the government. We're speaking in past tense, you know. Things will probably change. But sexual tension is considered dangerous for a fighter-pilot. So is becoming emotionally involved with a woman. A pilot is either at the top of his form or he'd dead. We have our women with the understanding that we will never choose the same partner twice."

"Maybe some of the stories weren't fiction after

232

all," Moore said.

"It's never worked very well. Men and women fall in love. They violate regulations. It used to be that a girl would just drop out of sight after getting involved with a fighter-pilot, but I heard about a pilot that rammed a city dome with a Cobra and killed a few thousand people because of a girl that who was missing. Not so many drop out of sight these days. If a pilot's reflexes fall below certain levels, he's retired. How about Lunan pilots? They handle themselves pretty well."

"We Lunans are supposed to be more compassionate to one another, but it amounts to the same thing. People are provided for the benefit of other people. I don't know why people treat each other the way they do."

Jon took the observation in stride. "There are too many people pushing for perfection and too many others letting themselves be pushed."

"I think there's more to it than that," Moore said. "It's almost as if humanity suffers the effect of both claustrophobia and agoraphobia at the same time. There's not enough elbow room in most of the colonies, but when you look outside, you're looking into infinity. Back on Earth, people got all excited about the plans to colonize space. Now we've been mapping the continents of planets twenty light-years from here. We're out here now, but we don't feel very secure about it."

Jon gestured back to the women. "Will they change anything?"

Moore nodded. "Sure, but they won't be remembered for what they did. They've kept a low profile."

Jon tended to agree. "They've handed us all of the answers to life on a silver platter. I could have accomplished the same thing by handing a handbook on fusion drive to the beach people. In the short term, it will accomplish about as much."

"There's nothing they can teach us without us having to unlearn an equal amount of garbage," Moore said.

Jon let the silence accumulate for a few moments. "We were on the subject of sex. Did you deliberately steer the conversation clear of one of life's most fasinating subjects?"

"Sorry. I didn't think you'd catch on so quick."

Jon shut off the warbling siren echoing through the confines of the cabin. He switched a screen over to a visual representation of long-range radar data.

"We have tailings from an old mining operation ahead, one hell of a swath of rocks in our path. It would make sense to lay an ambush where there's plenty of interference."

"How would you normally navigate it?" Lisa asked from behind him.

"Just pass through. It's almost radar opaque at this distance, but still just a sparse scattering of junk."

"Can't you detect a ship through it?" Moore asked, knowing the tailings to contain little metal.

"I'm getting a pattern of solid echoes, but it could easily be old mining equipment. I haven't any way to differentiate between a cargo barge and a Jovan warcraft."

"Then what will you do?" Lisa asked.

"I've got about twenty seconds to determine that. We can't afford to just chance it. I don't know what kind of shields we might have, but they can't protect us from a multiple missile launch."

Moore and the two women remained silent during the last moment of crisis. Jon considered his alternatives and at the last possible moment, settled upon one of them. He fired on one of the asteroids at the furthest limit of his range. The sky glared white, the filters blocking out the light of annihilation of matter. Within seconds, they rushed through the fading luminescence jamming the radars of any warcraft lying in ambush.

"A fleet ahead!" Jon cried out. "A full-scale warfleet!"

"Don't fire on them, Jon!" Lisa called out in alarm.

Jon suppressed the nearly irresistible urge to open fire on the geometric pattern of warships filling his screens. But the fusion engines of the entire warfleet were burning, every last ship swinging around to place the fusion burn between them and the Transtar—a universal gesture of nonaggression. The Transtar moved through the fleet within seconds. Jon held his breath, waiting for the telltale fusion burn of a missile.

"We're clear," he said at last. "That would be their last stand. They're not going to risk taking us on."

"Nobody died," Lisa said after a moment's reflection. "The radiation injured many, but nobody died."

"Why is that important to you all of a sudden?" Jon said, venting the last of his anger. "Billions have already died."

"It would be hard to explain."

"I'll bet it would."

"Then think about this, Jon. They consider us agents of alien forces. You refrained from wanton destruction. That forces them to reconsider the threat we pose to them. They also could have destroyed us in battle. That means that the cycle of destruction is broken."

It took hours for the tension to wind down.

"Would you have?" Moore finally asked.

"Would I have what?"

"Fired on those ships if Lisa hadn't stopped you?"

Moore thought that Jon needed time to think over the question, but Jon needed time to gather the courage to answer truthfully.

"That antineutron beam is like a laser in the hands of a child. Hell, yes, I would have fired on those ships.

235

Is that what you wanted to know?"

"Just curious."

"Haven't you ever killed anything? Doesn't an anthropologist get to dissect cadavers or something?"

"I stepped on a cockroach once. That's about all."

"Bastard! Three hundred million years of evolutionary perfection, the only creature with the guts to follow man into space and you step on it!"

Moore laughed. It came out tainted with hysteria.

They sat without talking in the darkened cabin, looking out at the glowing swath of the Milky Way. The planets left ahead in their path all lay elsewhere in their orbits. Nothing lay ahead but deep, unending space.

The stars were motionless, not even the constant burn of the engines disturbing the unsettling calm. But the engines would be shut down soon. They could continue to gain speed to a respectable fraction of the speed of light, but they'd have to decelerate at the end of their voyage and spend an equal amount of time and energy doing so.

At one time or another, the same thought occurred to all of them. The metallic hydrogen caressed by a low-powered laser would supply the reaction engines for a length of time difficult to imagine. Even the Transtar could reach the nearer stars, although not in any practical length of time. But the first interstellar voyages were already in the construction stage and had been for twenty years. The ship yards around Jupiter were filled with the skeletons of the caravan that would be exploring tens of the nearer stars over the next few centuries.

Now, man would depart knowing he wasn't alone in those endless skies. It had been thought that there were no indications of life within at least 200 light-years of Earth. But the nearer stars were indeed inhabited by a radio silent species of life difficult to imagine.

No one wanted to sleep as yet. Subjectively, suspended animation would last only a moment. Then, it would be time to awaken and confront the unknown. Jon and Moore weren't prepared for that confrontation yet.

"What are you thinking?" Moore asked of Dora.

"I am not thinking. I am experiencing. I watch sunrises and sunsets in deserts and in mountains. I sleep and awaken and together, my sisters on Earth and I experience inward, into realms of reality I couldn't describe to you. My sisters perceive through me the experience of traveling in space, the sensation of weightlessness, the appearance of the stars beyond Earth's atmosphere. The distance between us is so vast, but in important ways, it doesn't exist at all."

"How can you be aware of all that at one time and still be yourself?"

"Could you describe the stars to me if I were blind?"

"Maybe I'd try."

"You and I aren't really different, Ida Moore. There are parts of myself that are like you and parts of you that are like me. The universe is one and expresses itself in multitudinous ways. And yet, there is identity for all of its parts and an eternal becoming for each identity."

Jon and Lisa listened to the conversation weave and expand and backtrack. Then: "We should be alone," Jon said to her. "So should they."

"What do we do?" Lisa said with a regretful smile. "It is not convenient to take a walk out here."

Jon gave her a funny look. "The engines will be shut down soon. We'll be in freefall. Why not take turns taking a walk? Say four hours at a stretch?"

"What the hell are you talking about?" Moore

237

interceded.

"Going EVA," Jon said casually. "Taking a space walk."

"You're kidding."

"Not at all," Jon said. "Lisa and I can go first. I'll program the nav computers to rendezvous with us using the attitude thrusters. I'll show you how to activate the computer sequence to retrieve us."

"You'd trust me to do that?"

"Push a button? I'd sure the hell better be able to trust you to push a silly button!"

"I think he's serious," Lisa said, not fully able to interpret Jon's intentions.

"Why does it sound so outrageous? There's a magnificent view out there! We'll still have our radios for communication."

Moore gave Dora a furtive glance. Just the thought of being alone with her for tacitly acknowledged purposes made him feel queasy.

Dora smiled. "Zero gravity, Ida Moore. Or are you in the habit of suppressing your more interesting ideas?"

Moore turned beet red. Jon laughed. Dora and Lisa didn't seem to be at all perturbed by the idea. Moore wondered if anything could perturb a Valthyn.

"Jon, I can't do a thing like that," Moore said. "I'm liable to panic."

"The experience might surprise you," Jon said with a grin, but without its usually harassing quality. "You have no idea of what it feels like to float in the middle of all space and time. It's the most awesome experience man has ever known."

The idea did fascinate Moore. He recalled the skydivers back home. Using nothing but a pressure suit, a handheld computer and a rocket sled, they'd launch themselves from Luna orbit. Once confident of their ballistic trajectory, they'd abandon the sled and spend the next few days falling toward Earth,

238

whipped around the globe and back into a stable Luna orbit. Moore had always dreamed of undertaking that experience at least once, but had never gathered enough courage to do so. Occasionally, skydivers did not return. Moore had once dreamed of meteors screaming through the skies of Earth.

Moore met Dora's frank gaze. How could he bypass the opportunity?

"We'll go first," he said. "If I panic, you bring me back in immediately."

"Of course," Jon said.

"I just want to see what it's like."

"Of course," Dora said.

Moore fell into forever. The entire universe orbited about him once every five seconds.

"Jon, I don't know if I can take this!"

Jon's voice sounded tinny over the radio. "Has there ever been that much between you and the stars? A few millimeters of sheet metal and insulation maybe?"

"I can't see through it! I can't stop spinning!"

"If you don't stop spinning, you'll get sick. If you get sick, Moore, you won't be able to see the stars. I promise."

Moore touched his thrusters again. He succeeded in stopping the universe from rotating in one direction and initiated a rotation in the other. Dora appeared in front of him, fixed against the turning stars. She appeared to move without using her thrusters. Starlight gleamed from her faceplate.

"Show off!"

Dora moved in and hooked her legs about his waist. The spinning stopped.

"This is a new experience for me," she said, her face bright with delight.

"Coming from you, that's saying a lot."

"Even among the four of us there is a social

structure," Dora said. "Why have you placed yourself at the bottom of it?"

"This is silly, immoral, and probably illegal," Moore said, only half intending to soften his fear and anger with Jon's brand of humor.

"Perhaps, but who programmed your conscience for you? I'd like to know what outside agency is observing, judging, and intends to prosecute."

Dora let go and drifted away.

Moore continued to fall through the stars. There were individual stars in shades of different colors and clouds of stars like tendrils of glowing fog weaving among clouds as black as the night of infinity beyond.

"Isn't it strange," Dora said later when Moore had fallen into the trance of the universe's beauty, "how you defend yourself so vehemently against things as intangible as ideas? The defense is so stifling, life becomes unbearable. And here you are, falling among the stars, content and unmindful in an environment that would not support your natural life for a single moment.

"Who do you think you are to judge others by your standards or even yourself, to have taken them so seriously as to have limited your life by them?"

Sometime later, Dora swung him around. From infinity, the Transtar rushed up to him and stopped dead and silent beside him.

"Our turn, Ida Moore."

"Dora, I'm not sure. . . ."

"Now I suppose you're afraid to go back inside and want to stay out here."

The suspension equipment aboard the courier that Jon had hijacked from the Jovan S-5 had been emergency equipment. The Transtar was outfitted more elaborately. Moore had not noticed the six crypts lining the rear bulkhead of the cabin. If he had noticed them, he would not have known what they were.

The four of them stripped nude and carefully folded their clothing and personal effects and placed them in small lockers. Jon double-checked the instrumentation and initiated the suspension sequence. Dora chose the bottom crypt on the starboard side of the cabin, Moore, the upper. Any kind of nudity in mixed company had always been considered distasteful in Lunan society and Moore averted his eyes from the graceful, pale bodies floating alongside him, especially when Jon folded Lisa into his arms for a last affectionate embrace. Moore longed for the spontaneity that Jon displayed. He felt embarrassed by the conflict between unrealistic morals and the frightening pleasures that Dora had shown him. But his feeling of exposure went beyond simple nudity. Dora had dismantled and displayed for him, item by item, a complex structure of fear he would never have suspected in himself. He let Dora slip into her crypt without looking at her or saying the things he could not as yet express in the way he wanted.

Stretching out in the suspension crypt felt like being put to death. When the lid came down, a soft foam flowed to encase his body, solidifying to hold him in place. He almost panicked, thinking he'd smother before being put to sleep. He felt the needles enter his buttocks. They were the initial sedatives. He didn't feel the more intelligent probe of a needle seeking out a major artery in his leg and never knew that a whitish liquid began replacing his blood, a substance that would duplicate its functions and protectively permeate the cells of his body. Long before his body temperature dropped below freezing, he dreamed. The dreams ceased. The bioelectrical activity of his brain ceased.

He couldn't feel the air, nor the heat of the crimson

sun. There were broad-leafed, black plants waving about him on tree-sized stalks of interweaving chromium cable. Brightly colored insects danced in a ground fog shot through with muted, pastel colors that swirled and spiraled and flowed without blending. In the deep purple sky, two moons moved perceptibly from horizon to horizon, ghostly white and translucent in the hazed ocean of air. The bloated crimson sun quivered on the horizon, oblate and distorted by more than just the thin atmosphere. Massive sunspots twisted across its fiery, cool surface.

Dora observed from nearby, unseen but sensed. He required the illusion of his body, maintaining its detail all the way down to his uniform and boots. It would be a time before he'd be able to discard the structure and organization of a physical body. He remembered being like this many times before and knew it would happen many times again, but he'd never remember in physical, waking reality. His brain did not participate in this experience.

"I thought it would help if we could see their home world," Dora said without speaking in words.

"Something is wrong." He formed the concepts into words to be sure of making himself understood.

"You are confused by the size scale," Dora told him. "The plants the size of trees are only a meter high. This is their perspective. It is very cold, the air very thin, and the winds of high velocity just above the ground. The ground mist is dense, organic and thick with microorganic life. The smallest of the insectlike creatures you see are the size of protozoa."

Something loomed dark on the horizon, massive and indecipherable. Tentacles flowed from a body mass glistening blood red in the alien sunlight. It moved in slow motion and wrought destruction as it passed. Crippled insects spun and jerked spasmodically on the spongy soil where the creature's weight

242

had rested.

The landscape flowed and changed. Moore saw a different view. A city stretched across a flat plain. Masses of pod shapes and geometric ribbons interconnected them. There were spidery things moving in the air and artifacts rolling on the ribbons. Moore perceived a city, but with an organic organization that confused him. He turned away and it was gone. Darkening images turned into stars against a liquid quality to the blackness. Something white moved in a void, cold and lifeless. He did not remember or recognize the Transtar.

"The truly alien is indecipherable and untranslatable, but when the time comes, there will be some familiarity to guide your knowing, even if there is no conscious memory of what you have experienced. But look once more to be sure that what you saw is what you will see again."

Once more, the world of the red sun stretched around him. When Moore focused on what he had seen before, the insects moved through the air without support, drifting and trailing veils of transparency that sparkled electrically in blue. There were dangling tendrils and reflexes so quick, they brushed smaller creatures of the mist and tore them to shreds in a blur of movement. The plants moved to face the sun with veins throbbing in bodies that coiled in the ground.

The more carefully he focused on the environment, the more strange and unexplicable it became to his experience. He had always assumed that an alien world would bear similarities to life on Earth, but nothing of what he saw in this strange place matched anything in his experience. He became confused and frightened when Dora tried to move him into the consciousness of the life around him, to add to a part of his psyche that which had not existed before.

He fled in psychological distances and lost himself. At times, he'd forget and be a focus of consciousness. Drifting in cycles, he'd remember again and force-fit strange realms into the familiar. His senses were different in this nonmaterial realm. His consciousness directly touched and changed this fluid reality. From his vantage point, many of the things Dora had tried to explain became apparent.

He remembered Jon and found him with Lisa in a blue and quiet place. He could not relate to that environment nor communicate. He thought of Earth and observed panoramas of terrain from a great height. Associated memories took him from place to place, faster and faster.

"Ida Moore, you are not at all well organized," Dora said laughing. "Drift and dream then and be not concerned."

Jon awoke, thinking as always that the equipment had failed and that he had not as yet fallen asleep. He opened the panel to the crypt and gasped in the ice-cold air that washed across his bare skin. Within seconds, the air warmed, frost forming on the metal surfaces around him, turning to sparkling dew drops and evaporating.

The first to awaken, it was his job to verify their position and to awaken the others. He pulled on his coveralls and boots in the weightlessness and shoved himself eagerly toward the control console. Pulling himself into the pilot's couch, he activated the visual screens.

The starfields sprang into view. If there were alien ships out there, he saw no visual indications of them. In the rear screen, the sun glared bright, but little more than another bright star among uncountable numbers of them. The nav computer indicated that they were in solar orbit somewhere beyond the sun's family of planets.

244

He switched the screens to radar visual.

They were dead ahead, a fleet forming a vast, crescent-shaped, two-dimensional formation, the two cusps of the crescent pointed toward the sun with the Transtar almost dead center between them. When Jon switched back to visual for a second look, he could just see a transparent shimmering among the stars.

Jon waited for an hour to make sure the fleet wouldn't react to his presence. Then he activated Lisa's crypt and timed the other two to bring Moore and Dora to consciousness within an hour. He hovered near Lisa's crypt, watching the temperature rise to normal. A scope showed brain activity beginning. Heart and respiratory activity joined the symphony of life. Despite everything she had told him, a part of him firmly believed in death. He could see it before his very eyes and watch it defeated by human technology. Lisa had not been alive by any definition of the word, but she lived now, her flesh warm and pliant. She emerged from the crypt. Jon turned his back to her, pretending to check out Moore and Dora.

"The senses are not liars," Lisa said. "But they only give one picture of reality."

Jon turned to face her. He wasn't completely awake yet. He had forgotten about her first death.

"A smaller world is more comfortable," she said. "But its boundaries of life and death are oppressive."

"Old habits die hard," Jon said.

"Indeed," Lisa said. "But when their time has come, they die nevertheless."

An hour later, Moore emerged from his crypt.

"What went wrong? Nothing happened."

Jon waited for Dora to climb from her crypt and dress. She moved as implacably unconcerned as Lisa.

"We're arrived," Jon said. "We have our oddball friends waiting outside. What are we supposed to do

245

with them?"

When they grouped before the screen, gazing at the shimmering in the stars, Jon said, " They must know we're here."

"I don't know," Lisa said. "I sense a dormancy."

"Are they in suspended animation?" Moore said.

"They await," Dora stated.

"I suppose we'll just have to choose one of the craft and knock to announce our presence," Jon said. Despite the sarcasm, he suspected their next move would have to be a bold one.

"Precisely," Lisa said. "It appears that the first move is ours."

"They look so defenseless," Moore commented.

Jon sighed and took a moment to think it out. "They're packed fairly close together in a two-dimensional plane. Two or three Jovan battle cruisers carry enough firepower to wipe out a formation even that size. But they're not as defenseless as they seem, are they?"

Lisa answered. "They are not. There is grave danger should any hostile move be made against them regardless of how passive they appear."

Jon put his hand on Lisa's shoulder. "Don't let me make mistakes. What might be their concept of a hostile move? Maybe something as simple as approaching one of their ships?"

"No, it would be attempted destruction."

"I'd prefer that our intentions not be misinterpreted. Moore and I are prejudiced against pain and death, you know."

"You may approach them safely," Lisa said.

The process took hours—hours of silence during which the viewscreen gave no evidence of their progress.

"They're not supposed to be too far in advance of us," Jon said. "Is that right?"

"Roughly comparable," Lisa said. "They are different. They do not have your technology, no fusion propulsion, no electronics or nuclear weaponry."

Jon frowned. "What do they have?"

Lisa smiled. "How would I know?"

Their weight shifted from side to side as Jon accelerated, decelerated, and altered their trajectory by small amounts.

"I have one coming up fast."

It was hard to see at first, just a distortion among the stars, a flattened egg-shaped area within which the stars moved and twisted. It stopped dead before them, half filling the screen. Jon switched on a spotlight. But the light and a distorted view of the illuminated Transtar reflected from the curved surface of the object.

"A mirror finish," Jon said. "It's about a hundred meters in length, oblate in form. No visible protrusions, seams, surface blemishes of any kind. It's not emitting anything in the EM spectrum, not even infrared. It's not rotating."

Jon moved the Transtar around the alien object. It seemed to rotate once in the screen. "I have nothing else to work with," he said. "No way to determine its mass or composition."

"Why not take a look at another craft," Moore suggested. "Maybe they're not all the same."

"Good idea."

Jon moved the Transtar away. They could see stars shifting and flickering in the distance, evidence of the vast quantities of the objects about them.

"Anyone doubt that the next is identical to the first?"

It wasn't.

"Now what?" Moore said.

"I'll have to go EVA and take a closer look," Jon announced.

"Like hell you will," Moore said. "Pilot's aren't expendable personnel. Passengers don't like being stuck a few billion kilometers from nowhere with a deceased pilot."

"You volunteering?"

Moore hadn't had that in mind specifically.

"What do you suppose we're going to find inside?"

"Speculation won't work," Jon said. "About the only thing we can take for granted is that they've made some provision to handle contact with us."

Even Moore's logic boxed him into the inevitable. Jon would stay with the ship, responsible for the welfare of the two women. He would go outside—and what? Knock on the hull?

Jon looked at Lisa. "Are there other alternatives we're overlooking?"

"There will be no going back," Lisa said. "I can say nothing more."

Neither Jon nor Moore appreciated the finality with which she made that statement.

"All right, so my native cowardice is showing," Moore said as the three of them waited for his decision. "Do I get an ironclad guarantee that I'll receive a warm welcome?"

Jon grinned. "Like an atmospheric temperature somewhere around five hundred degrees?"

"That's not exactly what I had in mind."

"You're the perfect human specimen for a bunch of aliens," Jon said. "You're not just a tag-along anymore, Moore. I think this is your role to play in our little drama."

"But you were willing to go, weren't you?" Moore said. "You'd have no fear of what you might encounter. It was just the next thing to do as far as you were concerned."

Jon gazed at the alien spacecraft.

"I wasn't raised by the state to invest very heavily in life. I don't have a fear of death. Either it doesn't exist or it's repressed so well, I'm never conscious of it." Jon looked hard at Moore. "Lack of fear isn't the same thing as courage. Yeah, I'd like to go out there, but I have a sneaky suspicion I know why you're a part of this." Jon turned to Lisa. "How about one of your ancient metaphors?"

"Tell him it's his ball, to take it and run with it."

Jon nodded and grinned.

"Why do I get the impression I'm going to regret this?" Moore said.

"Maybe because you are?" Jon said, and laughed at Moore's expression of total exasperation.

Jon helped him on with one of the Transtar's pressure suits and a helmet.

"What exactly am I supposed to do out there?" Moore asked.

"Initiate physical contact with the object. Touch it. Move around and inspect the surface at close range. Report what you observe."

"Then you weren't serious about knocking?"

"Perfectly serious. Knock on the damned thing."

Moore spun slowly in the void, the Transtar passing vertically in front of him from top to bottom every few seconds. "I'm not very good at using the thrusters," he said.

"So we've noticed," Jon replied over the radio. "Stay calm and get stabilized before you move in. Otherwise, you're liable to spin yourself into oblivion."

Well aware of the possibility of panicking, Moore took his time adapting to the laws of inertia. After a few moments, he sent himself moving toward the alien object, but still tumbling slowly.

"Moore, stabilize yourself before you wind up shattering your helmet against the hull of that thing."

"I told you I wasn't very good at using these thrusters!"

"Not very good would be adequate. You're a whole lot less than adequate."

Moore caught a reflection of himself tumbling in

the hull of the alien object. With growing desperation, he tried again to kill some of his forward momentum, but only succeeded in accelerating himself toward the spinning reflection of himself.

"Moore, you're about to make history if you're serious about burying your head in the hull of that thing!"

One last attempt. Moore succeeded, miraculously applying just enough countering thrust to neutralize his spin. He cut most of his forward speed and looked at his own reflection slowly approaching.

He saw the blue flash when it hit and felt the sudden shock passing through him. In the next instant, he was sliding on his belly across the slick surface of the object and back into space.

From the Transtar, Jon saw the electric discharge and clenched his jaw. He watched Moore strike the hull, slide across the object, and tumble into emptiness.

"You okay?" Jon asked calmly.

"I'm okay," Moore said. "What was that blue flash?"

"It looked like a corona around you, static electricity maybe. Hard telling. No ill effects?"

"Not that I can tell."

Moore cut his forward momentum, turned smoothly, and started back.

"Something is wrong," Lisa said.

Jon glanced at the woman, trying to read the extend of the danger by her expression.

"What's wrong?"

"I don't know. Imminent danger."

Jon turned back to the screen. "Moore, look around. Does everything look okay? Is the object doing anything?"

"Nothing I can see. I'm moving back in."

Having crudely mastered the thrusters, Moore returned to the object and moved against it gently, braking his momentum with outstretched hands.

"Sure is slick," he said. "Nothing to hold onto."

Moore moved across the curve of the hull, sliding along on his hands.

"Perfectly smooth," he said. "I'd say microscopically perfect. I don't see the slightest distortion in my reflection."

"Moore, Lisa has warned of some kind of danger. If the object doesn't seem to be doing anything, start back toward the ship."

"In a minute. Do you suppose you could gain some idea of its mass if I tried to push it?"

"Push it?"

Moore braced his hands and knees against the curved landscape of mirror finished metal and used his thrusters to apply what felt like a substantial pressure against the object before beginning to slide across its surface.

Jon aligned the horizon of the hull on crosshairs in one of the screens.

"I detect no movement, Moore. It's too massive to be moved by the few pounds you can imagine, but I can at least calculate a minimum figure. Now move back toward the ship."

"Keep him at a distance," Lisa said, her voice soft and neutral. "Something is wrong."

Moore's image swelled on the forward screen. He moved like a pro now, showing due caution and well stabilized.

"Moore, stop! Keep a distance from the Transtar. Lisa keeps insisting that something is wrong."

Moore cut his forward momentum, drifting slightly.

"What's going on?"

Lisa pointed to Moore. "Something is wrong with Ida Moore."

"Moore, how do you feel?"

"I don't mean his physical health," Lisa said, her voice too low to carry over the radio.

"I feel fine," Moore said. "What the hell's going on?"

"I don't know! Moore, you're drifting. Maintain your position until I can figure out what Lisa is talking about."

From the moment Moore had left the Transtar, his heart had hammered hard and steady. At first, he had felt elated, the sense of danger sharpening his senses. Now, the fear had turned into something distasteful. Then, in a split moment, it turned into a flood of horror.

"Jon, for God's sake! The airlock's on the wrong side of the ship!"

"Moore, what the hell are you talking about?"

"The airlock's on the wrong side of the ship! The antenna, everything. Everything's turned around backward!"

"Moore, you're not making any sense. . . ."

Lisa spoke. "Jon, ask him to raise his right hand."

"Moore, Lisa asks you to raise your right hand."

Moore did as he was told without thinking, trying to find the reason for the perceptual distortion that had him bordering on panic. "Jon, it's like looking through a mirror. I don't understand what's happening!"

"Moore, I said your right hand!"

"This is my right hand, damn it!" Moore waved his right hand over his head. "What are you trying to prove?"

"Moore, relax and stay calm while we talk about this. It must have something to do with that blue flash. Just wait a moment until we decide what to do."

"Jon, I want to come aboard! Let me come aboard and we'll talk about it!"

"Tell him to stay where he is," Lisa said.

"Moore, just stay where you're at. I'll get back to you in a moment."

Jon cut off the radio and swung around to face Lisa.

Dora floated alongside her twin, holding on to Lisa's couch. "Do you know what's happening?"

"It's not just Ida Moore," Lisa said. "I sense extreme danger for us as well."

Jon turned back to the screen and magnified the view of Moore hanging free in space. On impulse, he focused the spotlight on the Lunan. Moore turned his head aside and raised an arm to block the light.

"The lettering on the helmet and arm of the suit," Lisa said. "It's reversed. It's not just a perceptual distortion on Moore's part."

Jon understood immediately. He switched the radio back on. "Moore, there's a small key for the emergency airlock in your utility belt."

"Key?" Moore fumbled along his belt and found the short piece of flat metal with a notch on one end. "I have it."

"Do you see Sirius, Moore? The star Sirius! I want you to throw the tool in that direction as hard as you can."

Moore craned his neck to search the starfield. Sweat stung his eyes. He shivered with the frigid cold of terror.

"The stars are all wrong, Jon! Jon, the stars are all wrong!"

"Don't panic, Moore! I think I know what's happened. Just throw the key as hard as you can off to one side. I'll be able to track it on radar. I'll explain what I'm doing in a moment."

Moore did as he was told. He threw the key as hard as possible and used his thrusters to stop his tumbling and to move back in position facing the Transtar.

Jon cut in a close-range radar, located the slowly moving object, and locked it into the navigational computers. He prepared a small instrument probe designed to explore potentially hazardous environments, anything from radiation levels to micrometeorite density.

"Jon, what's going on?" Moore pleaded.

"Good throw, Moore. How much air supply do you have left in that suit?"

"Six hours, Jon."

"All right, that's good. Just keep calm. I'll get right back to you."

Jon cut off the radio. "Lisa, where did the Isinti get the antineutron beam? Could it have been from these aliens? Could there have been some kind of mental contact between them?"

Lisa nodded.

"It's an incredibly dense beam, Lisa. When it interacts with normal matter, pure energy is emitted. It converts matter to energy."

Jon gestured toward the gleaming alien craft.

"What other form of energy could move a fleet like this? What other form of defense could be more effective? Antimatter is the key. I don't know what the symmetry reversal means, but I'm certain that the blue discharge we saw prevented Moore from making physical contact with antimatter. By some sort of dimensional inversion, it converted him to antimatter."

"Then it begins," Lisa said.

"It begins, but it's going to end on a sour note if Moore runs out of air. We can't bring him aboard and I still haven't the slightest idea what to tell him."

"You're in the process of testing your hypothesis," Lisa said. "Take one thing at a time."

Moore's voice sounded over the speaker. "Jon?"

"Relax," Jon said. "I've got things under control for the time being. I'm sending out a probe to make contact with the airlock key you threw."

"A probe?"

"We think it might be antimatter. I think the alien craft are antimatter. That blue flash protected you, but for the time being, you can't come aboard the

254

ship, Moore."

Moore said nothing. He either understood the implications of what Jon had told him or was suffering too much shock to react.

"Moore, are you okay?"

"I'm okay."

A low-priority warning signal warbled. Jon cut it off. At the far end of the range of the long distance radar, objects were moving toward the Transtar. Even on visual, the fusion torches of the approaching fleet of spacecraft were perfectly visible among the stars. Jon said nothing. Lisa could feel his thoughts and Moore didn't need to know. The Lunan had enough problems of his own.

CHAPTER FOURTEEN

Jon moved the Transtar around to shield Moore with its bulk.

"Countdown to contact, ten seconds."

Lisa pointed to one of the screens. The alien object had altered its appearance. A black rectangular opening marred its mirror surface.

"That solves Moore's problem," Jon said.

Sixty kilometers from the ship, the slow-moving probe made physical contact with Moore's airlock key. The ports and screens darkened. Jon watched the radiation detectors peg into the red zone and fall off slowly.

"Moore," Jon said. "Are you okay?"

"I think my faceplate blacked out," Moore said, his voice sounding flat.

Jon waited for Moore to question the fate of his key or the nature of the explosion. When the screens cleared, Moore had noticed the black rectangular opening on the hull of the alien object.

"Remember," Lisa said. "We're as alien to them as they are to us. They probably just deduced that we were having problems of some kind. They might have been trying to communicate with us all along."

Jon watched the screen, wondering how Moore

would react next. The Lunan appeared calm, but his voice had gone flat. Jon hoped he'd be able to function in a state of shock. The onslaught of events was just beginning.

Jon looked back at the two women. He spoke to Dora.

"Is he in danger?"

"He is no longer in danger."

On the screen, Moore disappeared inside the black rectangle. Then, it vanished, replaced by reflections of the universe.

Moore stood on the control deck of an ancient freighter. Red emergency lights glowed across a steel deck. Against one side of the steeply curved bulkheads all but hidden by plumbing and conduit arced a broad control panel with five crew positions.

Vintage 2200 A.D., Moore estimated. He had seen photographs and had visited mockups of such ships at the astronautical museum in the Lansing District on Luna. If the flight deck had been real, he'd be standing on the inside hull of a rotating section of the craft. Regardless of whether the mockup was rotating or not, he possessed his normal quarter G gravity.

Moore felt disconnected from reality. His hands shook and sweat trickled in beads down his face. He decided it would be nice to get out of his pressure suit. The gauges on his arm read normal air pressure and temperature outside his suit. He located a light switch. In brilliant, fluorescent light, he stripped off his suit and helmet, leaving them piled at his feet.

He explored the crew's quarters located off a main corridor that curved up and around, returning to the control room. His footsteps echoed in the silence. He found a working toilet and shower and bunks complete with rumpled sheets. He took note of the usual paraphernalia he'd expect of a museum exhibit, books, razors, diaries. The aliens had provided him with their best interpretation of a natural environment for a human being. Moore returned to the bridge and wondered how long it would be before they would attempt contact with him.

He heard voices. He turned, his heart beginning to pound again. But the voices were only coming from images playing on the large forward screen positioned over the control panel. The voices were distorted, the images of poor quality, ridden with static and odd, horizontal lines. They were in a bluish white, two-dimensional format, but strangely familiar. He had seen something like this before.

In the next moment, he recognized what he was seeing. The scenes were of the last half of the twentieth century, over five centuries old. The people were smaller and stockier than the Valthyn and dressed for an uncontrolled natural environment. Some scenes were of people moving about in snow. Cities of stone towered into a clouded sky and awesome quantities of personal vehicles rolled between the buildings. Primitive aircraft plied the skies, used in some scenes to depict primitive wars being fought between men and machinery tearing the very ecology apart in frantic efforts to kill one another. This was television, electronic scanning, illuminated phosphors, the ancient, popular means of communication. Moore recalled that it had been a one-way form of communication providing mostly information and entertainment. The little boxed viewscreens in the domestic scenes were television sets.

Moore's fear faded into a sadness and an affection for the aliens who had gone to all this trouble to demonstrate their limited knowledge of man. Did all of the alien craft in the fleet contain a similar set, each prepared in the same way for contact with man? Or had all of this been thrown together after the approach of the Transtar?

The screen went blank for a moment. The image of a woman who had lived centuries in the past appeared. She stood on a stage, gesturing and talking in a lively manner. But the words Moore heard were disconnected from her lip movement and inappropriate to her behavior. In fact, the speech consisted of bits and pieces of voices selected and spliced together to form an introduction.

"Hello," the voice said. "We are friends. We mean no harm. We wish communicate. We request, beseech. Be happy, comfortable."

"Do you understand me?" Moore said, speaking aloud for the first time.

"Yes, we understand you. Difficulty. Patience and calm."

"I understand," Moore said. He understood too well. The aliens had spent centuries in a blind attempt to isolate enough concepts and synthesize an archaic English in order to bridge the gap between them and man in this, their first contact. The communication hinted at an associative rather than logical method of thinking, but nothing that would give him much trouble. With time and patience and constant feedback from him, there would be proper communication.

Images began forming on the screen followed by words. Moore repeated the words, but amplified them with descriptions of this own and corrections of the more blatant misunderstandings. When he tired of the game after several hours, he rose from his seat and turned away. As he suspected would happen, the screen went dark. He sat back down to test the procedure. The screen came back to life.

Exploring the mock spaceship, Moore decided that it would support him. At least they had human biology thought out accurately. The water tasted flat and the food bland, but his first meal in a small, empty cafeteria had no ill effect and quenched his thirst and satisfied his hunger. When he lay down to nap for a few hours in one of the cramped, two-room quarters, the lights dimmed for him.

When he awoke, he investigated the airlock by which he had entered. It remained locked. Apparently, they would release him whenever they had accomplished what they wanted with him. For three waking and sleeping cycles, Moore worked with the screen. Using an incredible array of films and images that focused on twenty-second- or third-century life on Luna and Mars, periods that he could relate to without much difficulty, the aliens began their futile attempts to understand human logic. By correcting their errors and answering questions on increasingly subtle points of logic and grammar, the effort began to pay off. His unseen students began interrogating him on the nature of human life and the history of the human race. Moore began to do most of the talking with less-frequent interruptions for explanations. At first, a discussion over a concept as simple as *smile* or *flavor* would take hours, but eventually, Moore felt as if he conversed endlessly with an interested stranger—but not necessarily an alien one.

Moore began to worry about Jon. Jon would think him dead by now. How long would he wait for him to return? If Jon lost sight, even momentarily, of the particular craft he had entered, he'd never find him again among the uncountable numbers of alien craft in the fleet. Moore banged on the airlock, demanding to be released if only temporarily. He knew by now his hosts would understand. When they did not respond, Moore donned his pressure suit and helmet and stood before the airlock, stubbornly waiting to be released.

An image of the Transtar appeared on the screen. The sharp, three-dimensional view had to be a live one. Then, the view changed. Moore studied a bright, geometric pattern of stars, recognizing them finally in a sudden shock as an approaching Alliance warfleet. At the same time, he realized what he had been overlooking. Dora and Lisa would know what was happening to him. Jon would have an update of his progress whenever he wanted one.

Moore removed the pressure suit and his helmet, folding the suit neatly and placing it beside the airlock with the helmet placed alongside. It would be a time yet before he could leave. Nothing could be more important than developing the full potential of his ability to communicate with the aliens and their ability to understand man's behavior. Jon would stay put. Soon, they'd all have the common problem of coping with a premature confrontation with the outward-bound warfleets of humanity.

The inactivity tormented Jon. The alien craft fixed off the bow of the Transtar remained impassive, the Alliance fleet slowly crawling up from behind. If he had been alone aboard the Transtar, Jon would have assumed Moore to be lost forever, either dead, driven insane, or a permanent captive of alien lifeforms. But Lisa fed him a light diet of Moore's experience. They were like visual and audio hallucinations, not enough to gain a comprehensive idea of what was happening aboard the alien ship, but enough to know that Moore was alive, rational, and that he had his hands full.

"Humanity has scattered debris into his environment," Lisa explained. "At first, it was only radio and television signals expanding on a wavefront through the galaxy. Then it was garbage, derelict spacecraft, weapons, radioactive waste, and even an occasional human corpse. The alien species must have kept its distance for centuries, sifting through it all, learning as much as possible about man before attempting a confrontation."

"I didn't think that communication would be that much of a problem," Jon said.

"Language has its roots in our biology. Biology has its roots in the physical environment. And our physical senses are attuned to the most important aspects of the environment. An alien lifeform can have a different biology, live in a different environment and have senses that wouldn't perceive our environment in the same way we do. There would be no mutual, direct foundation of reference upon which to build a common means of communication."

"Does Moore understand this?"

"Perfectly. Moore is well suited for the task."

"And as for us," Jon said, "we have the Alliance to contend with. They might be out for blood this time. The craft visible on the screens are just the advance scouts. You should see what's coming up behind them."

Lisa smiled. "You are well suited to handle the situation."

"How? I could try taking them on with the anti-neutron beam, but they'd get me in the end. I have a sneaky suspicion that's not going to work anymore. I just hope they realize the same thing."

"Destroying and being destroyed is a cycle of stagnation that accomplishes nothing in the end."

At one time, Jon would not have understood what she meant. Now, it made more sense than he cared to admit.

"How long will Moore take to complete this mission of his?"

"Moore has resigned himself to taking what time he needs."

Dora spoke this time. Or at least Jon assumed that Dora spoke. The two women were almost interchangeable without Moore's presence. But it was too much for him to try to ponder the existence of two Lisas. Unconsciously, he imposed different traits upon the two. Only one had a depth of personality that he identified with Lisa, the other little more than a cardboard copy of her. He tried to keep the two of them separate in his mind.

"And he can be a very patient fellow, can't he?"

"He tracked us across the face of the Earth on a daily basis for years," Lisa said.

Jon sat at the controls of the idle Transtar and waited. He felt the slow drag of time passing. He wondered how it would feel to sit in one spot long enough to see the changes among the stars. He tried to grasp some idea of the length of time represented by a century, a millennium. If all time existed in an eternal Now a never-ending moment of becoming, what would the universe look like to an entity who could see the birth of a star and its death as a nova, all in some strange moment of time?

The next day he said, "This is the end of it. When Moore returns, regardless of what happens next, it'll be over for us. There's nothing left for the four of us to do."

"You've never thought that far ahead before," Lisa said.

"I never expected to survive long enough to have to. I've never had any future to look forward to, no past to look back at. It was one hell of a way to have to live, but even now, I can't imagine what might take its place."

"Life is just beginning for you," Lisa said.

"Why does that scare me?"

Jon looked at Lisa, really looked at her. He could still feel a barrier standing between them. He had loved her desperately when they lived on the surface of Earth, but she had died and life had lost what little meaning it had gained in her arms. She had come back, but he didn't dare open himself to that kind of risk again. The barrier protected him from pain, but it isolated him in a cold and unfeeling realm.

"You'll never love me in the same way until you learn that what life has to offer is worth the hurt.

There is still time for you to learn. My greater purpose in life has already been fulfilled. As an individual, nothing remains for me in life except you, Jon."

"What will happen to the Valthyn?" Jon asked.

"The Valthyn will breed no more. When the last of us is gone, we will have no more contact with your world. The children we bear until that time will be children of Earth."

"I can't go back to the way things were," Jon said. "I'm not a fighter-pilot any more. I'm not a Jovan citizen. I don't know what there is to take the place of belonging to that. What kind of future do we have together?"

"Your new foundation for living will be based on an open confidence that reality sinks deeper roots than you imagine," Lisa said, her voice soft and clear in the stillness. "Your old foundation was based on what you felt to be the certainty of death and oblivion. No man can build a foundation for life on death and futility."

Jon liked the sound of Lisa's words, but something else bothered him.

"What about everyone else? The whole solar system will have to live with the consequences of how we and the authorities handle this situation."

"The universe is not a hostile place to live," Lisa said. "When humanity gets to know the Isinti and handles initial contact with the aliens well enough to make new friends, many of the fears that have been covered over by arrogance and international rivalry will fade away. History may record this day as the end of a dark age. There has been little progress during the past five centuries, social or technological."

Jon watched the fusion burns of the incoming fleet.

"Look at those bastards brake. They must be decelerating at thirty or forty gravities. They've been in quite a hurry. Military forces don't like traveling in suspended animation."

"Don't misjudge their intentions," Lisa warned. "Two rebels from their own ranks have usurped the authority of the two greatest nations in the sustem, but would it surprise you to know that a few of those authorities have felt a secret relief at having the responsibility for all that has happened assumed by autonomous individuals free of social and cultural loyalties?"

"I'm not sure I understand what you said." Jon grinned.

"When they first noticed the alien fleet," Lisa said, "they knew for certain that they would fail to contain their fears. They knew they would destroy themselves. They feared that you and Moore were agents of the unknown and felt that we and the Isinti were invaders or traitors. But they knew that if they were wrong, we would most likely be the forces to prevent their suicide."

"Do we get medals?"

"At one time, you would have settled for posthumous honors."

Jon shook his head slowly, mocking a solemn rejection.

"I want mine now."

They wanted to examine him physically. The examination took place in an environment that turned out to be less of a concession for him than the fake spaceship. The walls of the chamber he entered off the corridor were irregular in shape, the texture of tree bark he had seen on Earth. Phosphorescent fungus provided a dim, bluish illumination. The air smelled corrosive and a dense mist swirled about his ankles. One wall glowed in white translucence that gave beneath a fingertip when he probed it.

The alien craft lived. The masters that the voice told him about were indeed masters of organic technology. As yet, he had seen nothing of the masters. The voice told him that it was not of the masters, but something artificial and subservient. Moore reasoned that the voice would be a biological computer.

Moore stretched out nude on a low dais set in the center of the chamber. He waited, suffering a constant low-level anxiety that he wouldn't have been able to tolerate indefinitely. He stared upward at the bluish glow, trying to ignore the black tendrils moving up alongside his body. He felt their touch and then their sting. They penetrated his flesh. Placing his faith in an intelligence he had grown to honor and respect, he did not move when he could feel them probing deep within his body. Once or twice he felt a twinge of pain or experienced an involuntary jerking of his muscles, but the tendrils jerked back when that happened, as if they understood the workings of the human neural system well enough to tune in and react to it. Finally, the tendrils withdrew entirely. When he sat up, Moore inspected his skin for wounds, but found nothing.

He showered and changed clothes and rested for an hour in his cabin, then returned to the bridge.

"Hello," the voice said to him.

"Hello," Moore said, completing the ritual.

"Did you suffer?"

"I am well."

"Summarize, please."

Moore took a seat in the Captain's chair set on a low dais overlooking the control positions lining the console. He sighed, thoroughly frustrated in his attempts to understand the specific requests the voice had narrowed down to making during their past several sessions.

"As I understand it," Moore said, "you take nourishment from the sun. You want my permission to approach our sun, to establish an orbit between the third and the fourth planet."

"That is correct."

"The rest is difficult."

"Difficult, yes."

"I don't have the authority to act in behalf of my people. You have my permission, but a few billions of others might object."

A question mark formed on the screen. The voice did not understand the concept of individuality. Or, perhaps, it didn't understand the lack of communication between individuals.

"Do you forbid?" the voice said.

"No, I do not forbid. Nor can I allow."

Again, the question mark.

The hour grew late, but the voice would not take Moore's explanation as a legitimate response. An image of the approaching Alliance fleet appeared on the screen followed by a question mark. Moore had his suspicions of what might happen when the fleet arrived, but he didn't dare tell of them to the voice.

The voice had told him that he could be free to leave when the alien fleet received permission to approach the sun and *unfold*. The voice had fed Moore images of men crawling across deserts in search of water, climbing mountains and collapsing with exhaustion at their summits, sprinting across finishing lines and dropping with fatigue to the ground. Moore took this to mean that their voyage had been long and exhausting, the fleet dormant and awaiting the nourishment of solar radiation. The voice had made it clear that the fleet would return to its point of origin if he so requested, but lacking Moore's direct orders, the situation had bogged down to a stalemate.

"What will happen when you achieve orbit?" Moore asked.

An image of an unfolding rose appeared on the screen in brilliant crimson against the black of space. He was shown images of armies returning home, streets lined with cheering throngs, images of returning astronauts showered with bits of paper as they rode down a canyon between buildings in an ancient Earth city. Evidently, the aliens took for granted that their presence would be a warm and welcomed event.

Moore, in turn, had learned little of the alien masters themselves. The masters had built and launched the fleet, although they were not aboard the craft. But the voice disagreed with Moore's use of the terms *craft*, *spaceship*, and *fleet*, using images of eggs, seeds, and formations of birds to symbolize them.

What kinds of communication did he know? Radio and verbal communication. The kind of telepathy that Lisa and Dora utilized. Then, Moore remembered the Isinti formation of one-person craft that had greeted him and Jon at their settlement, the beautiful double-helix maneuver that spoke of a kind of communication beyond his understanding. Solving the puzzle felt like pondering a koan of an ancient religion he had read about. What is the sound of one hand clapping?

The solution dawned on him shortly after he saw the fusion burns of the Alliance fleet shut down. Humanity spoke with individual voices. Except for the Valthyn and the Isinti, a common voice did not exist. To break the stalemate left a choice of sending the fleet back into interstellar space or into a close solar orbit.

"Hello," he said.

"Hello," the voice responded.

"I understand now. You have my permission to orbit our sun where you desire. May I leave now?"

Images of people shaking hands. An image of a boat departing a dock, people waving and shouting, steam whistles blowing. Moore thought he felt movement.

He suited himself and faced an open airlock. His final problem presented itself like a hand of ice down his back. He struggled to word his inquiry as accurately as possible.

"Is it safe for me to return to my own ship?"

A question mark.

"I don't understand the reason for the symmetry reversal I experienced. Before I entered, I threw a piece of metal. A device from our ship reached out and touched it. An explosion resulted. Is there danger now?"

An image of the Transtar first shown in normal perspective, then in mirror image.

"Yes!"

An image of tiny flashes of light against the hull of an egg-shaped craft.

"A meteoroid shield?"

An exclamation point followed by an image of a sunbather.

"And you absorb the energy?"

The sound of applause echoed through the bridge.

Moore turned back to the airlock. He launched himself through an opening into open space and recognized the stars.

The man of iron had grown brittle and fatigued by constant pressure. General Hester Alboran looked as panicky as Jon felt. Neither were in control of circumstances, nor could they bluff one another into thinking they were. The alien fleet was in motion, flowing like a liquid from one cusp of the crescent formation into a single file of craft.

"Honored Jon B-897Y," General Hester Alboran said in a quiet voice. "We meet for the third time."

Jon refrained from reverting to formalities. But he kept in mind that Alboran had been under constant fire for a solution to an impossible situation. He had slept for two years of the voyage to this alien fleet, but the Alliance fleet had slept for much less time, undoubtedly launched to high velocities by multi-staged, fusion boosters. There must have been many changes in the social and political structures of the new Alliance, changes in Alboran himself. But, the man had been his living death warrant for too long to trust completely now.

Still, the title surprised him. The honored were sacred. Very few were ever honored alive, a title generally conferred posthumously to individuals who had sacrificed their lives in displays of skill and courage in battle.

"The Alliance recognizes the commission of many errors in judgment," Alboran said. "We recognize the courage and sacrifice it required of you to contend with the injustice we have committed upon you. If we had paid closer attention to your warnings, we would have averted intolerable suffering. We do not fully understand as yet, but we acquiesce to necessity."

Some of Jon's old hatred still boiled within him. His body shook with it. But, for the first time, he could afford to let it flow from him without the need for a target or a focus. He sensed within himself its distant origin of hurt and bitterness. Alboran was not his enemy.

"What do you want?" Jon said, his voice cold and steady.

General Alboran hesitated. "The alien fleet is moving."

"Yes, it is."

"You have communicated with the alien forces?"

"Ida Moore has communicated. He is aboard one of the alien craft. We have not as yet heard from him since he boarded, but the Valthyn have kept me informed of his progress."

"I see."

271

"The aliens are not hostile," Jon said.

"We cannot be certain."

"Do you intend to attack?"

"That decision has not been made yet," General Hester Alboran said.

Jon made his final decision. "I will neither fight to defend ourselves nor run to avoid destruction. Not in the presence of the alien fleet. When Ida Moore is released, I intend following the alien fleet down into the inner system. If we awake at the end of our journey, we will meet a fourth time, General."

Jon switched off the screen. He heard a low-toned signal emitted by a pressure suit beacon. He turned sharply to Lisa.

"Where is he?"

Lisa pointed off to her left and up slightly. In a moment of cold horror, Jon had lost track of the alien craft Moore had boarded. The entire fleet was in motion now.

Jon swung a directional antenna in the vague direction Lisa indicated and focused on Ida Moore's tiny figure tumbling through interstellar space. He moved the Transtar to rendezvous.

An hour later, Moore stepped into the cabin of the Transtar with an ashen grin on his face. Without speaking, he stripped off his suit and moved to the rear of the cabin to the food and water dispensers.

"Welcome back," Jon said.

"Thank you," Ida Moore said. "Let me know if I act funny. I think I'm cracking up."

Jon locked the navigational computer onto one of the alien craft filing away from the main fleet and put the controls on full automatic. From the data he had to work with, it would take at least three years for the fleet to achieve its solar orbit between Earth and Mars. The four of them would sleep peacefully through the journey if they survived at all. But it

272

promised to be a nightmarish experience for humanity, a historic period that would determine the ultimate survival or extinction of the human race. If humanity survived the stress of watching a massive alien fleet spiral its way through the solar system, only then would they awaken at the end of that voyage.

Jon shut the Transtar down and prepared for their frozen sleep. Little could be seen in the screen, but on radar, a hazed, shimmering plane of return echoes slowly flowed into a delicate, rapidly lengthening thread.

"There are so many of them," Jon said. "What kind of civilization has the resources to build a fleet of that size and send it on a centuries-long voyage?"

"You're asking the wrong questions," Moore said. "Those ships weren't built. They're artificial organisms designed to function in open space. They're alive and intelligent. They have will and feeling. They weren't built. They were grown."

"What are they like?" Jon said. "The aliens, I mean."

Moore ventured a smile. "There are no aliens. Just the ships themselves."

A halo of light formed around each alien craft as it began moving. Jon checked out the Alliance fleet for the last time. Never in the history of mankind had a warfleet of that size ever been assembled in one place at one time. It carried more firepower than man had ever used in the combined total of every war fought in human history. But man stayed his hand. The fleet wasn't assembled in an attack formation. Scientific stations were being released from the bays of transports. In all probability, the fleet would be awake and active for the entire length of the sunward journey.

"What happens now?" Moore wanted to know.

"I don't think there will be any trouble," Jon

decided. "If the Alliance intended to attack, they'd do so now while a maximum distance from civilian populations. I might ask you the same question, Moore. What happens when those craft reach the orbit they want?"

Moore smiled. "What happens to a seed when it's planted in a fertile environment. Wait and see." He glanced toward the screen. "But it's going to be a nightmare waiting. I like the idea of sleeping through the waiting."

"Convenient, isn't it?" Jon said. "You get to experience the highlights of history and sleep through the dull parts."

Jon looked to Lisa, startled to note that the two women sitting side by side were impossible to tell apart. "And you two," he said. "Satisfied with the performance of your star pupils?"

"Yes," Lisa said, the one to the right. "Satisfied with the quality of your education?"

CHAPTER FIFTEEN

Moore lifted the lid to his crypt in time to see a classically beautiful female torso float by. Dora turned slowly in midair, aiming a shapely leg at a pair of utility coveralls.

"My but your thoughts grow bold," she taunted, her back still to him.

Moore reddened and pivoted up and out of the crypt, mocking silent anger. Jon glanced back from his position at the controls.

"You scientists are all alike. Repressed on the outside and a cauldron of perversity on the inside," he said.

"You'd be surprised at the quality of his imagination," Dora said in his defense.

"Thinking and doing are two different things."

"Opportunity must count for something," Lisa joined in. "Don't you think Ida Moore would make use of the same opportunity that you arrange for yourself?"

"Lisa!"

Moore spun around. "Jon, you bastard!"

Lisa and Dora burst into laughter. Jon's sheepish exasperation and Moore's indignation were hard to maintain for long. Moore shook his head and smiled.

Jon grinned.

"All right, so I'm a bastard," Jon said. "You three get strapped in and take a look at what our alien friends are doing."

Moore couldn't adjust that rapidly. He sought out the chronometer on the controls. "Four *years? Four years?*"

"You've got to see this," Jon said, making sure everyone was watching the screen before switching it on. "You'll never believe what happened when the first ship established solar orbit."

A gigantic rose burse into view, crimson petals glowing bright in the sunlight against the backdrop of stars.

"A rose!" Moore cried out. "That's exactly what they showed me when I asked what would happen when they reached orbit! I thought it was meant to be symbolic!"

"Looks more like solar panels to me," Jon said. "Rather unique, but quite efficient when you study the design."

"It's alive, Jon! Those things are alive!"

"All right, so it's a goddamned flower garden! Look what else we have to contend with."

Jon flipped on a second screen. They looked upon a solid wall of metal, the nose of a Jovan fortress. Jon backed the view off. An incredible armada of warcraft spread across the skies.

"Four years of around-the-clock shipyard construction," Jon said. "What else did they have to do with four years of watching tens of millions of alien spacecraft spiraling into the system? Every local orbital colony has been under power since they began moving, trying to put as much space between themselves and this fleet as possible. Society is in an upheaval. The economy of the entire system is paralyzed. But nobody's fired a shot."

How long had Jon been awake? How much time

had he given himself to learn the extent of the turmoil and to work himself into this state of anxiety? Moore glanced at Lisa and Dora. The two Valthyn had been strangely quiet since contact with the aliens.

"Jon, it's just about over. There's no danger."

"Tell that to the Alliance warfleet. As far as they're concerned, the solar system has been invaded and conquered without a shot being fired."

"Those people weren't exactly your allies a short while back."

"They're pathetic," Jon said, the tone of his voice quieting. "They're helpless, paralyzed by a confrontation with their own suicidal tendencies."

"Jon, you've become oddly sympathetic to those people," Moore said. "Why do I get the impression that you've been letting General Alboran cry on your shoulder? Have you been been talking with him?"

Jon gave Moore a sick grin. "It's that obvious? Would you believe that General Hester Alboran wants one of his former fighter-pilots to tell him what to do with a warfleet of sixty thousand ships. He had them built just in case. He doesn't have the slightest idea of what to do with them."

Lisa spoke. "The part of humanity eager to communicate with the alien fleet has always been a dormant, invisible part of humanity. It is time now for it to come to life."

Jon looked at the woman with a frightened, lost expression.

"One further thing remains to be said that both you and Ida Moore should thoroughly understand. In itself, this alien fleet has never been a direct threat to humanity. If a single shot had been fired at any time, the entire fleet would have withdrawn from the solar system. They would never have entered to begin with if they had known that the welcome Moore extended to them wasn't shared by all."

"They wouldn't have defended themselves?" Jon

said.

"There would have been no need. They are not vulnerable to General Alboran's armada."

"You've been holding something back," Jon said. "You're saying that if General Alboran had ordered an attack, the alien fleet would have gone away and left us in peace?"

"In peace?" Lisa said.

"I guess not in peace," Jon said. "Is there more?"

"Jon, if this initial contact fails, there will be no others, not from this species or any other aligned with it. Life is fertile. The universe is inhabited and man has never been alone. But for those who travel between the stars, both beauty and hazard are shared by all. The Valthyn have tried to prevent with a desperation from the depths of our very souls, the dying that would have happened should man have been quarantined by the civilizations that surround your sun. Humanity would never have survived the isolation. If humanity denies contact to the entities that sent this fleet to us, then the caravan of interstellar spaceships being constructed in the shipyards around Jupiter will be denied contact with the worlds they will be sent to explore."

A look of astonishment crossed Jon's face. He nodded in understanding of the obvious and simple logic that had been the key to the stress and the drama from the very beginning.

"When men suffer, they fear. Hate is built upon fear and anger. When men begin to take responsibility for their own suffering, they begin to empathize with one another. Maturity beckons for humanity, Jon. It is time to put aside the rage and bitterness of adolescence. Or haven't you bothered to question the source of your pity for a man who tried to destroy you?"

Jon shrugged, speechless. He flipped a switch on the console. General Hester Alboran appeared on the screen.

"Let's take it one more step," Jon said. "The last one."

General Alboran nodded once.

"Moore, you're making history," Jon said in the way of encouragement. Ida Moore floated to the rear of what he could only describe as a stemless rose facing the sun in the dark void. The more he thought about it, the more unlikely it seemed that the alien fleet had been dormant during their four-year journey into the system. They must have used the time to study human civilization at close range through the filter of the human analogue he had provided for them. This time around, he would meet the mysterious masters.

"I might enjoy reading about it some day," Moore said.

"Don't forget that you're wired for sight and sound," Jon warned. "Somewhere around eighty billion people have just discovered that you're reluctant to finish what you started. After all, you're the one who gave them permission for their visit."

With a twinge of shock, Moore realized he had forgotten about the open-channel radio and miniature cameras planted in his pressure suit. Incredibly, Jon continued his bantering despite the size of their unseen audience.

Moore located the entrance on the bulbous rear section of the artifice, a square of blackness against reflected starlight. "Welcome mat is out," he said.

"No blue flash, Moore," Jon warned.

"Let's assume our friends have the situation under control."

The black square absorbed him and deposited him on a deck of swirling mist. The creature he confronted would be a master, newborn, but old beyond human comprehension.

The being had a blood-red head and torso. Human

279

resemblance ended there. Tentacles lined the torso, supporting it in an upright position. The orifices and protrusions on the long slanted skull Moore could identify with no imaginable sense organ.

"We are different," the master said, the voice warbling and low-pitched, emitted from the air itself rather than from the creature. It flowed closer to him, the movement of the tentacles hidden in the mist. It stood a little higher than Moore's knee.

"We have adequate data available upon which to complete our analogical structure of the human mind," the master said. "The voice you hear is constructed of air vibration. It may not be accurate in every respect, but should be suitable for our purposes."

"I didn't notice the symmetry reversal I experienced the first time I boarded one of your craft," Moore said.

"That is a protective measure employed during the travel phase of our journey. We do not need protection now."

"I'm glad to be back," Moore said.

"We feared failure. We feared for your sake. We risked so little, you so very much."

"It has worked out so far," Moore said. He hesitated. "What do we do now? There are so many of us and so little coordination or cooperation or even agreement on how we should communicate."

"There are many of us to speak with many of you," the master said. "It is not a negative thing that we are different. You grow with frightening rapidity. We stand to gain enormously from your inert technology. Likewise, you suffer ignorance of the advantage of a living technology. There are many others among the stars who will appreciate your uniqueness."

Ida Moore knelt to put himself on an eye-level contact with eyes constructed so differently from his own.

280

"How much time do you and I have?"

"Time is of no consequence. Of what would you learn? I speak with words and with images. Soon, we will interface with your computers and transfer vast information."

There were no seats. Moore sat on the deck, ignoring the mist and the slime.

"Words and images will be fine. Especially images. Tell me of your voyage first, then of yourselves. Work backward from there and tell me of your world and history."

"Typical of humans," the master said in a chattering tone that Moore would learn to recognize as laughter. "Work backward."

Jon opened a visual channel to the Alliance armada. A startled officer seated behind a high-ranking command console within one of the fortresses looked up, startled by the intrusion.

"Honored Jon B-897Y!"

"I'd like to request the use of a couple items of equipment," Jon said.

The officer's mouth dropped open, then snapped shut. He swallowed and gave a firm nod.

"Of course. I'll take your requisition personally."

"One Transtar Model Ten. One Jovan atmospheric retrieval vehicle."

The officer blinked several times, absorbing the words, their meaning and implication.

"The Transtar is only a temporary requisition," Jon said to ease the impact. "I'll send this one back to the Isinti on automatic. It won't be interfered with, will it?"

"No, sir. We suspected your craft not to be a standard Model Ten."

"It's Isinti property."

"Yes, honored one."

"I want the standard Transtar parked to replace

this one until Ida Moore returns to his Valthyn companion. I and my companion will embark for Earth immediately using the Earth-lander."

"I've been instructed to cooperate with your party," the officer said.

"When can I have the two craft?"

"Within the hour."

Jon cut off the screen. He had no need to justify his behavior to Dora, no need to feel that he abandoned her. A mild guilt gnawed at him, regardless. He exchanged a knowing smile with the woman. He knew on an intellectual level that Lisa and Dora were the same person. On an emotional level, Dora belonged to Ida Moore.

When the Transtar and the Earth-lander arrived, Jon performed the multiple-docking procedure himself. Without a word or a glance back, Dora transferred to the standard Transtar and Lisa ducked through the emergency airlock to enter the Earth-lander. Alone in the Isinti Transtar for the moment, Jon programmed the ship to return to the vicinity of the Isinti colony. It wouldn't make it all the way back home without help, but he didn't doubt that the Isinti would be expecting its arrival.

From the cabin of the Earth-lander with Lisa at his side, Jon separated the three craft. They watched the Isinti Transtar accelerate and dwindle in the distance against the starfields.

Jon moved the Earth-lander away. The standard Transtar with Dora aboard waited for Ida Moore's return. He sent the Earth-lander on a slow, ballistic course toward Earth, the blue-and-white world visible to the naked eye as a tiny disk off to one side of the sun.

"We'll spend what time we have together," Jon said to Lisa. "Is there anything left standing in our way?"

"Nothing stands in our way."

Minutes later, despite the distance, the Alliance

armada glowed like a wall of lights against the stars. Only by using the telescope could he discern the line of crimson alien craft stretched in a line fifty million kilometers long. The armada did not try to restrict the thousands of individual, civilian, and scientific spacecraft from approaching the alien craft.

Hours later, Lisa said, "Ida Moore has returned to Dora."

"How is he reacting?"

"He is calling you a deceitful bastard this very moment.

"Are there any regrets?"

"There are no regrets."

TALES OF TOMORROW
RED DUST (illustrated)
By David Houston

PRICE: $2.25 LB921
CATEGORY: Science Fiction

From the popular TV series, TALES OF TOMORROW
becomes a series of exciting SF novels by award-
winning author David Houston. In RED DUST, an
Earth expedition to Mars is returning with a strange
and glowing red life form. If the ship lands, Earth
could be infected. If it stays in orbit, everyone on
board will die!

STARSPINNER
By Dale Aycock

PRICE: $2.25 LB973
CATEGORY: Science Fiction

AN EMPIRE FACES DEATH!

In the 27th century, travel over vast distances takes merely an instant—a terrifying, gut-gripping instant. Pilot Christopher Marlow must navigate spacecraft through a dangerous time/space warp called the "rim."